ANTONIO
THE BELOVED

CORY BLYSTONE

Kwirk
publishing

Vancouver, Washington

A Kwirk Publishing Original

Published by
Kwirk Publishing
Vancouver, WA

Kwirk Publishing Paperback Edition ISBN: 978-1-945931-18-5

Kwirk Publishing Kindle eBook Edition ISBN: 978-1-945931-20-8
Kwirk Publishing EPUB eBook Edition ISBN: 978-1-945931-19-2

Cover art by Cory Blystone

Interior tree branches art by Cory Blystone

Published in the United States of America

First Printing February 2026

Vampires of Ravenwood #1

Subjects: Vampires fiction. | Occult fiction. | Witches fiction.

Printed in the United States of America

For Greg: my past, present, and future love. Always.

ANTONIO

THE BELOVED

Alas, the words will flow as thick as blood, and just as red.

CHAPTER 1

Clinging On For Life

A red leaf watched Antonio as he stared out his bedroom window onto Song's End, a dead-end street capped by a crowded cemetery in the small town of Ravenwood, Washington—the bed he laid in a formality at best considering his condition—and waited for an answer to find him. He knew it wouldn't, but still, there he was, waiting nonetheless. If anything, he was like the fly who refuses to go out the open door, opting to cling to the window and imagine what life is like on the outside. Deep shit, man.

As his mind wandered, watching the wind blow away the leaves, carrying with it all the last remnants of summer and happiness and life into the death and decay of winter, the red maple leaves reminded him of Sam and the life Sam would never have. He imagined their life together, even in the ironic sense since he technically was not considered of the living, pretending like these leaves of change were bypassing winter and going straight for the new life of spring and all the joy and sunshine and warmth he never allowed himself to be a part of when he was alive, and couldn't be a part of now that he was vampire, and regretted his life choices and the choices made by others—or one other—that he never had a say in.

His maker.

Who was this other vampire who decided to give him the curse of everlasting life? Why? Why continue the chase over impossible dreams? What reason could this stranger, this other, Other with a capital O, this being have for kissing him and leaving him on his own like a toddler lost in the mall by a meth-addicted mother who walked off to chase something shiny that caught her eye? What right did he have? It was a he, right? It had to be a man. No woman (save the drug-fueled ones) could leave their child to his own devices after giving birth, leaving him alone to try and navigate a world that doesn't understand him or even acknowledge his existence. It was Mary Shelley's *Frankenstein* all over again.

The red leaf mocked him, dancing outside, begging Antonio to join him. He watched, waiting for it to move along, join his brothers and sisters on the ground, but it didn't. It hung around. Lingered. Patiently awaiting different company to join him on his journey. Swirling around, defying the wind that held it afloat while others just like it had been chased off the tree to their death, withering, decaying while he continued to defy the wuthering in the heights.

"Stubborn little bastard, aren't you?" Antonio asked the leaf, half expecting it to disappear after acknowledging it.

"Play with me," the leaf said.

"No," Antonio said.

"Play with me," the leaf repeated.

"Not gonna happen."

"Play with me."

Begging.

Pleading.

Pathetic.

But Antonio had to admit he was impressed by the leaf's persistence. While the rest of its kind fluttered away, he stayed behind. The lone watchman standing guard against evil. In a way, the leaf reminded him of his role in the coven that wanted him to join, and his reluctance over becoming part of a family he never wanted and didn't understand. After all, he may be a vampire, but what does that mean? Yes, he drank blood to live, but never from a living being.

No. That was a lie now. Sam was proof of that. So was Sam's death from his inability to control himself from succumbing to intrinsic needs his nature afforded him with. It was the same with sex. He never could stop himself from continuing to torture a guy's cock after he came while giving him head, continuing to suck in hopes of swallowing every last bit of cum, maybe even in hopes of causing him to cum again. It happened once with a kid he sucked off in high school, and ever since then it was a challenge he couldn't help but try to repeat. Random hookups at the nearby rest stop in Battle Ground, college guys who struck out at Ravenwood Bar & Grill, backroom glory holes in any number of night clubs in Portland. His quest for someone who had the stamina to satiate his needs and desires was endless. His disappointment was as well. But he could learn to accept the fact that it may have just been a random coincidence, right? A sixteen-year-old's overstimulation and impressive refractory period, right? He could control his urges, his desires, his irrational expectations? He could feed off a human without killing them? He could control the primal demon inside him that begged for totality? His past told him otherwise. Could it be truth from now on?

And so, Antonio watched the red leaf hold on. And now, as he stared out the same window on the same night ten years later, those same torturous thoughts danced in his head while a single red leaf danced on a branch, unwilling to go it alone as the wind knocked all the other leaves off the maple tree whose fallen leaves were browned and mottled with rain spots that created a harsher, uglier version of the beauty it was once capable of. He had long since given up hope of finding love, long since given up finding the elusive man who could cum multiple times in a row, long since given up ever being able to feed off a human without losing total control of himself. Yes, he had given up a great many things. But still, the lone red leaf begged for a partner in crime. Antonio was forced to admit that he needed a partner, too.

The coven still offered its protection, its family-like love, its guidance and acceptance of who, of what he was. Still, he didn't feel like he deserved their protection. He didn't feel like he deserved a family or love, and especially not the guidance they offered which was mostly of the how-to-dispose-of-a-body-should-things-go-wrong variety now that he had gotten to know them and their baseless threats over their own rules. No. He would not go down the coven road.

But he craved companionship. He craved knowledge. He craved the love and life and truth about the who what when where why how that he knew in the place where his dead and unbeating heart used to be, bound in the cavern, buried and forever unanswered. He craved his maker's companionship. He craved his maker's knowledge. He craved his maker's love and life and truth about the who what when where why how that only his maker could answer yet would probably remain a mystery for the misery of his eternal damnation as a bloodsucking fiend.

True, his town was quite accepting of his kind. Ravenwood was, after all, gifted with a horde of supernatural. It was also true that it was accepting of his kind before his change, when he was just another gay Chicano kid with a fetish for fellatio. His Catholic parents never understood him, thinking the gay thing could be prayed away with a few more Hail Marys and a hell of a lot of Our Fathers. His Catholic grandfather hooked him up with other good Catholic boys, only those good boys were good at all things decidedly not Catholic. Fucking, sucking, rimming, drunken orgies, poppers to intensify orgasms. Oh yes! those Catholic boys were good at all that. Antonio often wondered what the priests would do after listening to all those boys when they went in for confession. Did they jerk off? Did they lift the veil and beg for absolution by way of repeating the sin for them? Did they even care? One thing was for certain, and that was the celibate life was not for him. Antonio never considered himself a sex addict, but the thought of not having sex in any form for more than a few days was beyond insane.

The red leaf begged, "I'll let you do whatever you want with me, so long as you join me."

"You don't know what you're asking," Antonio told the leaf.

"I do."

"You'll only be disappointed with me."

"I don't care about me, I just don't want to be alone."

"There are a million other leaves just like you on the ground. Why can't you be satisfied with what you are?"

"I suppose it is for the same reasons you can't."

That truth hit Antonio like a backhanded bitch-slap of the 1980s prime time soap opera variety. Here he was, bitching and moaning about not knowing how to be a vampire, how to be his true self, and now a leaf was calling him out on his defiant position about taking up the coven's offer to teach him. Then a picture flashed before his eyes, and suddenly he remembered a glimpse of what his maker looked like.

It was time for Communion.

The shorter man laughed like a hyena in heat while the taller man snickered like a candy wrapper being pried off the prized chocolate inside. Antonio did not look amused as he waited for an answer. Well, he did find the shorter man's pathetic attempt at a mustache amusing as he counted the hairs. His laughter made the task take far longer than his patience allotted. Like, eight whole goddamned seconds that could've been cut in half, but no, the hyena had to cackle.

"Please, sir," Antonio said, wincing, immediately regretting the formality of his word choice given the company it was addressed to. "I just want to know if you've seen a man matching that description."

"Why you wanna find a man like that when what you really want is to suck my dick," the shorter man said, grabbing his crotch and aggressively rubbing his penis through tight jeans.

Antonio could tell the little guy was packing an impressive tool, but sex was not on his mind. Not since Sam. No. Not that he hadn't been having sex with hundreds of men since, but it was all meaningless. The connection he'd had with random hookups and strangers and back alley blowjobs all used to mean something. It was pleasurable. Exciting. Dangerous. But now it was just habit. No pleasure. No excitement. No danger. Just sex.

But he couldn't take his eyes off the shorter man's crotch. There it was. Growing. Waiting for him to kiss it. Lick it. Suck it. Fuck it.

"Edgar, chico's a chichi!" the shorter man told the taller man while he continued to rub just to the left of his zipper.

The taller man looked uneasy at this. He looked uneasier as the shorter man whipped his erect penis out of his jeans. Throbbing veins adorning it like a filigree sword, carefully crafted by artisans in immaculate detail. Veins pumping blood.

Delicious.

Viscous.

Blood.

"C'mon, faggot. Suck it."

"So, I take it you haven't seen him?" Antonio asked, resisting every urge his body was telling him to give into.

The shorter man just held his thick penis his stubby fingers couldn't even wrap around, giving Antonio a look of both disgust and disappointment. "Pipi chichi mi cabra!" he said as he stuffed his member back into his pants. It almost refused to be encaged again like the wild beast it was.

Antonio noticed he didn't wear underwear and suddenly started wondering why he didn't wear underwear and if he ever worried about skid marks on his jeans that smelled of week-old man musk and caused his hormones to completely assault his whole being like he was a cat in heat and the short man who laughed like a hyena with a dick the size of a Hillshire Farm Summer Sausage was the closest tom to fuck. He felt a little repulsed that he was mildly attracted to this depravity of human waste. The taller, quieter man was more his type. Lean, muscular, light skin that beautifully contrasted his own.

"Wait, did you just tell me to go fuck your goat?" Antonio asked the shorter man.

"Sí. Fucker speaks Spanish, Edgar!" the shorter man said, laughing again.

Antonio couldn't help but notice a wet spot soaking through the shorter man's blue jeans where the impression of the tip of his penis pushed. The smell of his precum intoxicated him for a second, momentarily removing him from the man who, after insulting him, basically wanted to fuck him as a sign of dominance. And yet, he wanted to give in. Let him have his way. Be his sub. Until the wind carried it away.

"Sí, fucker. Comprendo español muy bien," Antonio replied after the scent faded into the cold, damp night air.

"HahHhhahahahahahahaa!" the shorter man burst out.

The taller man nervously watched Antonio. Small moves. Twitchy thumbs. Random deep breaths. Antonio knew what it all meant.

"We should go, Sam," the taller man called Edgar said to the shorter man.

Sam. His name is Sam? If he wasn't such a hetero asshole, I'd make him my bitch. But he could never replace my Sam. My perfect Sam. Well, almost perfect. If Sam had a penis, I'd wish for him to have had one like this Sam. Well, maybe not that veiny, or maybe that veiny and massive, but damn, Antonio thought.

"Yeah, Edgar. If this fucker won't suck my dick, I still gotta find someone to. Where to next?" Sam asked Edgar, the alleyway only offering one way out.

Edgar stared at Antonio, hand in his pocket like he was juggling change. "I'm sorry, but we haven't seen him."

"Thank you," Antonio said, a slight grin forming.

"Eh, tú mama cama con perro!" Sam said, laughing as he grabbed his dick again before turning around.

Before he knew it, Antonio's teeth firmly dug into Sam's neck, sucking his sweet sweet blood he was certain would be bitter and have a nasty, fiery bite to it like habanero, ghost, Carolina Reaper. For a nanosecond he contemplated letting Sam go. Or making him one of the undead. His first. But his bloodlust overtook his senses. Again. Sam never had a chance. Even with a godblessed penis like that. And so, he sucked, letting the river of red flow over his mouth and down the front of his chest and halfway-unbuttoned shirt while his eyes chewed into the taller man who watched in horror and amazement as he sucked off his friend. Antonio couldn't tell if Edgar was frightened or aroused or both. When he had enough of Sam and Sam was on the verge of death, Antonio threw him to the ground, maintaining his dagger-like eye contact with Edgar as if trying to seduce him. Fuck objectivity, he wanted him.

Edgar's body was stiffening. Neck muscles pulsing like a Dodge Charger's engine. Hand still shuffling something in his front pocket.

"Don't be afraid, Edgar," Antonio told the man, never letting his gaze go.

"I'm not afraid," Edgar said, shivering ever so slightly.

Sam twitched on the filthy back alley, what little blood he had left oozed out of him like the last remnants of the toothpaste tube.

Edgar froze.

Antonio slowly walked closer to him.

Edgar's hand eased out of his pocket, revealing a fist.

"No need for bravado, Edgar. I know you want me."

Edgar smiled, almost causing Antonio to burst into flames from the radiation. His fist slowly unclenched. "Your gaydar needs a little fine tuning."

"Wait, what?"

A hundred sunflower seeds flew from Edgar's hand, causing Antonio to break his eye contact and concentration. All Edgar did was smile.

"Son of a bitch!" Antonio said as he diligently picked up the seeds and stuffed them into his pocket.

He never did see where Edgar ran off. Except in his dreams where his body was used for a brain transplant for his Sam so he could have a body that matched his mind and not the breasts he bound or the vagina he abhorred and didn't fit right with what his brain told him. Even after Sam's parents started him on hormone therapy, puberty had done too much damage. "My poor, sweet Sam," Antonio said aloud.

"You fucking rip my throat out and now you fucking calling me sweet?" Sam said with parched voice as he laid inches away from the remaining scattered seeds.

"Not you, fucker." He looked at the short man and briefly thought of giving into his previous demands as he saw the bulge still present beneath the halfway zipped opening in the musky jeans. "Why aren't you dead yet?"

"Too stubborn, I guess. Or maybe it's cuz I'm already a fucking vampire like you, dumbass chupa. Puta. Fuck, my throat."

"You are no vampire, but you are something powerfully delicious," Antonio said, licking his lips for any drops he may have missed.

"Shit, man. You got me," Sam said as he tried to pick himself up before collapsing back onto the chipped pavement and back alley refuse, a cigarette butt firmly stuck to his exposed esophagus. "Fuck! Edgar!"

"Edgar left," Antonio said as he continued pocketing the seeds scattered around him. "And this is by far the dumbest part about being a vampire. Fucking OCD bastard pieces of shit!"

The short Sam with the thin mustache tried to laugh, but the hyena had long since left the carcass, moving on to fresher meat. "Kiss me or kill me, faggot."

"Quit calling me a faggot. You're the one who wants me to suck your dick. You're the one who wants me to kiss you. If I had to guess, I'd say you're the faggot here."

"Got me again, fucker."

"You're stalling."

"No, I just want to be like you."

"But?"

"I can't. Fucking fairy blood on mi madre's side gone and fucked that up."

Note to self: fairies are the dessert of blood.

A trickle of Sam's leftovers dripped onto the ground and it took every fiber of Antonio's being to not lick it up after he picked up the last of Edgar's seeds.

Maybe a happy ending for poor Sam. If his blood tastes that good, I bet the rest tastes...

Sunflower seeds rained down all round him.

"Are you fucking kidding me?!" Antonio screamed, dropping the rest of the previous seeds he'd retrieved as his hands opened.

Then he caught eyes with Edgar again, who dropped the plastic bag, picked up his crude friend, and carried him to a car. Antonio, however, had seeds to pick up. And a goddamn bag. Fucking litterer.

"What will happen to my body after I change?" Sam asked Antonio, swinging next to him in Ravenwood Park's playground, the moon forcing itself through the midnight clouds, illuminating Sam's face in perfect light, but casting Antonio into eerie shadow.

For a moment, Antonio felt caught off guard. What question was this? He'd be a vampire! But then the reality of the situation confounded him. Sam would still have the wrong parts. Nature's cruel joke, making a boy have to build his own body because she screwed up. Sam should have pecs not breasts. Sam should have a penis not a vagina. But still,

Sam had the parts that made his parents name him Samantha, and only time would tell how long it would be before those parts were properly installed.

"I love you, not just the vessel," Antonio told him, immediately regretting his cold choice of words, but what else was he supposed to say? Tell Sam the truth? That he might never be able to fully love him because his parts don't match his gender? Tell him a lie and say that everything will be all right in the end? Tell Sam the heart-wrenching truth of the matter, in that should Sam have the surgery to correct his sex, the vampire virus would probably revert him back to his original state? So many questions. So few answers.

"Thanks, dick!" Sam said, punching Antonio in the arm, a burst of giggles escaping his mouth that seemed forever stuck between masculine and feminine.

Reeling back, pretending to be in pain when in reality the only pain he was reeling from was the hurt the change was bound to forever imprint on Sam, Antonio rubbed the punch away, and used the swing's chain like a shield against a future attack. *How could God do this to my Sam? Cause him so much agony and disgust with his own body?* Antonio thought while feigning a smile so as to distract Sam from them.

Sam swung forward and leapt out of the seat swiftly before turning back around and landing on his knees, inches from Antonio's crotch. "Well, I love you and your vessel," Sam told him quietly as his nimble fingers unzipped Antonio's jeans, freed the penis trapped inside, and began Hoovering like the in-laws were on their way over for an impromptu visit they'd just phoned moments before.

"Oh God!" Antonio cried, wondering just what Sam thought his penis tasted like considering only an hour before it was firmly thrusting itself in his tight little asshole, which only turned him on even more as Sam mumbled how delicious it was.

"Are you making a confession before the act is over?" Sam joked before his lips wrapped themselves around Antonio's shaft again, saliva dribbling over his balls, pooling between his ass cheeks where they teased him about something Sam could never give.

Part of him knew that whatever humanity he supposedly had left in his barren soul considered this wrong. Not the gay thing or the sex in public on a playground where children would no doubt unknowingly discover the remnants of their primal lust the following day thing, but Sam's age. True, Sam was on the edge of adulthood, but a seventeen-year-old nonetheless, and while he could pass that particular little inconvenience off as arbitrary in the grand scheme of things, he could not help but wonder if this is what all those middle-aged married men thought while he was blowing them at the Gee Creek Rest Stop when he was seventeen and horny as hell. Now he was the dirty old man taking advantage of a teenager's naïveté. That naïveté, however, was skillfully gifted in all things fellatio, and before Antonio could control himself, his cum was forcing its way out of his penis and down Sam's eager throat.

Sam pulled away and swallowed, a sly smile firmly planted on his face.

Antonio looked at the mess his hands had made, splattered across his chest and bed sheets and even on the ceiling fan over his head that was seconds away from falling back down to splash his face, and wept. Ten years to the day since Sam died, and all Antonio could think to do was masturbate to a pathetic memory of one of their sexcapades.

"Forgive me father, for I have sinned," he cried quietly, waiting for an absolution that would never come.

CHAPTER 2

Winds of Change

Transitioning is never easy. This much Sam was well aware of as he stared out his bedroom window and pondered how long it would be before his body matched his mind while watching the raindrops crash into the glass. He followed as many as he could as they dribbled pathetically towards their deaths. It was another typical wet and cloudy day in Ravenwood, with dark, gloomy skies and sporadic showers completing the picture. No chance of any of those "blue clouds" that some people have spotted on occasion, or the Giant Glowing Orb of Death that most referred to as the sun. It was, according to Sam, a perfect day.

Now if this seems odd to you, that a person would despise the sun and all the warmth it provides, well, it is obvious you have never met Sam Vader. Fiery red hair with a wispy curl; pale, milky skin resembling that of a porcelain doll; bright green eyes you would swear were a lush meadow while gazing into them. Oh, and a complete fascination with the night.

For as long as he could remember, he had been a night owl, staying up far past his bedtime so he could stare endlessly out his bedroom window at the sky, completely entranced by the moon and stars. His mother never understood why it took so long to wake him in the morning, until one night, by chance, she checked in on Sam sometime after he had gone to bed and discovered him sitting on the bay window seat, looking absolutely awestruck at the stars peaking between the clouds behind the window panes.

"Do you suppose there is a whole other life that happens when the rest of us go to bed?" Sam asked his mom without breaking his gaze.

Slightly stunned by her six-year-old daughter's insightful question, she answered, "If you mean owls, bats and raccoons, then yes."

"No, I mean people," Sam responded, shaking his head, his long hair an annoyance he wished his mother would just cut off. "Like, people who can't be out during the day, but they are able to walk around at night and do things like we do. You know, like drink coffee and pay taxes."

Folding her arms across her chest and firmly planting a scowl, Sam's mother asked, "Have you been drinking coffee again, Samantha? Is that why you can't sleep?"

"No…" Sam said slowly with a deep exhaling breath. "I take naps during recess at school so I can stay up and watch the stars play."

Now this would usually be the point where any reasonable mother would say, "I don't care. Get to bed!" But instead, she told her daughter, "If I have any trouble getting you up in the mornings from now on, I'll have that window boarded up and you won't be able to look out it again."

"Thank you, Mother," Sam said, smiling before turning his head back to the window. "Goodnight now, I'll see you in the morning."

So, from then on, Sam made sure to get up right when his mom told him to, which sometimes meant an after-school nap to fend off exhaustion. How he wished to know if indeed there was an entire world that only existed at night. For years he daydreamed of what it might be like, and who would be there and how everyone interacted together. What struggles did they endure? What triumphs did they celebrate? It all seemed so intriguing.

Even now, almost twelve years later, he still found himself sitting in his bedroom's bay window seat late at night, staring into the empty streets, and, every so often, thought he witnessed the very world he had imagined. The people carrying on their everyday lives in a completely different way than the people he knew. How graceful and swift they looked in the moonlight, and how he wished to be right there with them, dancing in the streets. But in the blink of an eye, they were gone, and he was left to ponder whether it had all been in his head, which decidedly was topped with much shorter hair. His room had also transitioned from pink to gray, like his wardrobe from dresses to denim jeans, and his name just Sam now instead of Samantha. However, hormone therapy could only do so much; there were still the parts he wished were never there, and the parts he wished he had instead.

Soon. Mom and Dad say it will be soon, Sam told himself, as if it was the only reassurance he had that one day he would be a real boy.

As he walked home from school one day—several countless days after promises were made, yet archaic laws forbid—in the pouring rain, dark clouds surrounding him, he smiled as thoughts of his night world people came to him. One by one, they all started to appear as if it was the absence of the sun that brought them out. Strolling about, he quietly said his hellos to those he walked past, smiling politely. Some would say hello back, and others murmured as if surprised someone was speaking to them.

And then he stopped.

Someone caught his attention.

Someone who took his breath away.

Berlin started singing in his head.

Standing before him was the most beautiful man he had ever laid eyes on. Masterly chiseled cheekbones; intense, jet black eyes; shoulder length ebony hair with a gentle waviness about it; tall stature and otherwise perfect terra cotta Adonis body. And that three-day stubble to die for.

"Hello," Sam offered when he regained control of his breathing.

"Hello to you, too," the stranger said back, coy smile that Sam basically read as, "I am planning on seducing you then fucking your brains out," to which he was completely receptive.

They continued to stare at each other for what seemed like hours, as people passed them by on either side, paying no attention to their existence. The rain had stopped and the sky had darkened, and there they were, alone on the lone stretch of sidewalk at the mouth of Song's End off of Main Street. It was all very reminiscent of a 1980s romantic comedy waiting for the tag line.

"My name is Saman…" *Goddammit.* "Sam," he finally said after catching himself fall into the trap he'd done for more years than he cared to count, correcting teachers and grandmas and aunts and uncles and cousins and basically everyone who ever knew him when he was timid Samantha who hated himself because he didn't understand why God made a mistake and created him female when he was supposed to be male while in all her cruelty also making his sister male when she was supposed to be female. Sam stretched his hand out involuntarily, like one goes in for an informal handshake, taking him back to Timid Samantha days rather than Confident Twink Sam.

Taking Sam's hand in his, an electrical current raced through them both as he said, "I am Antonio, and I apologize for not having a short name, but if you'd like to call me Ant…"

Sam laughed as an image of Antonio with six legs scuttled by carrying a red leaf much larger than him popped into his brain. "I'm sorry.

I didn't mean to laugh out loud. I have a pretty vivid imagination."

"I understand," Antonio told him, and something about the way he said it made Sam realize that he actually did.

It was then that Sam knew this wasn't another daydream.

He was real.

This was real.

And that could only mean one thing.

"You don't feel very old, how long ago were you turned?" he asked Antonio bluntly, one eye cocked while the other squinted.

Stunned to say the least, Antonio didn't let on to that fact, instead responding with a cool, calm, and collected, "So you are aware that I am a vampire?"

"I'm aware of a great many things. The fact that you're a vampire is just one of them."

"You're not going to kill me now, are you?"

"Why would I want to do that?"

"Because you know what I am."

"And that is what attracted me to you."

"You're attracted to me?"

Antonio's coy smile made Sam imagine getting an erection, but all he could conjure up was the poor excuse his vagina had to offer. The feeling, however, was a perfectly acceptable, though decidedly frustrating, alternative. "Of course I am." Sam blushed, cursing the fact that his super pale skin gave his emotions away every time. "And you're putting off the question I asked."

"Well, I'm a little off guard. Here I was thinking I was about to have an easy meal, but it appears you've got me at a disadvantage. You know what I am and therefore, know how to stop me if I tried to attack."

"You're not going to attack me."

Now Sam was utilizing the coy, seductive smile. The confident twink. The boy who knew what he wanted and how to get it. And his smile was all the pole he needed to cast.

Hook.

Line.

Sinker.

"And how do you know that?"

"Because you felt the same connection I did."

"How do you know so much?"

"How come you won't tell me how old you are, or how long you've been a vampire? If it helps, I'm seventeen and human." *And a fucking girl until I'm eighteen and my doctor will take off my tits and contort my hoo-haw into a dick and balls!*

"Three years ago. I was in an accident. Motorcycle flipped out of nowhere and pinned me to a tree. I guess some vampire took pity on me as I was inches away from death, turned me, and left me to fend for myself. I've been searching for him ever since, but every lead turns into a dead end." *What the hell? Why are you such a Chatty Cathy all of a sudden? And to this stranger, no less! This alarmingly attractive slightly underage pretty piece of flesh stranger!*

The last sentence hung in the air like the sadness of an old bassoon.

"So that would make you…"

"Twenty-three."

"Ah… I could live with that," Sam told himself.

"When I was turned."

Sam's eyes lifted as he shrugged. "So, judging from the direction you were coming from, I'd say you hit another dead end?" he asked, noting that Song's End was literally a dead-end street, flanked on either side by late nineteenth and early twentieth century houses and tailed by a cemetery where the road came to an abrupt stop.

"No, I'm afraid I live on this awful road," Antonio told Sam, the disgust in his voice evident on his face.

"It's not so awful. I live on it as well. Besides, I find it fitting that you would live on a street named after a vampire."

"Do you honestly believe that old tale of Chief Ravenwood's son being a vampire who slaughtered the entire Oaxaciian tribe?"

"Yes, and that entire tribe is buried underneath all of these houses. I wonder who my house is on? A tribal elder? Ravenwood's family? It's all so fascinating, don't you think?" *Please say yes! Please please please please please say yes! Oh, gawd… am I starting to sound like a naïve schoolgirl with a crush on the teacher? Pull yourself together, man!*

Not knowing how exactly to respond, Antonio just stared down the street, pretending to ponder Sam's question. Of the coven that had made the offer of family but Antonio never accepted, nobody ever spoke of Song's End, or the tribe that had been wiped out before E.W. Blaire's expedition party found a lonely Chief Ravenwood. It was all a mysterious Anglicized myth, floating, hovering over the town like mid-autumn fog. "Fascinating," he said out loud before he could stop himself.

Smiling, biting one side of his lip, Sam said, "It is. Only wish I could have been there to witness it all. Must've been a sight."

Antonio laughed. "Yes, must've been blood and dead babies everywhere." He swallowed quickly to prevent his salivating tongue from drooling out his lips. This boy was making him moist, his bloodlust pumping through his entire body, and he was willing to do all the bad things he promised not to do.

"Well, there may have been blood, but I doubt dead babies. Nobody has ever found the remains of any of the children, just the adults. Perhaps they were tender enough to eat whole? Just a thought," Sam said matter-of-factly.

"Morbid, but an interesting theory, assuming, of course, that any of that legend is true," Antonio said, at a loss that this human was carrying on a conversation about a vampire that even vampires wouldn't speak of in any detail, mostly out of fear that Song's End was still out there, hunting, preying, foraging for wayward children in the night. And from what little he knew, Song's End never turned anyone. He only slaughtered them, feeding and disposing of their lifeless carcasses in plain sight for all to see what he had done. Nothing like the vampire who rescued him, nothing like the vampires he knew, and nothing like himself.

Minutes went by without another word uttered, just glances as they casually walked together down Song's End toward Sam's house, but to Sam it seemed like hours. For the first time in Sam's life, he felt at peace, knowing that his nights of staring out his window were not just visions from a vivid imagination, but real. And there he was, walking alongside one of the very creatures that up until a few hours ago, he thought only existed in his head.

"I wish I didn't have so much homework to do tonight," Sam said, breaking the silence and the mood and hating himself for it. "I'd love to watch you hunt."

A little embarrassed by his forwardness, Antonio informed Sam, "I've never hunted before."

"What?!" Sam stopped in his tracks, confusion sweeping over his face like a wet blanket. "Then how do you feed yourself?"

With a goofy grin, no longer seductive and coy, but honest and real, eyes on the pavement beneath them, he told Sam, "The butcher shop downtown sells blood by the pint, so I buy it there."

Shaking his head, Sam said, "Antonio, you disappoint me."

"Why would I disappoint you?"

"You don't hunt! What kind of vampire are you?"

"The kind who was a vegan before being turned," he informed him. "The thought of killing and eating a person or animal is still ingrained in my psyche as something I can't do. If I could survive on anything else, I wouldn't even drink blood from the butcher shop. Although, I must admit, the sweetness of pig's blood reminds me of raspberry preserves."

Giving his response a moment to sink in, Sam told him, "I suppose you can be forgiven then." He paused. "Not for the vegan thing, though. I love meat too much."

I would love your meat in my mouth, Antonio thought, suddenly realizing the oddity of being vegan and loving cum, containing his desires from turning into actions he'd likely regret this early in the game, but knowing how seventeen-year-old boys worked, also hoped it would happen nonetheless. Something, however, about Sam's scent gave him pause. What was this aroma that seemed so unbefitting of maleness? He smelled like a man, but there was something else he couldn't connect.

Before Sam knew it, they were at his doorstep. The rain started again, and with it, a sadness swept over him as he realized their time, for that day anyway, had come to an end. "I must finish this paper," he told Antonio. "But tomorrow night, perhaps if you're not busy, we could continue our conversation?"

"Tomorrow night it is," Antonio agreed, taking his hand and gently kissing it like a gentleman even though he wanted to take another appendage and kiss it like a whore. *What is this? For God's sake, man! Is this love?* He lowered the hand from his lips and watched as they grew apart, ripping a piece of his soul away as Sam went into the house, the door closing on his face as he stared, smiling back at him.

Feeling lighter than air, Antonio walked back to his home as his body threatened to float away, forgetting he planned to eat, disjointed fragments of the Whitesnake song filtering through the air. There was still the uneasy lingering sensation he had never felt before. Perhaps this was the soulmate he didn't even know he was searching for. Perhaps this was the reason his conscience told him to leave his house when he felt like staying in until after nightfall. Perhaps this was the start of something wonderful.

Perhaps he should have stayed home and never met Sam.

Hours seemed to pass like days as Antonio sat awake, waiting for the time to come when Sam and he could resume their conversation. It felt like such a relief to him to find someone he could easily talk to without fear of retaliation. Even among his own kind, few understood his reasons for not hunting for his meals. They considered his butcher shop trips to be an abomination to all that is vampire. To hunt and feast upon fresh blood from a creature whose heart still beat like a steady drum, and drain it until the beat slows its pace to nothing, is what most vampires considered a decent meal. An honest meal. A well-earned meal. "Fast Food" they called buying blood, and it was frowned upon much the same way pretentious health officials look at the human world's endless streets of late-night drive-thru menus punching through the dark with artificial fluorescent and neon lights.

Checking the clock again, hoping that time had somehow sped up, Antonio found himself disappointed that only a few seconds had passed since he last looked at it. To stave off his boredom, he did what he used to do as a human: he ate. He also used to jerk off, a lot, but not tonight. Just in case. Not that he wouldn't be ready for another round or three. No. He wanted to save that part.

Opening the refrigerator, he removed a pint-sized plastic tub, took the lid off, and placed it in the microwave just long enough to take the chill off of it, a programmed setting as the appliance had only one reason for existing in his home, his domicile, one of his abeulo's houses he initially rented upon graduating high school, which he never really appreciated, but it came with a microwave already, and even though it'd be five years after he got the house before he became a vampire, it still took several attempts to program the settings to be just right for blood. Once, he made the mistake of heating it too long, at which point it had congealed into a grayish looking heap of matter, splattering all over the microwave's interior, looking about as appetizing as it sounds. While cleaning the mess, he slapped his forehead and rolled his eyes in realization of what had happened, remembering a time during his childhood when he defrosted ground beef from the freezer for his mother and it had cooked around the edges, leaving the same gray matter where any blood had oozed out.

He used to love cows when he was alive, their large eyes and quiet nature—often finding himself at the local dairy farm to stare at their beauty—but now only craved the blood inside the sinewy flesh. Admittedly, he used to love a lot of foods, all animal and animal by-product free after he turned seventeen and became vegan, but now he was reduced to pint and quart sized plastic containers of butchered pigs and cows and for a treat around Easter, lamb's blood. He'd become a vegan's worst nightmare.

Promptly removing the container from the microwave, Antonio began slurping the lukewarm thick red liquid, pondering if the pig's name was Luke and the irony of lukewarm life-force of Luke if it was, or if the pig even had a name, and how sad it would be for the pig to be nameless, so in his head he named the pig Luke and thanked him upon finishing the last drop of his blood, disposing of the plastic tub in the trash, and swearing he could hear his mother scold him for not recycling, so he quickly took it back out of the trash, rinsed it out and put it in the recycling bin located in the garage. It still surprised him how many thoughts could go through his head in such a short period of time since being turned. Then again, his mind always raced before, too.

Back and forth. His high school crushes he wanted to be gay like him. His teachers he wanted to be gay like him. His hopes that they weren't gay but still let him fuck them anyway. If only he spent more time using his mind racing for math instead of sex.

Sitting back on the sofa, Antonio once again took to staring at the clock, awaiting the moment when Sam would be in his presence for a second time. To him, it felt like the instances between tick and tock were slowing with every turn of the second hand.

Tick.

Tock.

Tick.

Tock.

Tick.

Tock.

In between a tick and tock, a passing thought strolled through his head from when he was sired. While all vampires have an innate sense of knowing they need blood to sustain themselves, a certain code is supposed to be transferred as well. The moral code by which nearly all vampires subsist by, allowing them to continue to exist without threat from the human world.

1) **Spare the innocent ones.**
2) **Do not hesitate upon the murderers, rapists, and child molesters.**
3) **No children no matter the reasons.**

These three simple rules, passed from sire to fledgling when the fledgling drinks the sire's blood, are the Vampire Code. And those who decide not to obey the code are usually hunted down and destroyed by their coven, which could be the one into which they have been sired into, or one of their own choosing. He knew chosen family all too well after coming out.

Antonio did not receive this knowledge during his transition.

Antonio did not have a coven to belong to.

But a coven lived nearby to explain these truths to him, and offer him their protection and guidance, as they sensed a newborn in their presence who was, as they termed it, a one-night-stand. Considering the innumerable one-night-stands Antonio had prior, he should've understood. Surprisingly, he did not.

Upon their arrival, they told him what he was and how to survive. They showed kindness as they picked him up off the ground, brushing off any debris that had clung to his clothing and hair, and continued to explain certain truths to him as they walked him home. And in return, he showed gratitude for their help and wanted to go home—not his actual home, but his family home—to his mother and father and sisters and brother—even though they'd somewhat abandoned him after he turned eighteen—but they told him that wasn't possible, for he could never be with them again, as they could never accept what he had become. To prevent any altercations, he verbally agreed to their rules and regulations, for they must have been put in place for a reason. But in the back of his mind, he knew that he would never be able to obey them. Never accept their so-called truth. Never be able to follow their rules, their regulations. There was something missing from his brain that he had to find first, and all those would have to be broken to find it.

So, he never accepted the offer to be part of their coven.

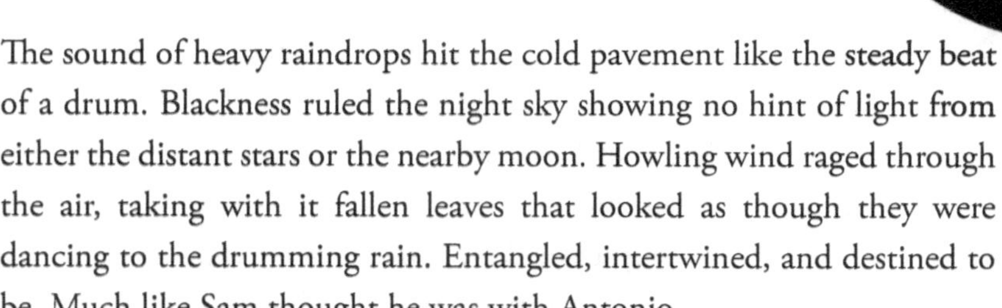

The sound of heavy raindrops hit the cold pavement like the steady beat of a drum. Blackness ruled the night sky showing no hint of light from either the distant stars or the nearby moon. Howling wind raged through the air, taking with it fallen leaves that looked as though they were dancing to the drumming rain. Entangled, intertwined, and destined to be. Much like Sam thought he was with Antonio.

Every time he looked into his eyes, he felt lost and completely at home and safe at the same time. So indescribable were his feelings for him that he dared not tell his parents or sister or friends of their relationship, for fear they wouldn't understand. And how could they? How could they know what he was feeling, how intense every moment they shared together was like? Even now, as they walked alone in the dark night, rain matting their hair and dripping down their faces, the wind whipping by and blowing their soaked hair and clothing in all directions, he was so happy to be where he was because he was with him, beside him.

As if someone had simply turned off the switch, the rain stopped and the wind died down, leaves settling themselves onto the ground until their next dance. Antonio turned to Sam, black, piercing eyes staring into his gleaming greens, which seemed to sparkle even without the help of any real source of light. Picking him up as if he was lighter than air, he twirled Sam with his arms around his waist and lips pressed firmly against each other, kissing him with such desire and passion, he told himself, *Tonight is the night.*

But could he do it? Could he possibly do what they had discussed for so long? The last month? What if something went wrong, would he ever forgive him? Performance anxiety raced through every fiber of his being, but subsided as quickly as it had formed as Sam put his warm hand on his cold, wet cheek, and gave him a reassuring look that everything was going to be okay.

That was all he needed to get his confidence back, and as Antonio kissed Sam again, their tongues behaved as if in a freeform ballet, performing pirouettes, frappe`s, and tendus in each other's mouths at near synchronicity. He could feel Sam's heart beating faster, the sound of which threatened deafness, and his breath getting heavy as it sucked every ounce of oxygen from the air, and he knew that now was the time. Quickly pulling away, he took in all that Sam was on the outside one last time before discovering everything he had to offer on the inside; his fiery red hair that seemed so wild and tame at once, impossibly green eyes that were about to be truly opened for the first time, and his clavicle. Sam had a magnificent clavicle, the line of which perfectly framed his neck. His beautiful, delicious neck.

With a forceful lunge, Antonio sunk his teeth into Sam's pulsating neck and drank with a hunger he had never felt before. And as he drank, Sam moaned, louder and louder he moaned, from both the pleasure and the pain. Blood started to drip from the wound, even though his mouth was still firmly upon it, flowing between his lips and down Sam's neck, onto the shoulder of his leather jacket where small puddles began to form before sliding like tiny red waterfalls to the wet pavement below. All those years of practice catching cum like a porn star and he couldn't handle the sheer amount Sam's body gave with abandon.

Sam began twitching.

Antonio stopped.

Something was wrong.

It wasn't supposed to happen like this.

"Sam! Sam, I need you to stay with me!" Antonio screamed as he held him in one hand, slitting his other wrist with his sharp, blood-tinged fangs. "Drink, Sam! You must drink quickly. SAM!!!"

But it was too late. Sam twitched his last twitch then simply fell over like a rag doll, limp and lifeless.

"Sam! Sam! SAM!!!" Antonio screamed over and over to no avail.

His one and only love was dead, and by his own hands.

Thunder clapped above, startling him enough to take his sorrowful gaze away from his beloved Sam long enough to notice that it was followed by that familiar drumming beat of heavy rain which began washing away the blood from his beautiful punctured neck.

Antonio stared at Sam.

His eyes closed. His lips slightly grinning. His face looked peaceful.

He's only sleeping, Antonio told himself, carrying him over to the grassy area of a nearby field just off the road.

As he carried Sam, the wind began to pick up once more, taking with it those restless leaves and once again allowing them to dance. Only this time the dance wasn't as poetic, it was sharp and punctuated. The wind vengeful and angry now, slinging the raindrops all over him like a spray of bullets. Fighting through the onslaught of stormy weather to find a quiet resting place for his love, he could hear the cracking of branches from the surrounding forest, but knew he had to keep going, no matter the cost. His feet felt like they were sinking into the ground with every step he took, the rain bullets not relenting their efforts, the wind nearly knocking him over at each move, all conspiring against him because of what he did. And why shouldn't they? He was a monster! But couldn't they at least wait to batter him down until he laid his Sam to rest?

A nook at the edge of the tree line, safe from most of the unforgiving weather's warpath, was where he finally placed Sam down, softly, taking care not to disturb his slumber. Looking upon Sam's face, he gently brushed his sticky hair out of his eyes, caressing his cheek, and smiling at him and all that he was just before the wind kicked up a fallen branch and plunged it into Antonio's back and through his beatless heart.

CHAPTER 3

Confession

Just as Antonio stepped out of his home, readying himself for a jaunt downtown to the back alley of the butcher shop for dinner, someone caught his attention. He immediately recognized Brendon, the awkward chubby neighbor kid who'd grown into a delectable young man. Tall. Thin. But not too thin. Dark hair. Brown eyes. Three freckles on his nose that looked like Hawaiian Islands and made him want to vacation on his face. The world around him was obsessed over gays twinning. How boring. He wanted someone just a little different from him, but also enjoyed the fantasy of finding someone like Brendon, the son of a DILF who was just as fuckable.

Their eyes met and time stopped.

"What power is this?" Antonio whispered as the air around him remained motionless.

Brendon walked toward him; his movements disturbing the quiet, oddly warm autumn night. Antonio was held captive to the seductive way the boy casually strolled, effortlessly flexing his muscles barely hidden beneath the tight t-shirt and tight pants that left nothing to the imagination about the trouser snake trapped inside. Was there underwear? It didn't look like it as Antonio traced the lines.

"Me," Brendon whispered back, continuing to close the gap between them.

"Are you trying to seduce me, Mr. Hollins?" Antonio asked bluntly.

"That depends, Antonio. Is it working?" Brendon asked, the half-smile his face sported almost causing Antonio to spontaneously orgasm.

Is it working? Is it working? Good night, man! You don't have to try and it would work on me, you delicious creature! Antonio thought, assuming his thoughts to be private.

"I may have gone overboard then. I was just hoping for a date," Brendon confessed, though the dimple carved into his right cheek said otherwise.

The world around them was still in a pause. In between breaths. Not quite holding it in, but not quite ready to let it out.

Edging.

Waiting.

"Wait, what do you mean about going overboard?" Antonio asked, suddenly aware of the unsaid words in his head that preceded the response in question.

I mean I probably should have just asked, not stopped the world to melt with you, Brendon's voice said in Antonio's head, causing him to shudder and shiver and tingle in places he'd forgotten about since...

"Do I want to know?" Antonio asked.

"Depends on if you think witches should be burned at the stake?" Brendon asked, cocked eyebrow causing Antonio's own cock to stiffen.

Brendon noticed.

"Well that depends on if you think vampires should be burned and/or staked?" Antonio asked, trying to cock his own eyebrow, but finding the task difficult to manage, and praying to his own personal Jesus that he didn't look like a stroke victim as he stood in front of a hot fellow local guy with a dimple he'd die for.

"Very few people in this world deserve to die," Brendon said stoically, smile fading into the ether. "I'm sorry, Antonio. I… I… I really should have thought this through."

"Thought what through?"

"Trying to make an us."

"You don't have to try."

The silence between them was deafening, especially with the absence of movement. A raven caught his attention; mid-flight, wings spread, mouth open, waiting for time to start back up. For now, it just hung there in media-res, waiting to be resurrected.

"I pulled that branch out of your heart the night Sam died."

The night burst alive, assaulting Antonio's senses with the suddenness. Brendon was gone, vanished as the world breathed in and out once more. Was he an illusion? Did Antonio imagine the encounter with him? The conversation? The hotness the neighbor boy had become now that he was a man? He was well aware of hunger hallucinations, but a twelve-hour fast was nothing. Those usually took months of abstinence, and if anything, Antonio could barely make it a couple days before the urges took over his train of thought, derailing any previous plans in favor of docking at the red liquid district, just where he was heading before Brendon stopped him in his tracks.

"Fucker never answered my question," Antonio said.

"The usual?" the butcher asked from the backdoor of his shop, the harsh fluorescent light seeping from inside doing his complexion no favors.

The fact that the butcher, a man Antonio had been getting his dietary rations from for over a decade, knew his preference for vegetarian fed pig's blood still amazed him. The whole veggie thing may not have been fair to the pigs as they're omnivores, but it was the closest his condition could offer his vegan sensibilities. Well, that and grass-fed beef blood. However, he preferred the gentle sweetness pig's blood had over the sharp bite of beef. He was also amazed that thirteen years later he had never asked the butcher his name and suddenly felt like an asshole. Here there was a man who had been servicing his needs for years and knew his name and his tastes and his timing and the fact that he was a vampire, but he knew nothing of the butcher other than his outward appearance that had changed drastically over time, growing more gaunt and pale and sickly and suddenly he wondered if cancer had riddled his aging body as he sniffed and took in an off odor about him or if this was just the normal aging process he was so far removed from. The man looked tired as he waited for Antonio's reply that, while in Antonio's head seemed like eons had passed since posing the question as it replayed—"The usual?"—nanoseconds at best had sped by.

"That would be great," Antonio told the butcher, who smiled slightly before disappearing as the door closed.

A minute later, the butcher came back with a plastic bag holding two quart-sized plastic containers and handed them to Antonio. As Antonio slipped a twenty to the butcher, the butcher told him, "No charge today, Antonio."

"Are you sure?" Antonio asked, the bill dangling from his fingertips like a passive smoker who only fashionably dons a cigarette while drinking with casual acquaintances.

"I am."

"I must ask why? I mean, you're running a business after all."

"True. But one day I may need a favor and I want to make sure you owe me one."

Fire raged in Antonio as the words escaped the butcher's mouth. A threat? Blackmail? *Who does he think he is, weak old man?*

"That came out wrong."

"How so?"

"I mean I only want to stay in your favor in case…"

"In case you need something I can offer?"

Though the butcher had a smile on his face, his eyes looked as if a sadness had flooded them. Again, the lighting didn't help his case. "Yes."

Antonio gave the man the twenty and said, "You have my word. No need to quid pro quo."

"Thank you. See you Tuesday, then?"

"Tuesday."

The door closed. Antonio suddenly realized the full intent of the butcher's cryptic proposal. He also understood all too well the vast emptiness of it as well.

A few nights later, Brendon walked from his car into the movie theater where he bought a ticket to *Kill Your Darlings*. Antonio followed, stealthily sitting in the very back row where he watched him eat popcorn and suck down soda like a pro, ignoring Daniel Radcliffe's portrayal of Allen Ginsberg, even when he was busy getting ass-fucked by some creepy older guy. The smell of butter and sweat filled the theater. And by butter, that fake shit barely worth the title. Admittedly, the scent was still intoxicating. Exhilarating, even. It was enough to make Antonio wish he could puke, but alas, the gag reflex he long prayed would go away finally did after becoming a vampire, and with it the ability to purge. If he wanted to empty the contents of his stomach, he'd have to rip a hole and pull it all out with his bare hands. True, he would heal soon enough, but still, ew. He was quite disturbed that, as Brendon left, he had to pick up all the unpopped kernels some jackass sitting in front of him kept launching behind her shoulders, landing near Antonio's feet and effectively blocking him from following the neighbor boy.

Brendon left the theater in his black late 1990s model poor-excuse-for-a pickup truck to meet up with his childhood friend Darryl at Ravenwood Bar & Grill for pool and beer and chitchat. Antonio watched from outside as he laughed and drank and lost two games before they called it a night an hour-and-a-half later, hugging each other in a way that Antonio wasn't quite sure was platonic or if there may have been a previous romance between the two which made him irrationally jealous and angry and want to rip the black man's throat out. But he didn't.

Brendon drove home where he saw through the front bay window that his half-brother Chad and Chad's husband Joel were visiting, and was about to go in the house to say hello, but stopped at the front door, hand on the knob, and said, "Antonio, I don't know why you're being so coy. Just fucking talk to me and stop being a creepy stalker."

But how? Antonio was certain he kept in the shadows and out of view. Fly on the wall. Inconspicuous. But there Brendon was, making the accusation that he was following him around town, which, albeit, he was. Still, Antonio couldn't help but wonder just what gave him away.

"Um…"

"I'm a witch, dumbass. I can sense you," Brendon said to the door as if looking at Antonio would cause him to spontaneously combust.

"Well, shit. I keep forgetting that little piece of trivia about you," Antonio said, his voice on the verge of laughter strangled by a noose.

"It's not little."

Brendon turned around, hand still lingering on the doorknob as if it was glued stuck, and smiled. It took every ounce of restraint Antonio could muster not to run up to the boy, rip off his clothes, and fuck him till the sun weakened him to invisibility and made him retreat back into his house until the sun went down and he could keep going, continuing until he drained him completely. But he didn't. Instead, Brendon casually strolled over the front lawn, brushed the inside of his hand over Antonio's cheek before sliding it behind his head and pulling him in for a kiss. Not aggressive or delicate, but passionate and meaningful and worthy of poetry and prose and diamonds, gold, pearls, and all the jewels of Agrabah. Oh Allah! Aladdin is so the most fuckable Disney character ever. Followed closely by Prince Eric, of course.

All Antonio could see when Brendon pulled away were the billions of stars dancing in the sky over his head. All he could feel were the sparks of a thousand suns bursting into existence. All he could taste were the lingering remnants of Black Butte Porter and Cherry ChapStick. And as he fell backwards onto the pavement of the street named after a long dead myth of a vampire who killed his entire tribe (save his father), all he could say was, "Whoah." It was all very Keanu Reeves circa 1999.

"As much as I'd love to continue, uh, this? My brother's apparently visiting and I haven't seen him in almost a year," Brendon told Antonio as he bent over him, fingers playfully intertwined with his.

Looking up at the stars, unwilling to look Brendon in the eyes, Antonio whispered forcefully, "I understand. I haven't seen my own family since…."

The emptiness around him was unavoidable. His words, the meaning behind the words, spoke volumes that needed no audibly articulated metaphysically historical representations to fulfill. There they were, lingering in space, floating in the windless night into the oblivion that would eventually gobble it up like a fat man's pork rinds, which made Antonio crave the delectableness of crispy pig skin like a celibate Catholic priest craved sex with the alter boys, but he would never be able to enjoy the indulgent snack he occasionally used to ignore his veganism in order to partake the same way as his bodily needs required blood to survive. Turning his gaze towards the boy he was passionately beginning to realize how much he wanted, craved, needed to have in his life, his body, to fulfill yet another requirement, he allowed a nearly imperceptible smile to escape his lips. The brown eyed boy with a gym-bunny body and dimples to die for and heart of pure heaven smiled back at him, causing his being to melt into the pavement and become one with the oil slick left behind from a recently parked little blue sedan that had seen its last days only weeks before when a tow truck carried it off to the graveyard.

"If you want, I can come over after they leave?" Brendon told Antonio with a hint of suggestiveness towards his intentions as his eyes peeled back layers of clothing to imagine a glimpse of what lay beneath, fingers still linked as if he was afraid letting go would break their connection.

"I will count the seconds," Antonio promised before dropping his gaze and laughing at his choice of words. "Wow, that sounds desperate."

But instead of mockery, Brendon responded with another kiss, another smile, and a reassuring glance that he would keep his word before he walked back to his house and disappeared inside where overjoyed shouts of his name graced the air before the door slammed shut, leaving Antonio outside by his lonesome with nothing more than his anticipating thoughts. Taking his time to stand, he looked into the window one last time before making his way home where he was met with menacing glares from two quite aged dogs, as if they were warning him about what they would do should he treat their human improperly. He assured them he had no ill intentions, but still, they appeared to have reservations.

"Fine, puppies, I'm going home," he said aloud before strolling a couple houses away toward his own dwelling where he realized how dirty his home was and immediately began the process of dusting, removing the layer of filth from everything he held dear. No matter how many times he cleaned off every object, inside every nook, cranny, and ledge, it never felt clean enough. As a human, he was a neat freak. As a vampire, his OCD had become beyond tolerable. The fact that he wiped the house down earlier that afternoon before following Brendon on his adventures never crossed his mind. The fact that Brendon would be in his home and sharing his bed and making sweet sweet love to him or, at the very least, fucking his brains out, was forefront.

Then a bag of pork rinds, his favorite ones back in his human days from a little taquería in Portland that fried and bagged the chicharrones fresh daily, smacked him in the face as he Swiffered the numerous books gracing his shelves. Did they fall from the sky? Manna from heaven? Hidden away for a rainy day in case the need arose? The smell was intoxicating. He let the Swiffer duster drop to the floor, scattering the clinging remnants across the hardwood floor and reached for the bag to rip it open.

He sniffed.

Heaven.

Pure piggy paradise.

"Surely just one taste would not be detrimental to my system?" he assured himself, a lie at best, he thought.

But the bag begged his tongue to reap the pleasantries inside, taste their salty seasoned dusting, crunch down on the thick meaty byproduct, and orally orgasm as the whole thing slithered down his throat. He expected rejection. To his surprise, his body asked for more. More and more and more until the bag was empty and he was left pathetically licking its insides, lapping up every last salty goodness like the greedy whore he was.

I see you liked that, Brendon's voice said in his head, seducing him effortlessly yet again, making him wonder how he never realized the potential in somebody so close, so available, so willing.

More than you'll ever know, Antonio told him back, hoping the message was received, not fully understanding this whole psychic connection or how it worked or why or really anything Wiccan or at the very least something Dionne Warwick would endorse in the early nineties. *Now I am waiting for my body to tell me how much it hates me for devouring all that deliciousness.*

You really don't understand what you are capable of, do you?

The question sounded like an accusation, but the realization that Antonio did not understand a great many things about his vampirism, the virus that gave new life to his dying body so many years ago, struck him as fanciful. He stood in awe over his indignation. He could feign ignorance, but the reality was that he never bothered to explore outside the tired stereotypical food his kind was supposed to require thanks to shitty books and movies and adaptations of shitty books into shitty movies. The kind his coven perpetuated with impunity. Admittedly, he found blood to be utterly delicious, much to his disgust.

Now I want you *in my mouth*, Antonio said bluntly, forgetting it wasn't just a casual thought to himself, but an actual transmission that made him wish he'd catch fire and have his ashes scamper away quietly.

Fuck me, Brendon's voice said.

Or that, Antonio thought back playfully, forgetting his previous thoughts of death.

There was no answer, which made Antonio furiously curious, fretting about his house in search of the boy, hoping to find him sprawled out naked across his bed and begging to be ravaged savagely before cuddling like an old married couple post-coitus. Alas, his search was in vain.

My sisters just showed up. Goddammit, it's ten o-clock! Who the hell decides to visit their parents at ten at night? Brendon's decidedly irritated voice pounded through Antonio's head like a herd of water buffalo.

Be grateful for your family, Brendon, Antonio thought to the boy, hoping it came across as genuine and not with an air of disappointment.

I am, but it feels like they are purposefully blue-balling me.

I can wait.

Thank you, but I don't know if I can.

Why?

Because I want you. I don't mean like a piece of meat, though I bet you'd taste delicious, but, like, I want to be with you more than I've ever wanted to be with another person, and I know how ridiculous that sounds, especially coming from me, you know, that fat kid you watched grow up two houses down from yours, but, I don't know, I can't explain why I have always felt a connection to you. It's like you are the missing piece to the puzzle that makes me whole. Fuck. Don't freak out on me because I just unleashed all that shit on you like diarrhea.

The sheer amount of time it took Antonio to process all that had been divulged in that thought nearly caused his brain to collapse into a puddle of goo.

"Forgive me father, for I have sinned," Antonio said through the dark mesh screen.

"Confess and be cleansed," a calm voice answered.

"I will never be clean."

CHAPTER 4

Principles of Lust

Forgetting to eat for a day is one thing. Forgetting to eat for a week and a half because of a one-track mind focused on seducing the neighbor kid is another. However, there Antonio sat on his sleek black leather living room sofa waiting for Brendon to enter his home, his bed, his life. His lustful thoughts stirred in the pressure cooker of his mind, but any minute the lid would blow and the contents spew out like in *The Exorcist*. Pretty freaky shit, yo.

Quarter mile away, maybe a little less, a jogger cut his shin. The smell brought him out of his trance, back into the real world, and made him forget about never drinking human blood again. The fairy he ripped apart was a fluke, but this? It was about as intoxicating as the time he was blowing a guy in the restroom stall during gym class and three others all gave him the most unforgettable bukkake of his life while he smiled like a glazed donut. He had no choice. He had to find the source of the blood and suck it dry.

The couch looked lonesome after he got up, the impression of his ass still firmly in place. How long had he been sitting there? Hours?

Days? Time got away from him. Again. A sweet-scented wind assaulted his face as he opened the door, daylight flooding his dark house, casting shadows that danced along the crevices like fire sprites. He didn't bother staying to watch them die as he slammed the door and bolted towards the jogger in the woods.

Something familiar about the smell tickled his brain, but didn't register as to why until he came face to face with the jogger and collapsed onto a log in a hollow to cry. Bloodstained tears raced down his face, puddling in his lap.

The jogger walked right up to him despite his invisibility, and said, "I thought this would get your attention. Why are you ignoring me?"

Attention? Ignoring? Who was this man?

"Antonio, you're delirious," the voice said like it was a million miles away as his leg plopped into his lap, the cut still freshly dripping. "Drink."

The wound looked angry. The blood looked delicious. Antonio finally broke his silence.

"I can't. I'll kill you," Antonio said with conflicting conviction, the blood tempting him like a Bel Ami porno. Lukas, Dano, Johan, hell, the whole goddamned gang of barely legal boy meat with insatiable appetites.

"You won't. I can stop you."

"You can't. You don't know."

"I've already got a spell at the ready to knock you out if you lose control. I don't even need to be conscience for it to work."

"Why?"

"You know why."

"I... I..." but Antonio couldn't find the words. Not because of the parched tongue grating against the roof of his mouth like sandpaper or the self-imposed fasting that made him quite ill, but because he did not feel deserving of the offer.

Brendon shoved his wound against Antonio's lip and said forcefully, "Suck on it."

And he did.

As Antonio drank, he felt his strength beginning to return. The wound, though small and decidedly not of the major artery variety, but merely a capillary that barely eked out a dribble at a time, was surprisingly fulfilling. Perhaps, Antonio figured, it was due to his ten-day abstention, diminishing his bodily needs from quarts to teaspoons. He continued to drink, forgetting about who it was he was sucking momentarily before pulling off the wound, pushing the leg off his crotch, getting up off the log, and planting his mouth firmly against Brendon's lips and began throat-fucking him with his tongue. Brendon returned his tongue in response, not so much like battling for supremacy, but definitely not delicately.

Reaching for the waistband of Brendon's shorts, Antonio swiftly slid them down as he went down and drank in the scent of his penis before swallowing it. For some reason, he half expected Brendon to protest the abruptness, but instead felt Brendon's hands grab the back of his head despite the whole invisible factor. Then again, his head was obviously located in front of the boy's penis, the delicious, hard, eight inches of man meat dripping with pre-cum and threatening release any second until Brendon's grip tightened around his ears as he came in Antonio's mouth with several forceful lunges.

The sweet.

The salty.

The flow.

Antonio held it in his mouth, reluctantly pulling away as his tongue licked the last drop off, and just as he was about to swallow,

Brendon forced his tongue inside his mouth and greedily took most of it back. Part of Antonio felt furious at this, and another part felt turned on, but before any part could react, Brendon shoved him back down to his still throbbing dick, and somehow with a look, told Antonio to keep sucking.

Could this be? Antonio thought, staring up into the light brown eyes that reminded him of chestnuts while the boys own nuts butted against his chin. Before the question could be answered, his penis was in Antonio's mouth, thrusting back and forth, over and over, while Brendon used his ears like handles, his chin like a paddle as his balls slapped back and forth.

Brendon's thrusts became faster, and soon he was cumming again, somehow even harder, bigger than the first blasts. Still, the boy kept thrusting long after, his penis never wavering.

Antonio had to pull away to say, "I'm keeping this one," and swallowed.

Brendon smiled. "Now fuck me."

"Here? Now?" Antonio asked.

Brendon turned around. "Yes."

"But…"

"The next words out of your mouth better be 'it's about damn time' or so help me God I will be sorely disappointed."

It was true. Antonio had wanted this for so long. Two weeks. But like this? The setting seemed wrong to him. But why? Would a bed be more appropriate for this carnal hunger that begged to be satiated? What could be more natural than nature? And here, with a child of nature, a witch, and child of the unnatural world, combining to become one, succumbing to the rules of attraction. He easily slid into Brendon's ass and began.

"Oh, gawd!" Brendon shouted, either forgetting that they were fairly close to homes with prying ears or not caring if anyone heard his cries of ecstasy.

The leaves that were left swirled. The cold air began burning his face with fiery rage. The ground enveloped his feet and sky swallowed his head and before he knew it, his whole world began violently shaking while galaxies danced inside his eyes while the sun sprinkled like glitter around him before he came with a low guttural growl that crescendoed into an, "I love you."

"Don't stop! Oh gawd, don't stop!" Brendon begged.

"As you wish," Antonio said, picking up the pace once again without waiting for the world to regain order.

"Yes, please stop," a woman's voice said.

"Oh, gawd," Brendon said, snorting quietly before laughing.

"Seriously, Brendon? On the jogging trail behind Mom and Dad's house? And with a vampire? I mean, he's super hot, but really?" the woman asked rapid-fire.

As Brendon pulled his pants up, the awkward boner still ever-present despite being caught, he said, "I hate you, Sheree."

"Wait, your sister can see me during daylight?" Antonio asked Brendon quietly, whispering into his ear before sneaking in a gentle nibble of his lobe.

"Yes, she's been unmagicked," Brendon said matter-of-factly.

"What the fuck does that even mean?" Antonio asked, face perplexed as he stuffed his penis back into his black jeans painted with blood, spit, and a couple dribbles of missed cum.

"It means I can see you, sexy," Sheree said, side-smile full of mischief. "And as hot as I think two guys fucking is, not so much when one is my little brother and no amount of bleach or bricking will claw that vision out of my mind. Blech!"

"Whatever. You'll just replace my face with Jeff's," Brendon teased as he walked towards her, dragging Antonio by his invisible hand that only Sheree could see.

I have no idea what is going on, Antonio thought.

Sorry about the postponement of our fuck session, but I guarantee it is not over, Brendon said via the Psychic Friends Network.

You've already blown two loads.

I'm not done. And neither are you.

"True. But still, you've got Dad's body. Not sure what kind of magic that took," Sheree said bluntly.

"Of the genetic variety," Brendon said.

"Who is this Jeff?" Antonio asked.

"Her dead boyfriend," Brendon told him.

"Oh, I'm so sorry," Antonio said.

"Don't be. I just have to wait a few more years," Sheree said jokingly.

"Huh?"

"Oh, her dead boyfriend came back a while ago. He's our nephew now. Just go with it," Brendon said nonchalantly.

"Creeper," Antonio said playfully as he gave Sheree a wink.

She winked back. "It's not really a thing. Just something he teases me about. Easier to play it off as hope than think about what could've been."

"Still a creeper," Antonio said, realizing his own creepiness in underage boys, or one boy.

Sheree just smiled, shaking her head, knowing Antonio would never understand the relationship she had with Brendon went beyond just siblings. She owed him her life. Several times over.

Brendon refused to let go of Antonio's hand as they walked, and Antonio didn't understand why. Was he afraid of letting go? Did he think

Antonio would be just another fuck and dump? Wasn't he there for the earth-shattering blissfulness? Didn't he feel the connection? He had to… right?

Calm your tits, Ant!

How do…?

I can read your mind. Yes, there are a million reasons that is a violation of privacy and blah blah blah bullshitty bullshit blah, but seriously, man, I've never ever ever felt anything that powerful before.

Ha! My Glock packs quite the powerful cartridge unload.

No, not just that. I mean the swirl, swallow, galaxy, glitter becoming one cliché.

"Anyway, Mom wanted me to tell you that Rex and Deschutes pooped in the house. Clean it up," Sheree said.

Brendon's face reddened. "You interrupted me losing my virginity to tell me my dogs shit in the house?"

"Uh, you're a virgin?" Sheree asked, sounding more like an accusation.

"Well, not anymore," Brendon told her, stopping just outside the Hollins's backyard that butted up against the forest.

"Fuck, I'm the worst sister ever, and totally deserved the Jeff thing" Sheree said as she pulled Brendon in for a hug. As she did, she gave Antonio a peck on the cheek and forcefully told him, "Break his heart and I'll kick your ass."

Sheree pushed away from the hug, her eyes never leaving Antonio's. Brendon turned towards his face's general direction and half-smiled.

"Don't listen to her," Brendon told Antonio.

Don't listen? Don't listen? Good God! I've taken something precious from you and you want me to not listen?! I'm a monster!

You're not a monster.

I am!

I wanted it. I wanted you. No, I want you.

You… you…?

"Tell me I'm yours," Brendon said out loud with authority.

"You…?"

"Tell me!" Brendon shouted demandingly, somehow void of anger, just sheer forceful pleading.

Do I really want this? Of course, I want this! I've wanted this for so long. Did I even tell him I love him? I did, didn't I? Oh my gawd, after I shoved my demon seed up his ass, I said the words. What kind of idiot does that? Waits until after orgasming to pledge their love? Meaningless words! So easy to say, and yet so difficult to articulate. Fucking kangaroos, you're listening to my inner dialogue, aren't you?

Silence.

Brendon waited for an answer. Sheree looked impatient and distraught and then suddenly in her own little world as she seemed to spot something in the distance, which, as Antonio struggled with his inner demons he heard the doe and soon-to-be-on-its-own fawn nibbling on the dwindling fall foliage that hadn't died off despite the late November date.

"I need you to see me, to be able to look me in the eyes before I say the words," Antonio said to the ground that made him stop because a scattering of sunflower seeds from a nearby feeder had been blown away by the wind, trapping him in place until he could pick them all up. It took every fiber of his being to not let go of the boy's hand and get to work.

Brendon's head fell to the ground as well, immediately spotting the seeds. "Seriously?"

"Yes," Antonio said.

"I know, but seriously? Sheree, help me pick these seeds up off the ground so Antonio can move," Brendon asked, knowing it wasn't the right time to inform Antonio he had the power to ignore them.

"Oh, so the mystery man does have a name after all?" Sheree said slyly. "Wait, you mean, like, our neighbor?"

Though it may have come off better when she was a teenager instead of the thirty-year-old woman still living at home with her parents (or more accurately, back home), Antonio felt this person was good. Kind. Mean girl on the outside, yes, but harmless. The type of person who would give up her life if it meant saving yours. The type of person you want to take home to Mother. The type of person whose one true love died, was reborn, and somehow has chosen to move on despite the possibility of resuming once he's of age. The type of person who could pick up seeds just about as fast as he, and though he felt a jolt of pain letting go of Brendon's hand, he joined the woman in collecting.

"Thank you, señora," Antonio said, pocketing the seeds.

"I'm not married," Sheree told him.

"You ain't no virgin either, honey, therefore, señora," Antonio said, one eye cocked while his voice was full of cockiness and lined with cock juice.

That line punched Sheree in the gut. It was true she wasn't a virgin, but little did Antonio know that the reason why was beyond her control. Not that she hadn't dated and fucked others since then, but the prospect, the pain, the punishment for things beyond her control never left. The uneasy look in Brendon's eye told him that was a total dick maneuver.

"I apologize, Sheree," Antonio said, putting a hand on her shoulder. "That was uncalled for."

The hurt in her eyes was more than he could handle, so he looked away.

"I'm fine, just, you know, personal shit," Sheree said quietly, faking a smile that even a blind man could notice wasn't genuine. "That and my fiancé and I broke it off about a month ago, so really shitty timing."

The dying sun peeked through the quickly forming clouds one last time before being swallowed up. Antonio hoped that would be enough to shed his invisibility cloak, but alas, the clouds were white and fluffy and still radiated what little light the setting sun had to offer. Antonio reached over and took Brendon's hand in his own, suddenly forgetting where he was and who was watching as he took in the young man's scent.

"Down, tiger," Brendon told him through chuckles.

"I'm going in. You're welcome to join us, so long as, you know, you don't eat us all," Sheree teased.

"All?" Antonio asked.

"She means herself and my mom and dad and sister and sister-in-law and brother and brother-in-law and brother's mother and brother-in-law's father and brother and brother-in-law's sister. Oh, Jesus. My family is a mess," Brendon admitted.

"I am so confused."

"Oh, you don't even know," Brendon said. "Shall we?"

"But they won't see me!" Antonio said, stating the obvious.

"Won't that be better? That way you can judge them all and only Sheree will know."

"And I won't say nothing. Promise. Judge all you want, Antonio," Sheree admitted. "Besides! After the sun goes down, we can play games! Ooh! Ooh! Queers against straights! Well, straight-ishes. Our numbers are equal now!" Sheree jumped up and down like a little schoolgirl who just won the spelling bee. Shut up, it's a thing.

CHAPTER 5

Is This Love?

Could I really be falling in love? Again? For the first time?

Antonio wasn't quite sure what to make of the thoughts swimming in his head, confusing his emotional state that swirled somewhere between bliss and suicide.

Love.

Death.

Sam.

Brendon.

Was the new boy bound to suffer the same fate as the old? The notion wrecked him. Brendon had advantages Sam never did. Brendon knew who he was and what he wanted, but so did Sam, right? But Sam did not have the parts to make him whole and should the virus have taken hold instead of reacted poorly, though admittedly Antonio had to take most of the blame, refusing to consult an older, wiser vampire on the art of sire. Eventually Sam would have been miserable. Not at first. Maybe not even after years and years, but at some point, the disappointment over not becoming his true self had to surface. But Brendon was different. He already had the right parts... oh, gawd did he ever! He also had, at least never vocalized or hinted at, any inclination whatsoever of becoming one of the undead. He was perfectly comfortable as himself.

But what will I do as he ages and withers and dies? I've already taken his precious virginity, could I really be selfish enough to take his life as it is? Oh! but that ass that dick that heart that soul that delicious beautiful pure soul. No. he could never truly love me back. I am a monster! A demon! An aberration whose only solace will come by my true death! But my Brendon. My sweet Brendon, who years ago saved me when he was just a kid by taking the tree branch God struck me with after murdering my Sam. Murderer! What wretched soullessness have I become?

"Stop torturing yourself," a voice said in the distance, trying to navigate through the floodgate of his thoughts so far offshore.

It was the boy. The beautiful boy. Antonio swam back to shore.

"Brendon!"

His call was met with a kiss. Light. Airy. Careful and daring all at once.

"I am so sorry about earlier," Brendon told him.

"You are sorry? I stole something you will never get back!"

"Hehe, you took nothing I wasn't ready to lose for years. Besides, for you, I was more than ready to give."

"But why? I have to know. Tell me!" Antonio cried, blood tears streaming down his face.

"Because I love you. I've always loved you."

A stake to the heart.

Bon Jovi flooded his brain.

The branch was back, slicing his insides that should have killed him forever but didn't. All because a thirteen-year-old kid pulled it out of his unconscious and dying carcass on a dark and stormy night filled with more clichés than he could count.

"How could you love me?" Antonio begged.

"If I knew how love worked, trust me, I'd let you in on that shit."

Clutching the space where his heart used to be, Antonio silently pleaded. Brendon knew what was burning through him. Should he tell? Should he lie? Why lie when the truth is not so awful?

"I don't exactly know how, but when that branch struck you that night, I... I..." Brendon hesitated, but didn't exactly know why. "Don't laugh, but I felt it."

"You felt it?" Antonio asked for clarification.

"I felt it like it impaled me," Brendon admitted, fist pounding his chest.

"You... you did?"

"Yes."

"I don't... are you fucking with me?"

"Not yet." Brendon winked.

"Then, what, I, well huh."

"Yeah, huh."

Silence.

"Part of me wonders if there is a connection between us that transcends logic," Brendon said, breaking the reticence.

"What does the other part wonder?" Antonio asked, expecting something sexual.

"If my great-great-great-grandpa set me up with you," Brendon revealed.

Antonio looked floored. "I'm afraid I have more questions with each answer."

"Tell me about it! One minute I'm playing *Super Samurai Slugs* and the next I'm pulling a hunk of maple out of your chest."

"But you were so young!"

"Oh, I didn't pull it out with my bare hands. I carefully extracted it with my powers. Being a witch has its advantages, the least of which is not having to worry about ruining my well-manicured nails." Brendon busted up laughing, shaking the house. "I'm sorry! I'm gay, but not that gay!"

Antonio didn't know if he should laugh or cry or both as Brendon crawled on top of him, kissing him fervently. Brendon pulled away, got up, took him by the hand as they made their way to Antonio's bed. They scarcely left it for a week like strict Catholic newlyweds doing the Lord's work.

"Cerveza," Antonio ordered, questioning the authenticity of the bar's decor as a velvet painting of Mexican Elvis caught his eye. Or was it a matador? The harsh glow of amber-covered fluorescent lighting cast a depressing shadow over the figure's face no matter who he was supposed to represent.

"Huh? What's that?" the bartender asked.

He was paler than vanilla ice cream and looked just as bland. His uniform beyond racially offensive, complete with garish satin fringes that would cause Tammy Faye Bakker to go into conniptions and cry her fake little eyelashes off while her mascara raced down her cheeks like creeks.

Shit. Should've guessed Los Rainbow Hermanos was an old white guy's interpretation of a latin gay bar. "Uh, beer?"

"We've got Coor's on tap," the bartender said, tapping the tap to the beat of Gloria Estafan singing Miami Sound Machine's "Conga" as it blared from tinny speakers that made her sound as fake and synthesized as the rest of the bar.

"Uck. Anything else?"

"Coor's Light!" the pale boy said, beaming like sunshine.

"You've got to be kidding me."

"Nope. It's super popular."

"For white people."

"You should try it."

"No thanks." *Jesus, get me out of here!* Antonio said in his head towards the blond blue-eyed statue bleeding his mother-loving heart out just to his right.

Jesus, all six inches of plastic and paint, however, had no response.

"We don't usually get any exotics like you here," the bartender blurted out.

Exotics? EXOTICS?! "I'm like a fourth generation Washingtonian, ass clown," Antonio said as he stood up off the stool, nearly toppling it over as it pushed back.

"Awkward."

"Yeah."

"So, I take it the stockroom is out of the question?"

Well son of a bitch. Looks like I'm gettin' laid tonight after all.

Years later and Los Rainbow Hermanos had changed hands about a dozen times, but the bland twink he fucked on top of a case of gallon sized cans of nacho cheese sauce and who squealed and cried like a little girl as he came still worked behind the counter, suddenly sagging and balding and bulging around his midsection. Fourteen additional years did the boy no favors, not that he had much going for him to begin with. Poor soul. He still had the seductive stockroom twinkle in his eye as he wedged a thin lime slice into a bottle of Corona and handed it to a kid who obviously either had a fake ID or slipped the bouncer a large bill and didn't notice the unsaid offer that twinkle stood for.

"I see you finally got better beer," Antonio said.

He nodded. "I see you haven't changed a bit. Fucker."

"Still bitter I never called you? Pretty sure we both knew that was a one-time deal."

"Pretty sure I've never had better sex since. You've ruined me."

"Sorry."

"You should be. People like me don't usually get people like you. Wanna beer?"

"Nah. Maybe. Sure."

"Coor's Light?" His smirk that fiddled into a giggle clued Antonio in to his factitiousness.

"That Corona looks fine."

"Lime?"

"Duh."

The balding bartender squeezed a little of the wedge into the bottle, a small amount dribbling down the side where his hands grasped, stinging a paper cut he'd gotten earlier while opening another case of overly processed mild nacho cheese-like-food-product. He cringed as the bottle slid towards Antonio, sucking his finger as he turned around.

Antonio pushed the lime wedge into the bottle and watched the bubbles rise to the top. He could see someone approaching him through the amber lens his Corona offered.

An overly processed drag queen squeezed into a lime green dress pushed past Antonio, sat on the stool next to him, rubbed her greasy fingers complete with Lee Press On nails (which, Six-Inch Plastic Painted Jesus, they still make that shit?) along his upper thigh, and announced in a husky voice reminiscent of Kathleen Turner, "You ever fucked a real woman before?"

Antonio didn't even flinch, just casually took a swig of beer, slowly set it down on the counter, and asked back, "Have you?"

"Honey, does this look like it's made for a woman?"

"Honey, does this?" Antonio asked, using his free hand to gesture his body like Vanna White.

She burst out laughing so hard Antonio prayed to the plastic Jesus just to his left now to keep her dress firmly in place. A few seams busted and he prepared himself to be blinded for life over the impending disaster about to unfold before him. Alas, Plastic Jesus came through. Thanks, Plastic Jesus. Plesus.

"Well this queen is on in five. After the show, stud?" she asked, her plump lips obviously filled with collagen, and her makeup impeccably on point, especially the bright red lipstick covering those luscious lips.

"Sorry, Honey. Taken," Antonio said as Brendon walked through the door.

The drag queen followed Antonio's gaze and said, "Damn, boy! I just came in my panties lookin' at that fine thing!"

"Calm your tits, Honey. Or don't. He's all mine."

"Fucker," the bartender said under his breath as Brendon saddled into the stool on the other side of Antonio before planting a kiss.

"Hey," Brendon said.

"Hey," Antonio said back, continuously surprised at how the boy was able to calm his nerves and excite them all at once.

Tight blue jeans. Tight black t-shirt. Black low-top Converse. No jacket. Must be December in southwest Washington.

Sometimes memories are the worst form of torture.

Sam's fiery red hair danced in the wind as he readied himself for his impending transition. "I can live with my body the way it is if you can," he said, green eyes preparing for rejection and pain.

Antonio smiled and lied. "I can."

"Besides, even if we wait until after the surgery, chances are I will revert to the parts I have now."

It didn't take a detective to clue into the hurt those words conjured. True, Sam was supposed to be male, and true his mind was that, but it was also true his body was decidedly female beneath the suffocating chest binds and lack of external genitalia. Still, Antonio braved his face, lied through his teeth, let Sam believe that he was enough as is. But he knew it would only be a matter of time before he strayed to get fucked by a real man, suck the dick of a real man, drinking up cum like he was back in high school again at the rest stop. Maybe he should tell Sam? Come clean about his needs, his desires. Surely he would understand, right? But that hurt in his eyes would only deepen. That sorrowful gaze would break. Could he really live with himself if he didn't tell Sam the truth?

"And you are certain this is what you want?" Antonio asked, unable to ask what he really needed to.

"I have never been more sure of anything in my life," Sam said, inching closer, sliding his hand down the back of Antonio's jeans until his middle finger reached the sphincter. "Besides, I can always wield a strap-on instead of my packer."

Antonio's smile told Sam that would help, but hid the fact that it would not be enough. Didn't let on that he could not promise straying while Sam slid his index and middle fingers in and out of his ass. Couldn't be honest about his bodily craving for dick his biology demanded. Shouldn't he stop Sam from making this decision until he's in a better frame of mind? Sam just turned eighteen, surely this is the rash decision making of a naive child. But he didn't. He gave into the pleasures of the flesh. And what lovely flesh Sam was! Maybe he could get over the fact that a vagina sat between Sam's legs instead of a penis. Maybe he could learn to love the parts that didn't match Sam's mind, but would forever be a part of his body. Maybe he could, one day, but today, right now in this moment where Sam added a third digit to his fervent fingering, all Antonio could think about was how completely dedicated Sam was to pleasuring him.

"Sam?"

Antonio wept as the red hair faded into the sea of bodies at the club. Sam was long dead. Brendon was his now. Why couldn't he let his guilt stay hidden in the past where it belonged? And Brendon? He knew with every cell in his body that Brendon was his true match. At least, his true match while the boy lived. After all, while Sam desired life among the undead bloodsuckers, Brendon had no intentions of becoming a vampire. Brendon, whose mind and body matched perfectly. Whose wants and needs Antonio could provide and vice versa. Whose shirtless and sweaty body was making its way over to him, eyes begging for closeness, finger motioning for Antonio to join him on the dance floor.

"You can't deny me," Brendon said.

"I am bewitched by you," Antonio responded.

"Well, I am a witch."

They held each other's gaze, not daring to be the first to flinch. It wasn't about dominance or pride. It was much more than that.

"As much as I want you all to myself, there are just some things I can't offer," Brendon said.

Antonio blinked. "Goddammit. What do you mean?"

Brendon stared back, deciding it was safe to move his eyes towards other parts of Antonio, like his black hair that casually wrapped around the pillow and billowed out from his face where they were pressed together, the effortlessly manicured stubble that he prayed never left, the flawless reddish-brown complexion that instantly made him conscious of the zit forming on his own chin, and those obsidian mirror eyes. Gawd, he could stare into those eyes for hours and get lost and never once feel guilty about the time. But alas, he had to answer the question.

"The coven."

"What? Really?"

"Yes."

"But we've been down that road. I mean, not literally. Okay, literally since they're on this road, but, well, you know what I mean."

"I still think you should ask to join."

"It won't help."

"Why not?"

"I don't belong. I'm… different."

"I know."

"You don't."

The smile faded from Brendon's face as he finally allowed a blink to filter through. "I do."

How could he know? How could Brendon, little Brendon who, yes, now a man, but was just a boy when their fate became intertwined after he saved him from true death? Antonio battled with that question, knowing that without a heart, even a dead and unbeating one, he should not exist any longer, but there he lay, in his bed, next to the man he loved, staring into his sad brown eyes that hid a truth he wasn't sure he wanted to uncover, but knew deep down he had no choice but to discover it.

"Tell me."

"The coven suspects you're different because they can sense it, just like I can sense it. Scratch that, like I know it."

"Your vagueness is exhausting."

"Like your stamina."

"My stamina? I've never met anyone who could match mine, but you? Gawd, it's almost work to keep up."

"Hehehe... sorry about that. Dad says it's from him."

"Oh gawd, you and your father have discussed...?"

"Sex? Hell yes!"

"Mine wanted to know nothing."

"I've known too much for too long."

"Alas, I am at a loss. I will never be able to look Frank in the eyes ever again. The man is going to think I hate him."

"For me talking about our sex life? Ha! I never told you that my older half-brother Chad is a year and a half younger than my full sisters and that my mom was in on the whole thing because they were carrying on a threesome with the nanny and holy shit that was an awkward family meeting with his mom and all of us which basically boiled down to finding out that Sheree and my dad are the only two straight people out of the whole lot of us."

"Now I am for certain never going to be able to. Bastard."

"We're tangenting."

"I don't mind the tangent."

"But it's keeping you from the truth."

The truth? The truth? "Do I really want to know the truth?" *Of course I do... don't I?*

"Probably not, but you need to."

Pause.

As Antonio's Angel and Devil ping-ponged the pros and cons, the thought of finally knowing something true, something he could hold onto and grasp other than the concept of love that, at that moment, was beyond his comprehension how he could so fully love another being, a human, a witch, a flesh and blood living creature like Brendon in a way that he never thought possible, nearly overtook his fragile emotional state. Their gaze once again took hold, longingly awaiting the next words to escape Brendon's lusciously moist lips. How could he love while he was dead inside? How could he feel when there was quite literally a hole inside his chest that never healed, never grew back the lost heart? And yet, heartless as he was, the void had filled with love for Brendon he could never fully express because of stupid metacognitive limitations his brain still suffered from, a leftover human aspect the demon could never dismantle and unlock to its full potential. Or could it? He never thought to try. But what was the use? That useless jumble of Jell-O the human world called brains was nothing more than a pile of fused neurons and dendrites and axons and fat sitting inside his thick skull.

Brendon's eyes widened.

Antonio sensed the fear behind them.

"What is it?"

"I need to go. Now," Brendon said, leaping from the bed in search for his clothes he knew had to be somewhere nearby.

"What is it?"

"I just need to... I have to leave."

"Brendon, tell me. Don't shut me out because you don't think I can understand. You know me better than that." *Does he? Does he know? What does he really know about me? I keep my secrets and lies hidden, locked, buried, but for what? Why hide anything at all from him, especially since he can hear my thoughts?*

"Fuck this, I don't have time," Brendon said as he stood naked one moment and gone the next with a snap.

A pair of black running shorts and heather grey t-shirt caught his eye under the lounge chair, along with a cell phone. Tossing the bed sheets aside like a matador teasing a bull, he walked over to the pile, picked it up, and folded the shorts and shirt, then lifted them up to his nostrils and sniffed until they unfolded themselves as his senses took in the powerful scent that made him melt into a puddle of goo back onto the bed. But there was the phone, and he was unable to resist the urge to pry into the secrets that lie within. His Angel and Devil continued their Ping-Pong session, rapidly firing back and forth with their paddle tongues.

No.

Yes.

You shouldn't.

You should.

It's private.

Who cares? He'll understand!

No, he won't!

But he loves you. There should be no secrets.

I haven't told him hardly any of mine.

But you will.

Will I?

Of course, in due time.

In due time? What the hell does that even mean?

It means that you will have time to tell him, but for now, you should look.

Look? For what?

What begs to be seen. Look. Find out.

I can't.

Oh, you most certainly can.

The argument stopped as Antonio's fingers unlocked the phone to find an unread text message from a man named Jonathan. He started shaking, becoming irrationally angry over his lover receiving a message from another man. Who was this Jonathan and what did he want with his Brendon? Another press and the message opened:

> **Urgent. Meet me at the park alone.**

"Oh Jesus, the clichés I'm conjuring," Antonio said aloud as he threw the phone onto his bed, dressed, and sped toward Ravenwood Park to find the possibly clandestine lovers in a compromising position. But he didn't find clandestine lovers. He found an older but still decidedly attractive gentleman who felt out of place and time with the one they were in; a silver fox from another era. And a vampire, he realized, as he listened in on their conversation, which made him realize he knew the voice. Not some restroom creeper or inappropriate college professor or closeted married guy who begged for anal in the coat check room while his wife ordered a third glass of wine and told the kids to stop playing with their food and just eat it, but particularly singularly familiar nonetheless.

"He cannot know," the older man said.

"I have to tell him," Brendon pleaded.

At least he's clothed, Antonio thought.

"I beg you to reconsider."

"He has to know why... why... why he's... not like the others."

"He is here."

"I know. Do you think he...?"

"I haven't heard your voice since the day I was turned," Antonio said as he glided out of the shadows.

"Antonio, this is..."

"Jonathan."

"Yes," Jonathan answered, expressionless.

"…my great-great-great-grandfather," Brendon confessed to the ground.

"Well slap my ass and call me a bitch."

"If you will not, I will," Jonathan said with a smirk across his alabaster face.

"Really, Jonathan? Really? Ugh! See what I have to deal with?" Brendon told Antonio as he reached for his hand.

The voice? "You're not my maker, are you?" Antonio asked quietly, suddenly shy and scared and not really sure he wanted to know the truth after all now that he was so close to finding it. But why? Why now timid when the quest has been nearly all consuming for so many years? He chocked it all up to fear. Fear of rejection. Fear of denial. Fear of the unknown made known.

"I am not."

Fear.

Fear.

Fear.

Rejection.

Denial.

Unknown.

Error code 004C.

The dreaded blue screen of death.

"But if you are looking for someone to blame for your condition, then I am guilty."

"My… condition?"

"Your vampirism."

"What are you? You're so much more than vampire."

"He's a vampire witch, which, yes, I realize should not exist as the vampire virus supposedly overrides all other supernatural gifts and curses and alterations, but alas, my multi-great-grandfather is both," Brendon told Antonio calmly, realizing he may have shared too much when, somehow, Jonathan looked paler than usual. "Crap. I said too much, didn't I?"

"Perhaps, but it is too late now. The cat is, as you say, out of the bag," Jonathan said.

"Perhaps you're bit late on that. Nobody says that anymore," Brendon said.

"Like, since last century," Antonio added.

"In my defense, I am from the previous century before last, and therefore, stand by my comparison," Jonathan said, an ever-so-slight upward curl of his lip threatening a smile.

The next moment dragged forever while they all stood in some sort of awkward circle or triangle depending on how you choose to view such a coordination of three people, and stared at each other, waiting for the next person to speak. But nobody wanted to be first. Nobody wanted to break the ice that had already cracked. Nobody wanted to divulge or discover the truth of matters, surprisingly least of all Antonio who did not understand how he was so close to the answer he craved yet frightened over the impending disappointment. He would be disappointed, right? He had to be. True, this Jonathan was an anomaly, an otherly othered Other of sorts, but still, what connection other than being somehow involved in his change did he have? He already knew, truly knew that the man was not his maker, but failed to reject the null hypothesis and thusly failed to be prepared for life. Not that he was living, but even that notion was somewhat up for debate as, true, no heart and alas no heartbeat, which meant the heartbeat laws so many states tried to pass were null and void, but he was in motion, able to feel complex emotions to the max, and, to this day he still did not understand, could fuck and climax even better than he could as a human.

"There is a rumor floating around town, and we need to kill it. Quickly," Brendon said, his eyes a mess as tears started falling out of them uncontrollably like when a dam can't hold back the river anymore and the whole thing starts to spill over the ledge so the engineers pull a lever or press a button and open a few portals to allow the flow to drain more smoothly through predestined portals.

Antonio decided Brendon's cry face wasn't as abhorrent as he once imagined. Actually, it made him almost more adorable as his dimples filled like swimming pools of tears while he tried to smile off the pain. Still, what rumor? Who was spreading it? *Oh shit, that fairy? Sunflower Seed Man? Both of them? Please don't be the butcher, the goddamn butcher I still don't know the name of because I am a horrible, useless monster! Stop. Stop! STOP!!!* "It would help if I knew the rumor in need of quelling."

"That…" Jonathan started, but choked. Not one of those shitty fake-chokes "reality" television housewives conjure up for ratings as they clutch their costume pearls, but an actual, honest-to-God choke like his voice was being strangled, like an invisible hand gripped his esophagus and cut off the air. The only problem was that vampires didn't require oxygen, or at least not in the same sense that humans did. In essence, oxygen served about the same purpose to vampires as it does to steel. It coats the outer layer in an effort to protect it. But unlike like steel, where the rust will eventually corrode the entire product until the earth reclaims it, it hardens and shields and over centuries and millennia creates a nearly impenetrable statuesque skin, similar to the toddler-like skin Jonathan had acquired after over a hundred years… still in his infancy, practically.

Squeezing his hand, Brendon waited until Antonio held his gaze once again before finishing what Jonathan couldn't. "Song's End is your maker."

CHAPTER 6

Forgive Me for My Sins

"Forgive me father, for I have sinned."

"Confess, my child," the priest said behind the thinly veiled screen of sanctimonious salaciousness his ears lusted for day after day.

"I drank the bodily fluids of another man today," Antonio confessed to his lap.

"Continue, and be cleansed from this," the priest said quietly, calmly, decisively.

"He tasted so sweet. So delicious. I couldn't stop swallowing. I drained him so completely," Antonio admitted, blood tears gliding down his cheeks.

"Yes. Good. Yes," the priest said methodically.

"Good? Are you listening to me?" Antonio asked, louder than the little more than whispers he'd been speaking before, furious at the hidden man of God begging for climax.

"It is good to purge these internal conflicts from your soul," the priest told him, same soothing tone.

"Agreed, but I fear I have no soul," Antonio said, quieting down to his former decibel.

"No soul? Surely you have a soul, my child. If not, where does your guilt stem from?" the priest asked.

Checkmate. The priest had Antonio's queen cornered by a mere pawn and there was no way to win. He had to admit defeat so quickly into the game.

"I fear my soul has been tainted by uncontrollable desires," Antonio responded.

"Then learn to control them. Find a way to distill those desires with someone you trust. Someone you can love. Someone with similar passions," the priest told him.

"But I am gay. A monster. A demon of society," Antonio confessed.

"You are a child of God. Make no mistake, your desires are part of his plan for you."

"Which ones?"

"All of them."

"All?"

"All."

"But..."

"Child, please listen. God does not punish love. If you find love with another man, then love has found a way to break through your hardened heart. Cherish it. Make it grow and in doing so, God will shower you with His love which will be bounteous when you meet in heaven."

"How can you know?"

"Our continuous dialogue, my child. Our continuous dialogue."

"I doubt I am bound for heaven."

"Oh, my dear child. All are."

"And Hell?"

"A construct."

"A construct?"

"Child, this life is Hell. In deciding to be better, to love and live, that is Hell enough. Once you pass, the Kingdom is yours."

"And if I never pass?"

"Never pass? Why, we all are but mortal beings!"

"No. Not all. Not me."

"Surely, my child, you may think you are a god among men, but assuredly your heart will cease one day."

"It already has."

"Poor child, so cold so soon?"

"I have no heart."

"No heart? Why, you must have one, for where could all this grief come from?"

Antonio couldn't take it any longer. He ripped off the metal grate window, pulled the priest's head through, and slammed it against his chest holding one ear while the other pressed against the void. "Do you hear it? Do you hear my heart, Father?"

"I hear nothing. But how?" the priest asked, eyes begging for absolution as they slowly lifted.

"I fear for that answer I must ask my own father. Not the one whose body helped create mine, but the one who made me the way I am today with nothing more than a kiss."

"And then you will tell me, child?"

"Promise."

"Do you think you will ever change your mind about turning?" Antonio asked Brendon, partly wanting an answer and the other part dreading the inevitable realization that eternity is not for everyone, even if his fate was part of that curse.

The twinkle in Brendon's eyes flew away like a migrating bird simply making a rest stop. "I'm twenty-three."

"So am I."

"But with a few years of experience added to that age. Plus the fact that you weren't given a choice. I have a choice. I can decide right now if I want to live forever."

"But you don't," Antonio said, deflating into despair.

"I don't…"

Antonio slumped as if he were nothing more than a slug that just crossed a salt path; shrinking inwardly and frightened of the inevitable. "I understand."

"…right now," Brendon finished with a side smile.

Hope. There was hope and Antonio latched onto that hope like a rope and held it in his hands and pleaded with his body they wouldn't chafe from the friction that undoubtedly would ensue. Intertwined in his fingers. Dangling from his wrist. Begging for a tug. A smile escaped before he could stop it. He let it linger like bait.

But then Brendon's demeanor changed just as unexpectedly like a shit-bomb; the kind of shit that comes on quickly and weighs you down like you're filled with bricks until you find a way to let it go, be it a toilet or discreetly behind a tree, and takes forever to finish. Each push that falls another log sending yet another to take its place. Smaller and smaller, but thicker and thicker with fiberless density.

"What?" Antonio asked Brendon, sidling up to him, sliding his fingers until they melted together with his, foreheads making their way towards connection.

"Maybe later."

"Why later?"

"I still haven't fully explored my humanity. I want to experience everything I want to experience as a human before deciding if I want to, you know, alter that reality."

"But you are already different."

"Being gay isn't all that different."

"I meant being a witch."

"Oh, yeah, well, there's that."

Silence for what Antonio perceived an eternity, despite the blaring techno music pounding their ears, vibrating through their feet. He waited. Patiently he waited until he realized that Brendon was not going to be as forthcoming about the obvious, the real question, the undeniable truth of the matter that, as a vampire, he would no longer be gifted with wiccan abilities he'd grown quite accustomed to. But he knew there had to be a way, as there were two examples he could name off the top of his head who hadn't lost their witch powers, but who had actually enhanced them by becoming vampires. "You might not lose it all."

"Antonio, I love you. Can't that just be enough for now?"

Blank.

"So, what if we wait a little while until I figure stuff out?"

Blank.

"Besides, you… can't… be the one to turn me."

Blank.

Shock.

Silence.

"Antonio?"

"I'm pretty sure I heard you, but what did you say?" Antonio asked, internally combusting with irrational rage about to set the world on fire.

"If and when I decide to become a vampire, it can't be you who turns me."

Brendon's words were cool, icy cold against the fire that burned inside Antonio as they penetrated his soul, or the vacancy left behind where his soul once occupied. He sat, still as possible, using every ounce of concentration to not rip the boy's throat out and suck him dry. The boy he loved more than anything. The boy he would die for if it meant his life would be spared. The boy whose pieces fit into the ones missing from his own puzzle. "Why would you say that?"

A loud sigh fell from Brendon before he could stop it. "I don't know if I should be the one to tell you this."

"Tell me what?"

"About Sam."

Sam. The boy he thought would be his forever. The boy he swore he could never live without. The boy he killed. "What about him?" Antonio growled.

Brendon started tapping his feet against the barstool, methodically bouncing like when one has to pee but doesn't want to get up because then they'd miss out on the riveting conversation, or because they have an irrational (or rational, depending on the reason) fear of public restrooms. But Brendon seemed comfortable in his skin, at least now that his skin was soft, supple, smooth, slim, and sexy as hell rather than when he was a child whose excess weight invited teasing by those less comfortable with their own bodies. Sometimes the horrors we inflict on each other are scarier than those depicted in books and movies with monsters.

"Sam wasn't your fault. You didn't know."

"What? What are you talking about?"

"You can't… you can't do it."

"I… I… I don't understand?" Antonio asked as the room spun like some horribly cliché scene in a poorly produced movie when a character suddenly drops the plot twist.

"You couldn't have known. I mean, nobody told you what you are."

"I'm a vampire. Nobody had to tell me what I am."

Tears slowly traversed Brendon's cheeks, trickling down, carefully treading the hills and valleys his young face held. "Not just any vampire."

"I'm not a vampire witch like my maker."

"No, but your maker is not just any vampire either."

"I know. You know I know. Jonathan told us, both of us about Song's End."

"Jonathan has a way of only letting in a little bit of the story and purposefully leaving the fine print out."

"Then what? What is it then?"

"You have to promise you won't be angry."

"I can't make any promises."

"Please."

"Why are you covering for some coward?"

"I'm not."

"It feels like it."

"Antonio," Brendon said before kissing his lips, hoping to soften the blow he was about to deal. It didn't. "You will never be able to turn anyone into a vampire."

"What?!" Antonio flew off the stool, garnering the attention of a few clubbers close by. He quickly sat back down, ignoring the scene he'd just created which in turn made the guys who turned to see what the commotion was about resume their promiscuous flirtations that would lead to dirty bathroom stall blowjobs and rashes in a few weeks that'll require antibiotics to clear. "How can you know that?"

"Sam."

"Sam was an accident." The bluntness of his words caught him in the end, surprised by how cold he could be.

"Sam was an accident, but not one that you caused. You didn't know. Nobody told you. Nobody prepared you."

"I sought the advice from the coven across the street from me. From many of them. True, they were all younglings, but had done it before. They all said the same thing, told me how, what I needed to do, what Sam needed to do. Only…" Antonio paused, choking. "Only I couldn't control the hunger and took more than I should have."

"Even if you didn't, were you any other vampire, you might've saved him or turned him."

"I don't understand. I am a regular vampire."

"No, Antonio, you aren't. You are the sire of Song's End."

"A vampire."

"A vampire witch who literally birthed himself into existence when he was a week old. Think about it. How many newborns have the power to cast a spell at the moment of their death, a death by fire that should kill anything, especially a witch or a vampire, and become a legend?"

"I'm sure he can't be the only one."

"The. Only. One."

"Really?"

"Really. He accomplished what no other witch could accomplish before him, which is truly become immortal."

Antonio guffawed. "Immortality is overrated."

"You say that now, but think about it. Where is your heart?"

"Gone. That branch you pulled from me ten years ago pushed it out."

"And how do you kill a vampire?"

"Stake through the heart."

"But you have no heart."

"So, I shouldn't be alive?"

"No. If you were any other vampire you'd be…"

"…dust in the wind," Antonio sang, doing a fairly abhorrent Steve Walsh impression.

Brendon snickered. "Cheesy, but yes."

"I always assumed part of it must still be in there somewhere," Antonio said before putting his hand over the area and continuing with, "Even though I can't feel it."

"It's not. I took it. If you want it back, it's in a jar in my parent's basement."

"That's creepy."

"You stole my heart. Only fair I stole yours."

"That's creepier. You were thirteen."

"What can I say, I've always had a thing for older men."

"And now I feel dirty."

"Don't. We're the same age now."

"Same age, but I still have many more years."

"Which is why I'm not quite ready yet."

"I didn't have a choice. Song's End turned me against my will."

"Because my great-great-great-grandfather begged him to."

"Why?"

"For me."

"He? He knew our future?'

"It's a witch thing."

"Yet another anomaly in this crazy equation I have yet to solve."

"Which all leads back to Song's End."

"I must know the truth. All of it."

"I'll tell you, but please, you couldn't have known what would happen to Sam. You've lived with your guilt long enough. He's moved on and wants you to as well."

"You can't know that."

"But I do."

"How?"

"My friend Anna is a medium. We've been in contact."

"You… you've talked to my Sam?"

The way Antonio made Sam possessive—"My Sam"—stung Brendon harsher than he expected, but he knew the pain wouldn't be as quick and simple like peeling off a Band-Aid. Still, the freshness of something that happened a decade ago still lingered on Antonio's breath. After all these years, the guilt only dug its way deeper, pushing its barbed tentacles into every crevice, abscessing.

"Don't be angry. I only needed to make sure he was okay before I told you the truth."

"And if Sam said he was not okay? That he was trapped in Hell because I sent him there?"

"I still would have told you the truth. And try to figure out a way to fix it. You need to know that you simply did not know it would never work."

"Sam and I?"

"Antonio. You. You can't turn anyone into a vampire. You just… can't. You don't have that curse."

"Curse?'

"Yes, curse!"

"I'm listening, but confused. Small words."

Brendon rolled his eyes as a chuckle managed to slip out. "Got it. I'll pretend you're my sister. The strain most vampires have is based on a curse. That's why most vampires we hear about are, to put it bluntly, evil. And yes, I know the ones here in Ravenwood are a bit more, shall we say, restrained in their bloodlust due to the slightly more open-minded nature of our town, and also the fact that some have learned and continue to teach others how to live amongst the living, but that is not the norm."

"I know."

"I know you know. But you aren't normal. You were created not by a curse, but by a being who cast a spell on himself to become a vampire."

"I don't get it."

"Simply put, new rules for his strain."

"New rules? Meaning…?"

"Meaning, basically, none of Song's End's sires can procreate without his gift."

"Awesome. The whore becomes a eunuch."

"I mean, it's a hell of a lot more complicated than that, but still, all boils down to the fact that, even if you wanted to make me a vampire, you couldn't."

"I only want what you want." Antonio couldn't shake the sadness from his voice as he let those words spill out.

"I know. I just, uh, I just wanted you to know before, well, before you…"

"…get my hopes up?"

"Yeah."

"Too late."

"I'm sorry."

"Don't be. Painful as it is," Antonio started, lifting Brendon's chin up and forcing their eyes to meet, "I appreciate the honesty."

As they kissed, Brendon could sense Sam's presence. Not physically, but within Antonio's psyche, permeating the kiss and tainting it. And although he knew that Sam was Antonio's past and he was Antonio's present, suddenly he couldn't foresee the future and that frightened him. Antonio was not just his first love, but his true love, his one and only, once in a lifetime, call the fucking Lifetime or Hallmark Channel love and make a goddamn Christmas movie love. The love he patiently waited for as he watched countless men walk in and out of Antonio's revolving door. The love he fantasized over in masturbatory bliss. The love he carefully saved his own virginity for because he knew only one person was worthy of taking it, and if he didn't play his cards right, it might all be for nothing.

"Mind if I join you?" a familiar voice asked, though without any hint of expecting an answer or courtesy in his tone.

"Actually…" Antonio started.

Brendon cut him off and finished with, "Maybe you can explain better than I can, Jonathan."

The silver fox. The boy's great-great-great-grandfather and life companion to his maker. The vampire responsible for his special brand of vampirism.

"Did you know?" Antonio asked, malice unintentionally present.

Jonathan briefly averted his eyes, but brought them back up to respond. "Yes."

"Why? Why can I not create another?"

"Because you are not cursed."

"But I am!"

"No." Jonathan smiled. "No, my dear, sweet Antonio, you are no curse."

"What am I then?"

"A beloved gift."

"What good is a gift if it can't be shared?"

"It is a gift that can only belong to you."

"But I want to share it?"

"If the time comes for you to take a companion who wishes to become immortal, we will know."

"And?"

"We will come."

"And?"

"If that person is worthy, Song's End has agreed to sire a third."

"A third?"

"A third like him. Like me. Like you."

"You mean I am only his second vampire he's sired?"

"Yes."

"That's why you can't sire, Antonio. You're not a curse," Brendon said, putting his hand over Antonio's thigh. "I need you to understand that."

"But why was I sired in the first place? He didn't know me?"

"Because I asked. Because I saw you as I prepared for my own death I was certain would happen but did not because I did not know, neither of us knew, that we, our line, our very small line, does not exist within the accepted rules, but I saw you and looked into your soul and realized that you were meant to be for someone very dear to me."

"Brendon?"

"Brendon."

"See? Like I told you, my grandpa set me up with my boyfriend," Brendon said, hoping the sarcasm would help keep the air from suffocating the room.

"I need some air. I can't breathe."

"You cannot breathe. You are dead," Jonathan said.

"No, metaphorically. It's a lot and the cool night will help and…"

"Go," Brendon urged, kissing Antonio's forehead before he quickly made his way towards the exit.

You never told him the truth about Sam, did you? Jonathan asked in Brendon's head.

I wanted to, but I can't, Brendon telepathically responded.

Why?

I'm afraid.

Afraid of what?

How he'll take it. He might do something rash. Something he'll regret.

He should know the truth, no matter what.

Like you told him the truth about being unable to turn anyone into a vampire?

I deserve that.

You do.

But I did not know.

Did Song's End?

Only after Sam died. But he would have died nonetheless.

Maybe not that night. Maybe another vampire could have…

"That very night, that very hour, that very second while Antonio began draining him of blood, Sam most definitely would have died on his own," Jonathan said out loud instead of through thoughts as Antonio walked back up to them, as if on purpose.

"Jonathan!" Brendon shouted.

"What are you talking about? What do you mean Sam would have died anyway?"

Brendon put his hands around Antonio's face which, had he been able to create heat, would be hot with the fiery coals of Hell itself. "Sam didn't die because you failed."

"I don't understand!" Antonio cried. "Tell me so I understand! Tell me!"

"The reason Sam could see you, see vampires when others couldn't, like during the daytime, is because he had an aneurysm pressed against part of his brain, the part that magic shields humans from seeing vampires during the day. It hemorrhaged. An aneurysm killed him, not you."

"How do you know? How could you possibly know that? I killed him! It was me!" Antonio shouted so loud it should have caused the rest of the people in the club, the dancers, the bartenders, the casual sex seekers, to notice, cause their ears to bleed, pass out, but Brendon put their voices in a bubble to prevent it.

"We should go somewhere more… private," Brendon suggested.

"Brendon is right, Antonio," Jonathan added.

"No! Here! Now! The truth!"

"I snuck into my dad's office and looked at the autopsy report," Brendon confessed quickly before his conscience intervened.

"You're dad?" Antonio asked, confused.

"Yes. He's a medical examiner. His official ruling was not, as he's lied about so many times, an animal attack, but an undiagnosed brain aneurysm."

"And you trust that? You've admitted he's a liar!"

"I trust that if he wanted to say it was merely another vampire killing, he could have left it alone at that and nobody would have blinked except maybe some vigilante hunter willing to find some random wolf and kill it and say that it was the culprit. If he said it was a subarachnoid hemorrhage, then it was a subarachnoid hemorrhage."

"I want to see the report."

"You don't."

"Yes, Brendon, I must see it with my own eyes."

"My dad's going to kill me."

"You're twenty-three."

"I know."

"Do you think your father will talk to me? Let me ask him questions? Do you think he'll remember the case from so long ago?"

"Remember? He never forgets."

"Never?"

"Never. They haunt him."

"Jonathan, I…" Antonio started, but Jonathan was nowhere to be seen. Vanished.

"He likes to ghost."

"Well that's shitty."

"Easier than saying goodbye."

"I feel like we're saying goodbye."

"We're not. I'm not going anywhere."

"Promise?"

"Promise."

"So, you will allow Song's End to make you into an immortal?"

"I will consider it. Why don't we come back to this when I'm… thirty?"

"Thirty? But that's seven years away! You'll regret not maintaining your youth!"

"Wow. Shallow much?"

"Yes." Antonio cocked his right eye before quickly looking Brendon up and down.

"Liar. Besides, you've seen my dad and he's in his fifties and looks like he's thirty. I'm basically his clone with brown eyes instead of blue. I'll still be hot enough for you."

"Thirty?"

"Thirty."

"I can live with that."

At the urging of the casual acquaintances Antonio had kept in his life over the last three years since turning, the other bloodsuckers who begged like stereotypical Bangkok whores to join their coven, join their underground lives, join their private slash public club where he could dance and drink and suck and fuck and basically be himself without judgement, he caved after Sam died and went to Communion in 2003.

The dim backroom lighting that basically silhouetted the backs of heads blowing random strangers in the hall leading to the bathroom was oddly comforting. That or the scent of cum and sweat and piss that coated the floor and walls and bodies made him feel at home. And the blood. The delicious, flowing arteries, open necks, wrists, thighs, all up for the taking in any of the rooms if the price is right. That price could be as little as just the chance to be sucked by a vampire to as high as ten thousand dollars for a half-pint. One thing was for certain: Antonio had never paid a cent for human blood, and never would. Or so he told himself.

Suddenly the sweet sweet aroma he'd found in the back alley a few weeks prior caught his attention. It had to be Sam. Not his sweet Sam but the crude Sam with the big dick. Fairy Sam. Sure enough, veiny sausage dick firmly stroking with both hands, sat the man in question as two vampires, one on either side, drank from his neck while another approached to take one of his inner thighs. Antonio watched, counting the mustache hairs. He counted twice just to be certain before entering the room.

"You healed well," Antonio told Sam, who immediately recognized the voice and opened his eyes to magnetically lock.

The trio of suckers side-glanced, but kept their smooth, steady, calculated sucking mouths on the prize. The bulge in Antonio's tight pants also did not go unnoticed by any of them.

"Told you, man. I'm a fucking fairy. Now fuck me," crude Sam said.

"What?" Antonio asked, although he heard the words crystal.

"I said fuck me," Brendon demanded, hand firmly planted on Antonio's dick.

"You're awfully bossy all of a sudden," Antonio said, slight smirk after realizing his daydream was just that.

"Fine. Then turn around and I'll fuck you," Brendon said, eyes welling like a dam about ready to burst.

"What is this all about?" Antonio asked before adding for clarity's sake, "And don't give me any of that hormonal horny as hell shit."

Brendon released his grip on Antonio's penis, folding his arms across his chest and proceeded to pout on the sofa as if he was Jan Brady and Marcia got away with something she never could. It would have been adorable if he was still the ten-year-old kid he first saw all those years ago after being turned, but decidedly not-so-much as a twenty-three-year-old post collegiate man. Who was Antonio kidding? Brendon was adorable any mood or tantrum or innuendo he played.

"I know you have to go to Communion."

How does he even know about Communion?

"And I know you have to talk to Sam."

How does he even know about Sam?

"And I know what Sam wants in return."

How does he even...

"And I can read your fucking thoughts, so please just talk to me if you want to know how I know shit, asshole."

"Well that's one way to kill the mood."

As much as he tried not to show any emotion, Brendon snickered. "Fucker."

"Not now. Limp as Pillsbury biscuit dough. Sure, it'll pop out of the can, but then it'll just sit there in a puddle of flattening flesh."

"Stop trying to make me laugh."

"Sorry. Nervous. I don't want to talk to Sam, but I fear he knows something I don't know but need to know, you know?"

Brendon gulped, long and hard. "I know. But what he wants in return..."

"To be a vampire?" Antonio asked, face scrunched in a most unsexy way. "Impossible. He's a fairy. Can't happen."

"The problem is that it can, only not by any normal vampire."

Normal? What does Brendon mean by normal? Like me? An abnormal vampire? The blender of Antonio's brain swirled on high speed, cutting though every possible scenario and meaning and suggestion and possibility, but all that happened was a conglomerated mess of nonsense filling his brain, making it as useless as a punctured grocery sack.

"It's like being a vampire witch," Brendon told him.

"Vampire witch? Like Jonathan?"

Antonio's confusion was beyond frustrating to both of them. Like he wasn't paying any attention to their conversation just a couple hours ago. Like his computer failed to save the most updated version and he was back to page 30 while the rest of them had moved on to page 54.

"Yeah... and Song's End."

"But that is different. Witches and fairies are..."

"Different, yes, but, c'mon, you know the vampire virus wipes out witch abilities, and fairies are naturally immune to it. The problem is that these rules only apply to the common strain."

The common strain? The common strain? "The common strain?" Antonio asked, mind and mouth stuck on repeat.

"Oh gawd, seriously? We just had this conversation," Brendon said, annoyance filtering through his words without conciliation.

"What do you mean?" Antonio asked, begging to understand.

"It means you are no ordinary vampire, my child," a voice said from the shadows. As it billowed out into the light, shaping into a humanlike form, Antonio was struck by his beauty. Masterly chiseled cheekbones, flawless skin, obsidian mirror eyes flecked with gold and red, straight black river of hair that stopped abruptly mid-back, and a godlike body to match. He was Hollywood's Native American.

CHAPTER 7

Truth Will Set You Free

It didn't take long for Antonio to realize that he was at the wrong place at the wrong time, but since he was there, he figured he might as well see it through. He stared down at the man who'd mistaken him for some other guy, some other Mexican man because, you know, they all look alike, right? That was the reason for the mistaken identity situation that had escalated to a cold gun between his eyes, right? Whatever the reason, the young man pointing the gun started wavering as he looked into Antonio's eyes as his own adjusted to the dark December dusk and realized his mistake. Antonio's smile didn't help the situation.

"The fuck you smilin' at?" he asked, finger firmly on the trigger even if the gun shook like he had Parkinson's.

"I know you," Antonio said, sly smile making his eyes look a million times more mischievous.

"What?" he asked, face contorted.

"I said," Antonio started, penetrating through the man's retinas as he finished, "I. Know. You."

The man's buddies started laughing. They all looked like tough guys, the three of them. Leather and denim jackets dangling from one hand off their shoulders, greasy hair purposefully slicked in Rockabilly fashion, sleeveless shirts to show off their abundance of tattoos with names and dates and naked women and crosses and the Virgin Mary. You know, macho asshole thirty-something dickwad types desperately trying to hold onto their youth as time continued snatching it away one hair at a time to increase forehead real estate while adding it to the back for frequent mowing.

"You don't know me, asshole. You know nothing about me," the man said, lower lip stuck out as if he was pouting over his mommy not getting him that new Transformer he wanted for Christmas.

"I know you're a swallower not a spitter," Antonio spewed. "Or at least you were in ninety-nine when you sucked my dick during the homecoming game."

Antonio didn't realize it was possible for a face to drain of blood so quickly, but there he stood in front of a man whose face had paled in a flash, a face he'd never forget, sweat beading at the hairline. Checkmate. Or so he thought.

As the bullet pulsed through the barrel of the gun, Antonio paused to ponder whether or not to vacate the cartridge's trajectory. *If I stay, well, that's all folks. If I go, well, then what? Brendon. My Brendon. My love. My...* he thought before, at least to him, he slowly took a step to the left and watched as the spinning cartridge shattered as it hit the brick behind him, sending pieces scattering across the ground, showering them with sandy particles that pierced flesh like glass in the ever-so-glamorous back alley security lighting. The tiny droplets of blood were intoxicating, but Antonio kept his cool. He couldn't figure out why he bothered, but did anyway. He also couldn't help but wonder why he continued frequenting back alleys when they seemingly always caused him trouble. Alas, he felt most at home in them. He was, after all, a back-alley sort of fellow, if you catch my drift [wink].

"Well that's awkward," Antonio said to the cowardly swallower.

"What the...?" he asked the barrel of his gun as smoke swirled out in that cliché way it always does in the movies and rarely in real life.

"May want to work on your aim," Antonio said as he stared at the hole in the brick behind him.

"You may want to work on..." but he stopped. Froze. Along with the other two guys.

The only other time that happened, *Brendon.*

"Please tell me you are about to rip those fuckers' throats out?" Brendon asked Antonio between the tick and tock.

"I can't. I'm just toying with them." Antonio chuckled.

Brendon's face burned red. "Okay, then you need to stop me from doing it."

"Why?"

"Fourth of July two-thousand. Fort Vancouver. I was ten for Christ's sake."

Fire raged through Antonio. "What did they do to you?" he asked, praying it wasn't the first place his brain went to because that was too painful and horrible and unforgivable, recognizing the year as his own second birth, still not knowing that Brendon knew something more about that fateful Labor Day.

"They beat me up."

"Why?" *Whew! Not molesters. Still, who the hell beats up a kid when they're like, what? Twenty something?*

"I wore a shirt." Brendon remained cryptic, possibly over embarrassment, possibly over his shortened temper that was about to go supernova on the Douche Patrol, probably both.

"You'll have to be a little more, uh, descriptive than that," Antonio said with a short, punctuated laugh that was regrettably mocking.

Silence.

"You don't have to tell me if you don't want to," Antonio said, taking Brendon's hand that immediately latched on like a newborn to his mother's breasts, which, ironically, Antonio suddenly realized he never latched and had to be bottle fed from birth because his mother gave up after three weeks of trying, and he'd lost too much weight, and basically he was dying, which made him realize even then he knew he wasn't into boobs.

Brendon smiled, almost reluctantly at first, but turned into a genuine version before he answered, " 'That's Mr. Faggot To You!'."

Antonio burst out laughing like someone lit a barrel of gasoline, the explosion of which nearly caused the frozen moment between tick and tock to tumble. "You're shitting me?"

"I even made it myself," Brendon confessed.

"Ha hahaha! And your parents let you wear it?" Antonio couldn't stop laughing no matter how much he tried, but the guilt could not be overtaken by the shock.

"Let me? My dad thought it was the coolest thing ever." Brendon side smiled.

That dimple is going to be the death of me. "That's, huh? That's pretty cool. I mean, I knew Frank was cool, but now, I don't know, I kinda wanna..."

"If your next words are 'fuck him' then I'm going to cry."

"Then I won't finish... son of DILF."

"Son of a bitch."

"Hey! You don't even know mi madre!"

"You know what I mean."

"I also know what I want."

"Yeah?"

"You."

Then Antonio leaned in and kissed Brendon and everything else melted away until the next thing he knew they were back at his house, in his bed, furiously making love. I shit you not, it was all like some cheesy 1980s music video and he was the slutty whore fucking the lead singer. There may or may not have been actual 1980s butt-rock power ballads to boot, but in the blur, Antonio wasn't quite sure. Still, even with a perfect memory thanks to the vampire virus (or so he thought), even the uncommon strain his body was infected with that basically made him literally unable to forget a single moment—though frustratingly, not able to recall the more confusing details as well as he'd hope, especially when he was still recovering from the shock of Sam—every time he was with Brendon, the rest of the world didn't matter. He prayed to whatever god was listening that this wasn't just another infatuation. Even though he was like 99.999999999999999999 percent sure, there was still that 0.000000000000000000001 percent chance that he was going to find some fault in this one true thing and fuck it up like everything else he touched.

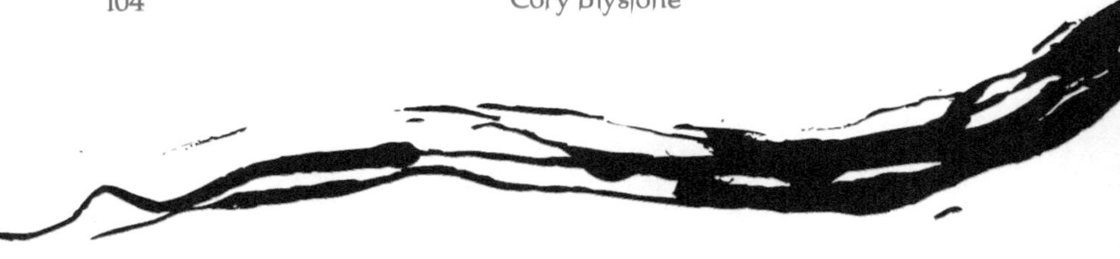

"You are not bound to most rules," Song's End began, jumping right in without any lube as the bass of an old Ace of Bass song pounded every orifice.

"Like which ones?" Antonio asked, not wasting another goddamned moment of his undead life on unanswered questions when the encyclopedia in front of him held nearly every answer he needed, and he sure as hell wasn't going to wait any longer in case that encyclopedia decided to up and disappear. Again.

Song's End sprayed him with answers like rapid-fire twink cum. "There is no code to abide by for killing people as you can kill whoever you want whenever you want, no need to drink human blood unlike your common counterparts who need it to survive, no reason to belong to a coven for your survival but also no reason not to, no need to fear werewolf bites like common vampires whom will perish from such wounds, which leads to yes there are werewolves among us, and no need to pick up…"

"…seeds?" Antonio finished.

"Precisely," Song's End informed him, an all-knowing smile and mischievous twinkle in his eyes relaying even more visually than words ever could.

"Son of a bitch. I knew it. Goddamn coven across the street ruining my life for the past thirteen years," Antonio fumed, folding his arms across his chest like a child having a tantrum.

"Do not blame them, they are creatures of habit," Song's End said.

"I'm a pretty despicable creature of habit myself, something you might have known had you stuck around," Antonio said, regretting the words after he spoke them, but leaving them to dangle in the club's air until they tickled Song's End's ear drums to register the malevolence behind them.

I wish Brendon was here to comfort me, but I know why he left us alone.

"I deserve that. Nobody prepared me to be a father, and my own burned me while I still had breath even though he thought me dead," Song's End confessed.

"Still…" Antonio started, but Song's End interrupted.

"Still, I realize my mistake now, as Jonathan has helped me reclaim what little humanity nature endowed me with. I understand your anger, though, admittedly, you have handled yours quite admirably compared to how I did," Song's End said, continuing his confession.

"I apologize for my anger," Antonio said quietly, eyes falling to his knees.

Song's End lifted Antonio's chin. "Never apologize for that. You have every right to be angry with me, and every right to voice that anger to me."

"I do?"

"Of course, my son. My beloved son."

Antonio didn't know whether to be comforted by this or further push him into the eternal damnation of anger's black hole of narcissism he'd become since losing Sam. Both seemed viable options. Couldn't they coexist together?

"Thank you, Father," Antonio said, shocked it didn't sound inauthentic.

"One word of advice, however," Song's End said as his smile faded while the DJ transitioned from one song to the next.

"What's that?"

"Don't kill your entire tribe to get back at me."

"Promise."

"Thank you, Son," Song's End said with a slight smile that faded nearly as fast as it came. "It is but my one regret, and haunts me still."

Antonio sat on the barstool, heels digging into the metal rung. "So, I can kill anyone without others hunting me down?"

"Antonio, be cautious. Taking a life is not something to make light of."

"I'm not making light of anything, just want to be clear."

"Alas, I fear it is so."

"Don't fear. But also can't make any guarantees. I sense someone from my past has found me here and must, in a sense, make sure he stays in my past," Antonio confessed.

"I know," Song's End said before disappearing, like literally disappearing right before his very eyes which, had Antonio not seen Brendon do the very same thing after making love to meet an old man in the park, he might have chalked it up to delusion, but now it was already older than that proverbial hat people are trying to make a thing.

"Why are you here, Drew?" Antonio asked accusingly, arms decidedly behind him, hands locked together.

The man smiled before saying, "To see you."

His voice brought back memories of dark rooms and broken bones. Cold floors and no blankets. Old urine and fresh feces.

"Why shouldn't I kill you?" Antonio said with an insanely calm demeanor considering what the man in front of him, the monster in front of him, did during his childhood.

"I heard about your... condition."

"And?"

"I was curious."

Antonio noticed Drew fumbling with something in his pocket, and if he hadn't been all too familiar with what the man's genitals looked like at the tender age of six, might have mistaken it for nothing more than adjusting his package due to his underwear riding uncomfortably. The size. The shape. The smell. Wood. Real wood. Hickory. Carved. Polished. Pointy.

"Curious enough to stake me through the heart so the world doesn't find out about the real you?"

"I knew you would never tell."

Antonio took out his phone and filed a police report faster than Drew could blink. "Too late. Just did. They know where to find the others. The ones who didn't make it."

Why didn't I do that earlier? Why did I let Drew control me long after he no longer had the power to? Why am I still the chickenshit, scared kid I was back then even now as the asshole in front of me looks weak and old and about as threatening as broccoli? Broccoli? Really? That's what your goddamn brain conjures for nonthreatening? Jesus, no wonder he grabbed you and... and...

"I don't know what you're talking about," Drew said, still fidgeting with his pocket wood, a bead of sweat slicking down his right temple.

Antonio watched the bead fall down Drew's cheek, freefall onto his shoulder, and soak into his jacket. Sad. Slow. Sweat.

"Yes, you do."

"Is this any way to treat your tío?"

His words stung with the venom of a thousand wasps. Stabbing over and over in rapid succession as Antonio replayed the words over and over in the moment between tick and tock. Swelling with pain until he felt numb.

"You are not my uncle."

Even if the man in question may have been treated as such by his family, even to the point of his parents insisting that he was, indeed, his uncle, there was no blood or kinship of any kind linking them. In fact, Drew was just another one of his father's projects. No job. No family. No home. Nothing but a past his father never spoke of and a future that took away Antonio's childhood.

"C'mon, Tony."

Nobody called him Tony. Nobody. It was not his name. Not his nickname. But that was what Drew insisted on calling him after he kidnapped him. Locked him in the basement. Used him. Threw him away.

"Antonio."

"Excuse me?" Drew asked, slowly walking forward.

An unconscious flinch escaped Antonio's being as he took a step back. It took him a moment to remember what he was. Who he had become. He was no longer the scared little kid begging for his mother and father as he lay in his own piss and shit. He was vampire. Now he had the power.

"My name is Antonio, fucker," he told him, taking a decisive step towards Drew.

Drew pulled out Mr. Pointy from his pocket, along with a handful of sunflower seeds. Antonio watched as they scattered in the air, dispersing like a goddamn dandelion blowing in the wind, settling on the pavement at his feet.

Seeds.

Antonio shook his head and laughed.

"Are you serious?" Antonio asked, staring at his shoes as he continued laughing.

Drew didn't say anything, just ran up to Antonio, pushing the hickory stake deep into his chest. "I should've killed you years ago."

Antonio kept laughing, the stake obscuring his gaze towards the seeds around him. "I guess I'll have to tell my boyfriend you ruined the shirt he just got me."

"Why aren't you dead yet?" Drew asked, staring at the stake he felt certain he had properly placed.

Antonio picked him up and carried him over to a ditch. "Can't stake a vampire who no longer has a heart."

Drew mumbled something incoherent. Antonio dropped him.

"What was that?"

"Seeds? How did you walk past? I've done that dozens of times to your kind. I know it works!"

"I am not just vampire."

"What?"

Antonio picked Drew up off the road by the leg.

CRACK!

"Aaaaaaaahhh!!!" Drew cried. "You broke my fucking ankle!"

"Well, for good measure, I may as well break the other one. After all, it's only fair to repay you for doing it to me. You know, so I wouldn't run."

Another *CRACK!* and another primal cry screeching from Drew as lights of red and blue flashed in the distance long before human eyes could register them. Antonio dropped him. One last *CRACK!* Sadly, just an elbow this time.

"Rot in hell, asshole," Antonio told the broken old man before grabbing the stake from his chest. He stared at the craftsmanship in awe. This was not its first staking. This would not be its last. "Thanks for the gift."

And then he disappeared, leaving Drew in the dark with nothing but pain and broken bones until the cops found him lying in a puddle of his own piss.

Karma.

CHAPTER 8

Karma Chameleon

"Stacy, why did you change your name?" Antonio asked his old school friend after running into her on a sketchy corner in downtown Portland outside a sketchy bar where sketchy people went to get away from their world.

"I didn't legally change it, honey. Just, you know, girl's gotta work, and Stacy makes people think of "Stacy's Mom" and that song needs to stay in 2003 where that bitch came from," the friend said, her blue eyes catching a twinkle from the streetlight as she readjusted her blonde hair made even more golden by the lamp's hue. "Besides, there's something charming about Karma."

"Charming all right. Like 1983 charming and annoying as hell," Antonio told her.

Karma kicked her heels into the pavement, her gold sequined skirt barely hiding what lay beneath. "You know I love me some Boy George. Damn, he was like the epitome of fine back when we were kids."

It was true, Antonio realized. Stacy had been in love with Boy George since kindergarten, and never really grew out of that fascination, even after "The Crying Game" and that whole frighteningly familiar Audun Carlsen scandal.

"You and I have very different taste in men," Antonio said, shaking his head.

"Not so different these days," Karma said, one eye cocked as she motioned behind him.

Her finger pointed straight towards Brendon who patiently pressed his ass against Antonio's car while he pretended to be on his phone. He looked up from it, gave Antonio a mischievous smile that said he'd had more to drink then he should have had and that he'd be up for anything kinky Antonio had in mind. Not that it took much convincing for Brendon, as his years of pent-up sexual frustrations were finally getting release. A lot of release. More than he ever could have hoped or dreamed for.

"Careful, Stacy. That boy is mine," Antonio said as his face turned around back to her.

"Damn, sweetie! That is one fine piece of ass I'd love to sink my teeth into," Karma said, biting down as she bared her pearly whites, wrinkling her nose.

A car slowed down just behind her, nearly stopping. Karma winked, flipped her blond hair behind her shoulder, turned around, and was about to bend forward so the driver could get a good look at her tits about to burst out of her red top, but it sped off. "Fuck me."

"It appears he didn't want to take you up on that offer," Antonio said.

"You're an asshole, Antonio," Karma said as she flipped him off.

"I know."

"I know you know."

"Why do you do it?"

"Work the streets?"

"Yeah. You're smart as hell. Surely there has got to be something else you could do that would be a little more…"

"Respectable?"

"I was gonna say safe, but since you said it, yeah."

"Honey, when I can make five-hundred dollars a night doing something I love, why wouldn't I do it?"

"Danger."

"You mean like hanging with a fanger?"

"Precisely."

"Please, Antonio. We've known each other too long. I'm not your type. My clients on the other hand…."

"Any with questionable pasts they're trying to hide?"

Karma Chameleon turned white so fast Antonio thought she had become a chameleon, or worse, Republican.

So pale.

Frightful.

Like she'd seen a ghost.

"Stacy?" Antonio asked, putting his hand on her shoulder.

"That man over there by your boy. Him. His friends coming up behind him. Too many of my girlfriends and I have had dealings with them. Tanya'll never work again thanks to that fucker. Mary Jane had her last dance with him," Karma said, her voice quivering like Jell-O as her finger pointed to each of them, naming their victims, her friends.

"I'm sorry, Stacy. Why haven't they been prosecuted?" Antonio asked before he realized he knew the answer.

"We're whores. Who's gonna take our side?" Karma asked, eyes full of rage.

"Still, you're human first," Antonio said.

"They're also not too fond of faggots either, so if your boy is of the less-than-coy variety, you may wanna do your thing," Karma told him.

A short-bursted laugh fell out of Antonio's mouth before he said, "My boy can handle himself."

"He looks like he's not lacking in the muscular department, but there's six to one," Karma said. "Never underestimate numbers."

"You know how math and I have never been friends."

"And I've lost more friends than I care to count to them and people like them."

Her words stung with truth, and Antonio knew he had to do something.

"What should I do?" Antonio asked as his fangs lowered and eyes bloodlusted.

"Too late. You were right about your boy," Karma said, laughing as she watched the six grown men scream like babies.

"What'd I miss?" Antonio asked as he turned around, seeing the last of the men disappear into an SUV before it drove off in the opposite direction.

Brendon winked at him, then looked back at his phone.

Karma forcefully pushed out her laughs in steady breaths before saying, "No idea. One minute they're just talking and your boy's just smiling and then those guys look like they're about to pummel him and I shit you not, they all grabbed their dicks and ran."

Antonio smiled.

"What'd your boy do?"

"Brendon. His name is Brendon Hollins."

"Oh shit! You mean like the Hollins family? Like Sheree and Kayla? Like serious?"

"Like yes? You know them?"

"Not well, but been around town long enough to know that Kayla's a W-I-T-C-H," Karma spelled quietly.

"So's my boy," Antonio said, side smile creeping up out of the shadows on the left side of his face.

"Cool," Karma said before shouting towards Brendon, "Hey Hollins!"

Brendon tried to play it cool, but his clumsy dork slipped out instead as he dropped his phone, cracking the screen. "Son of a bitch!" they heard as his words slowly made their way down the street towards them. He picked it up, brushed it off, and walked in their direction. "Yeah?"

"Just curious what kinda spell you put on those dicks?" Karma asked.

"Uh… Uh…." Brendon fumbled.

Antonio caught the ball and told him, "She knows you're a witch. Knows Sheree and Kayla apparently."

"Well slap my ass and call me a bitch," Brendon said.

"Gladly, darling," Karma said before taking two steps in her green heels and doing just that.

"I love her! Can we keep her?" Brendon asked Antonio.

"I've known her since I was four, my only true confidant. Besides you, of course," Antonio told Brendon before kissing him.

"Awww… how sweet. Now spell, kid. Spill," Karma demanded.

"Um, I uh, well, kinda made their dicks shrivel up?" Brendon confessed with more hesitation than even he expected.

"Ha! Serves those fuckers right!" Karma said.

"I mean, it's only temporary, but they don't know that," Brendon said.

"Damn it. Should be permanent. They're the worst," Karma told him.

"Like, pretty much bottom of the barrel deplorables," Antonio said. "At least based off what Stacy, I mean Karma has told me."

"Stacy's fine," Karma said, pushing out her hand for a shake. "I doubt he'd ever need Karma Chameleon's services when he's got you to satisfy his needs, Antonio."

Going in for the shake, Brendon said, "No offense, but you aren't my type."

"I see that," Karma said, noticing his and Antonio's interlocked hands.

"So, how exactly do you know Brendon's sisters?" Antonio asked.

"Oh, you know my baby sister Angie? She's friends with them, or was back in high school," Karma told them.

"Angie! Kevin's best friend! Oh, my gawd, Kevin. So hot. Milk did that boy's body good," Brendon said. "Sorry, Antonio, but when I was ten I thought Kevin was the dreamiest and wanted to pet his Moobs."

"Wow, that seems like an overshare that I'd feel far too much guilt trying to compare based off my history," Antonio admitted.

"It's not. Kevin's still pretty hot. And I got to pet his Moobs," Karma said.

"Okay, why is petting a man's boobs a thing?" Antonio asked.

"Moobs was one of his bull calves," Brendon said.

"Kevin's a dairy farmer," Karma clarified.

"I can't tell you how many times I masturbated to him in nothing but his cowboy hat and boots and a tall glass of milk," both Brendon and Karma said like a goddamn country duet of unlikely pairing.

"And with that, we really should be going," Antonio said, suddenly uncomfortable about where their conversation was going, even if it was more in-sync than 'NSYNC, which is saying something. Oh, Justin Timberlake and your ramen noodle hair we all wanted to eat up in our younger days!

"Oh, Antonio! You know we're just joking," Karma said, playfully shoving his arm as she did, a heavy-lashed wink and toothless grin accompanying it for good measure.

Looking at his watch, Brendon said, "Actually, we do need to get going. Karma, it was a pleasure meeting you. Maybe Stacy can come play with us some time."

"I'd like that," Karma said.

"You sure you don't want me to kill those assholes?" Antonio asked.

The offer hit Karma like a backhanded bitch slap caught her off guard. After the initial stun and sting wore off, she said, "No, don't kill them. Then I'd be no better than they are. Karma's a bitch, but she isn't of the asshole disposal variety."

"Let me know if you change your mind," Antonio said, hugging his oldest friend.

"Will do, sweetie," Karma said, squeezing tighter than usual but knowing Antonio could take the extra. She let go, and just as Brendon turned around to walk back towards the car she yelled, "Hollins! You hurt him, I hurt you!"

With just a smile, Brendon let her know her message was received loud and clear as a Seventh Day Adventist church parking lot on Sunday. He grabbed Antonio's hand and held it until they forked around the car, reconnecting with their opposite hands once inside. As they drove off, Karma stepped into a sporty black Jaguar coupe.

"Biggie Smalls ain't wrong," Brendon said.

"What?!" Antonio screamed.

"Fuck bitches, get money."

"True dat."

CHAPTER 9

I'm Yours

"Please, tell me I'm yours," Brendon demanded quietly as they lay in Antonio's bed.

"Why do you need me to say that? Isn't my love enough?" Antonio asked, brushing his fingers through Brendon's short brown hair.

But it wasn't enough. Antonio was unable to fully grasp Brendon's demands. Couldn't understand why Brendon wanted him to quite literally take possession of him. People should not be slaves. People should have free will! So why did Brendon, a young man so sure of himself and what he wanted in life want that taken away? Some BDSM fantasy? A Master-Slave complex?

"Please," Brendon pleaded again.

"Tell me why?" Antonio asked as he searched Brendon's eyes for answers in case words failed as they often do.

He found none.

"You've marked me," Brendon confessed, diverting his eyes.

"Marked you?" Antonio asked, pulling his hands from Brendon's hair, sitting up slightly. "How?"

"Sex," Brendon said bluntly, almost blushing like a ten-year-old girl with a crush on the teacher.

"Sex?" Antonio wore confusion like it never went out of style.

"Yes, sex," Brendon repeated, sans blush like when the teacher's significant other shows up to class one day and is prettier than you'll ever be so you give up your unrequited quest for pre-pubescent romance based solely on self-doubt.

"I don't understand." Confusion by Calvin Klein, lingering long after everyone has left the room.

"I know." Brendon's voice suddenly small and mouse-like.

"Tell me." Antonio's voice pathetically pleading and clueless.

"I will," Brendon said.

They sat in silence for days as Antonio waited for Brendon's promised explanation. Days and days and days until months and years passed and still not another word, an explanation, a reason for this request, no, not request, demand was being made of him. Brendon had asked once before mere minutes after their first tryst, but then it was dropped as soon as Brendon's family began with the sixty-four questions about the invisible man in the room.

After a gentle kiss Antonio hoped would put Brendon's mind at ease, he softly said in barely a whisper, "Please, Brendon, I must know why."

Brendon smiled and his cheek dimpled and then in a flash they both disappeared. "Virgins are typically spared vampire attacks because their DNA hasn't been infused with another's and thus is less potently odiferous."

"Wow. I mean, that makes sense, just..." Antonio started, but Brendon cut him off like one of those small penis mobiles during rush hour traffic.

"There's more. When a human and vampire, you know, have sex? That smell is tenfold," Brendon said, avoiding eye contact.

Antonio's face, had it actually been able to convey anger in color, would've burned red as coals. "Have others tried to...?"

Looking straight into Antonio's eyes, Brendon assured him with, "No."

"Good." Antonio's coals turned to ash.

"But only because I've been holding in my scent through magic. Twenty-four hours a day. Seven days a week every second since that day in the forest."

Slap.

There it was.

The slap Antonio felt that never was but was real nonetheless.

"Why didn't you tell me?" Antonio asked, selfishness filling the empty void where his heart used to be, sandwiching itself between the guilt slices.

"I didn't want to pressure you when you wouldn't tell me I'm yours right after. I didn't want to force you into something I wanted," Brendon confessed.

"But... but... This whole time?"

"Yes."

"How have you not exhausted yourself?"

"Trust me, my weakness is unraveling quickly."

"And if I say it, what happens to you?"

"Protection, nothing more."

"Protection?"

"Protection from the horde of vampires waiting to feast on all this," Brendon said, motioning his hands all over his naked body, finishing with a playful squeeze of his dick and balls which he shook for good measure, causing an awakening that turned Dick into Richard.

"And saying those words will prevent... that?"

"Kind of. It binds us."

"And others will know?"

"They will once the words are spoken."

A violent knock at the door followed by a continuous series of doorbell rings shattered the air. Muffled through the solid door they heard what sounded like, "Open up! Hurry!"

Antonio didn't even take time to dress as he swiftly leapt out of bed, ran to the living room, and opened the front door with a swoosh. "What?"

"Oh, Jesus, wow, um, okay, uh, thanks for the show again, but I need you and Brendon now," Sheree said, unable to take her eyes off Antonio's dick.

Brendon was at the door covering the peep show before she could squeeze out a quickie. "What? What's wrong?"

"Dad's freaking out," Sheree said, shaking her head once the snapshot in her mind reverse-Polaroided.

"But Dad doesn't freak out. Like, ever," Brendon said, eyes wide. "Jesus, Antonio, put some pants on!"

"Or don't, I mean, that might help ease the situation. I know it's helping ease..." Sheree started but Brendon put his hands up as he interrupted her.

"Stop mentally masturbating over my boyfriend!" Brendon shouted so loud a raven fell from the sky, splattering on the street just in front of Antonio's house.

Squish.

"Fuck," Sheree said as she turned to see the bird, or what remained of it. "Yeah, I'm pretty sure that's bad luck."

"Fuck. Fuck fuck fuck fuck fuck!" Brendon said, voice shriller with each repeat. "Goddammit, Antonio! Pants!"

"I'm putting them on!" Antonio said, dressing faster than the speed of light, and finished clothing himself before his mouth finished uttering.

They ran to the Hollins house a couple doors down and further from the cemetery that flanked the dead-end street. When they got there, Mr. Hollins—Frank—paced the living room, etching the ancient hardwood floor. Mrs. Hollins stood in place leaning against the kitchen counter next to a set of barstools that had seen better days, a half-filled glass of red wine in her hand threatening to waterfall onto the floor and showing lipstick signs that it'd been filled more than once.

"Stop freaking out, Dad," Brendon said calmly, knowing it'd do nothing to ease the apprehension but maybe enough to break the trance-like pace his father kept at even though he couldn't even bother looking in their direction when they walked through the front door.

"Yeah, that's not gonna work," Mrs. Hollins said before gulping down the rest of her glass. As she refilled it, she continued with, "Already tried that."

"Beth, I realize we don't know each other well, but how many of those have you had?" Antonio asked soft as Angora kitten fur.

"Not enough," Mrs. Hollins responded quietly into the glass.

"Just tell me what the hell is going on," Brendon demanded.

He's awfully bossy lately. I hope part of that isn't me, but I know it is. Stress. The stress of him and I. Us. Keeping up that barrier wall all the time. Stop being a pussy and tell him what he wants to hear? Antonio battled in his head. *Crap, you can hear me can't you, Brendon?*

There was no reply from Brendon, confirming his suspicions. Part of him felt relieved. The rest felt like a sad pit of depression with a side of pendulum of doom. Was this the beginning of the end of their short romance? Was this love? Was this just another lust-filled fuck frenzy only disguised in monogamous relationship clothing? As the questions swirled in his head, the pendulum swinging over the pit of his stomach nearly made him hurl.

"These fucking quote animal attacks unquote have got to stop," Mr. Hollins said.

Yes, he said "quote unquote" out loud.

Antonio sat. "There's been an increase?"

"Nine so far," Mr. Hollins said.

"Since when?" Antonio and Brendon asked simultaneously.

"Today. Nine so far today," Mr. Hollins said bluntly.

Brendon sat down on Antonio's lap in the armchair. "Shit."

"Shit's right. I can't cover that much up. Goddamn vampires are getting out of control. No offense to you Antonio. I'm sorry, but this is so out of character for our town," Mr. Hollins said.

"None taken, or at least none yet because I'm still in shock. Any word on if this is a local issue or if there are out-of-towners on an all-you-can-eat bender?" Antonio asked.

"I was hoping you'd know the answer to that," Mr. Hollins asked.

"That's why I grabbed you," Sheree said.

"No. Nothing. I don't know what this is all about, but I will. Maybe Song's End or Jonathan have a clue about…" Antonio said, unable to finish because…

"Oh! You've met my great-great-grandfather and his lover?" Mrs. Hollins gushed, her wine dribbling down the side of the glass, droplets splattering like blood on the floor.

"Yes, Beth. Song's End is my maker," Antonio confessed.

"Well then you already are family and that makes you and Brendon a little awkward though decidedly not as awkward as some of our dirtier little secrets we have. I should shut up now," Mrs. Hollins said, taking a large gulp of wine, some trickling down her chin before she caught it with her free hand, licking the finger after.

It made Antonio think that he and Mrs. Hollins were kindred spirits, only instead of wine, he guzzled cum like a greedy snatch. And while this oddly comforted him, he realized he had to do something else other than think of his glory hole days. His mind, however much he tried to persuade otherwise, wasn't having it as he turned his attention back to Mr. Hollins who, even in his fifties, pumped his nads. And then all the guilt bricks started stacking in the hollow space where his heart used to be, so he slipped his fingers into Brendon's and lightly squeezed.

"I promise I will find whoever is responsible for this," Antonio said assertively.

"And?" Mr. Hollins asked.

"Judge, jury, and executioner all in one. I will end him," Antonio assured.

"Or her," Sheree piped in.

Antonio smiled. "Of course. And if we're being equal, a gender-neutral pronoun like them might better suffice."

A midnight stroll through Ravenwood Park was just what the doctor ordered. Literally, Mr. Hollins, the city's chief medical examiner, and thus a doctor, albeit doctor for the dead, said all the bodies were found in the park. More precisely in the forested areas skirting the park. However, as Antonio and Brendon walked a well-worn path where Antonio's heightened senses told him to go, the blood sifting through the air like chimney smoke, their conversation just as lofty, Brendon became more and more rigid, and not where Antonio wanted the rigidness to reside.

"You know what's sexy? A real conversation," Brendon said bluntly.

Antonio didn't know what to say. They'd only been together a few short weeks. And with all the death paths they were following, he just wanted to lighten the mood. Take Brendon's mind off their work. Keep up the empty talk that filled their mugs so he didn't have to think about the undue stresses of Brendon magically holding his shit together. But the bag was open. How could their relationship stale so quickly? "What do you want?"

"Us. A real us," Brendon said, cold as ice.

Unintentionally shivering from the coldness behind Brendon's words, Antonio asked, "We aren't real?"

"You are distant, and I realize I'm beginning to sound like one of them clingy gay clichés I bitched about in middle school when I was the living embodiment of one, but we need to have an actual discussion about our future that involves both of us, not just me making decisions and you blindly copiloting."

It was as if someone stitched in a new heart inside Antonio, ripped it back out, stomped on it with six-inch stilettos, and walked away as the still beating organ power walked down the street before getting kicked into a sewer drain. "Wow. Bossy much?"

"That too," Brendon said, crossing his arms like a child and realizing it before rolling his eyes.

"I'm sorry about earlier," Antonio told him, eyes following a red leaf as it blew down the path they were heading down.

"I know. Me too." Brendon loosened his stance slightly.

"And I'm sorry for how far away my brain has been these last few days since Drew." Antonio said, still focused on the leaf.

Brendon noticed he didn't have Antonio's full attention, even now. "Just talk to me."

"It's something that Song's End said," Antonio said as the leaf dropped to the ground.

"What's that?" Brendon asked, a fledgling of hope sticking to his soul like flypaper.

"That I can kill with impunity," Antonio revealed. "That has shaken me more than I care to admit, both from the terror and the thrill."

"You're not a monster," Brendon said, connecting his forehead to Antonio's as he tried to interlock their fingers.

Antonio didn't lock. "You never met Fairy Sam. He might say otherwise."

"Fairy Sam is a monster who preyed on your weaknesses and forced himself on you like some Hollywood hot shot telling Corey Haim all boys have sex with fat and balding old men," Brendon said as he pulled away.

"Wow, that's a twisty excuse for me eating him and leaving him for dead," Antonio said, unable to shake the image of a middle-school aged Corey Haim getting raped in the ass by a creepy middle-aged man, sadly making his overdose death that much more understandable and tragic.

"Twisty but true. Never underestimate the fae."

"Fuckin' fae."

"We're tangenting."

"It's kinda our thing."

"I'm going to go. When you're ready to talk, really talk about real shit, I'll come back." Brendon turned around, walking back towards the meadow space of the park.

"Brendon, please stay," Antonio half-assedly pleaded.

Brendon stopped, turning so part of his face was barely visible.

"Antonio, I fear I'm only holding you back right now. You're not ready to let me in fully, and I am all in."

"Wilt thou leave me so unsatisfied?" Antonio asked, hoping Brendon would fall for the trap.

He did.

"What satisfaction canst thou have tonight?" Brendon asked back, cursing himself for falling for the Shakespearean bait.

"I'm sorry, now we're Romeo and Julieting. I love you, but I need to figure out what is holding me back, as you've discovered all on your own, before I let you back in," Antonio confessed, shocked by the ease at which the words flowed even though they were thick as molasses.

Brendon turned around, walking back towards Antonio. "I love you, too."

Then they kissed, not hard and furious, but soft, gentle, still full of wanton desires and unfulfilled lust and passion and sweetness that lingers like honey. Then Brendon left, and Antonio was left with nothing more than his misery for company and a red leaf begging him to follow.

CHAPTER 10

Down the Rabbit Hole

As Antonio went deeper and deeper, Darkness's blanket spread over him, surrounding him in black. Still, the red leaf spun around, moving ever forward along the path less taken, pulling him with an invisible leash towards… towards what? Towards answers? Truth? The beginning of the end of his damned existence he prayed would never end while equally begging Life's perpetual edging would push him over, make him cum, painfully orgasm through blue balls, spur the little death that morphs into physical death? Black death. Death of the Moon, whose rays he knew had to be hidden somewhere above on this uncharacteristically clear mid-December night. Night of sadness and want and needs and desires all rolled into one chaotic recipe for disaster. Disaster wielding her whisk, beating him into cohesion with all the other ingredients until only the batter remained, smoothed by hegemony and torture. Torture filling his void like Taco Bell's Fire sauce and succumbing to the eventual anal destruction mere hours after consumption. But oh! the nibble!

The red leaf turned a corner and disappeared. Antonio ran after it, expecting to find him just around the bend, but he didn't. The red leaf was gone. Instead what he found was a hole in Darkness's blanket, light spilling out so vibrantly against the black like the proverbial light of heaven welcoming you into its warmth. He didn't feel the warmth. No welcoming love or acceptance or angels singing on high or street-side sign wavers urging him to the finish line. Nothing but like he was shit, worming its way through the lower intestines while an open and awaiting sphincter pushed him out into an obscenely large toilet bowl.

And then he passed.

It'd been years since Antonio last trekked through the woods to the giant basalt plateau centered by a huge cliff nearly perfectly round and hundreds of feet deep in the middle of the forest. He felt out of place, out of time and space, and assuredly out of his element as the forest hid him well. But this place, this open space, exposed him to an eternal vulnerability he didn't but should've expected. After all, he followed the rabbit down the rabbit hole like Alice towards a life of hoes and gigolos like Adam and came face to face with a truth he never saw coming like Donnie.

Song's End awaited him with his long black hair and arms spread out and eyes, though ebony, shone bright as sunlight in the night while galaxies danced in them. He looked like the crucifix. Like the stereotypical portrayals of Jesus as a Middle Eastern man, not some blond and blue-eyed Aryan concoctionated standardized bastardized version of beauty tainting the truth with greed and dominance and fat stacks of cold hard cash in the hands of the Lord's men doing the Lord's work on national television. Antonio's own personal Jesus telling him to reach out and touch faith.

So, he did.

"Drink me and know," Song's End offered, his wrists at the ready.

Antonio didn't know if he was ready for the offer. Did he really want to know? Did he want to truly understand what little he could about himself? What little Song's End told him the week before about his specialness? His differentness? His rare preciousness? After all, Song's End was no superstar, he was just another father who abandoned his child and showed up at graduation to tell others how proud he was.

Antonio's conflict pulsated. Song's End felt the vibrations. Instead of explaining, Song's End merely kept his wrists out, hoping Antonio would take the bait, drink him, eat him, know him, and in doing so, know himself more truly. And honestly isn't that the dreams of most fathers, for their children to know their authentic selves? If not, shouldn't it be?

"All will be answered with a taste," Song's End assured, voice calm and velvety as VElvis.

Hesitation blew away with the wind, and Antonio plunged into the ecstasy of forbidden fluid, sucking like his mouth was a goddamned Hoover. His eyes widened with realization. Knowledge. Power. Truth. Real truth, not that bullshit stuff investigative reporters shove down our media-riddled throats so hard our uvula gags and we try not to vomit. Eyes black, full black holes devouring everything in their path as his mouth devoured all Song's End had to offer him until he could drink no more.

"Whoah!" Antonio said as he fell back, head hitting the solid rock ground with a sickening crack that split the basalt where the base of his skull smacked. Slowly moving his head, his eyes caught Song's End, blood dripping from his wrists and looking like a corpse. "Oh gawd, what have I done?"

Slow as death, Song's End folded his fingers into his palms, closed his eyes, and healed his gnawed raw wrists. As he did, the emaciated man he had become while his life force literally drained out of him and into his beloved Antonio also began filling, healing, back to normal, whatever that means anymore. Sunken eyes became plump. Bony fingers became caressable once more. His sharp features were no longer jarring and nightmarishly gaunt, but polished and sexy as hell.

"Do you understand?" Song's End asked quietly, staring straight into Antonio's soul that moments before he questioned the existence of.

"I will," Antonio said, bathing in moonlight as his true self filled every crevice his body held.

"Then goodbye, my son," Song's End said.

The tone was sad. Lonely. Desperate and honest and heartbreakingly painful to hear. It wasn't that he didn't want to stay, to help Antonio along his journey, it was just that he couldn't. He had to stay hidden. He was, after all, a wanted man in more legends than he could count. But more than that, he was the singularly most powerful vampire who'd ever created himself into existence. The longer he stayed out in the open, the more he exposed himself to people who'd want to do very bad things to him, even if he had the power to make them not. He had decided long ago, just after meeting the love of his life, that love was more powerful than hate, and he hated himself for that more than he cared to admit.

"Must you go?" Antonio asked, almost unable to move as his body swam with forbidden fruit.

"Yes. You should go back now," Song's End told him.

"I can't go back to yesterday because I was a different person then," Antonio said.

"And so, your adventure begins," Song's End said.

Then Song's End bent over Antonio's frozen body, kissing him so gently on the lips that he thought that had his eyes been closed it would have felt like nothing more than a breeze passing over them. And then he was gone, and Antonio was all alone, waiting for his body to play catch-up as the data computed at quadrillions of bits per microsecond.

Snow fell from the clear black sky; the moon's dandruff. Each frozen flake that hit Antonio's face burned like molten lava, instantly vaporizing as he lay steaming. Vampire sauna.

How long had he been lying there? How long did Song's End leave him for the last time? How many hours or days had passed since he drank the blood and ate the body of his creator? Or was it merely minutes? Seconds? Time failed. Hell, even space failed as he saw no clouds, just a full moon and abundant stars and a ribbon stretching from one end to the other he registered as the spiral arms of the Milky Way. But there was snow covering the ground around him, the trees surrounding him, brightening the night quickly into blood red beauty.

As Antonio sat up, he suddenly felt the **weight** of his body, like all that infusion of

and knowledge held *heft.* Struggling to stand, he urged his body onward, focusing on only the next step of **standing up.**

He fell back down, and the **spiral arms** of his body matched the *Milky Way* as he flailed

down,

down,

down,

back down the *rabbit hole,* watching the little oysters get conned into giving up their very lives to feed the

FAT WALRUS who convinces the working man carpenter into collecting them all for him—corporate greed at Lewis Carroll's finest—watching the Cheshire Cat smile his wicked smile and snicker as he tells him, "We're all mad here." —a truth he never would be able to argue against— watching Wonderland pass him by, spiraling out of control, still falling down, down, down until he hit rock bottom.

SQUISH

CHAPTER 11

Come Undone

Blackness ruled.

Where am I?

Suddenly he was six, and the stench of stale cigarettes and buttery urine-like odor of microwaved popcorn flooded his senses, seeping into every sealed pore, climbing into his nostrils, clawing at his eyes, touching him in places he knew was wrong but couldn't understand why he was even there in the first place, being told it was okay, being told it was normal, being told to put his mouth around it and pretend it was a large thumb. Popcorn and tuna fish. The butter had gone bad. Bitter egg whites that hadn't been cooked yet. If he could've, he would've made himself as small as possible, grow wings, fly away, but he also knew that even with wings, he wouldn't know how to find his way out of this, not when all he wanted was his mommy and daddy and abuelo to hold him and tell him it was all a nightmare, a terrible, terrible nightmare that never wanted to end.

He prayed for numbness so he wouldn't feel what the man was doing.

He prayed for silence so he wouldn't hear what the man was saying.

He prayed for death so he wouldn't have to feel the heaviness of every breath crushing him like stone, the dryness of tears that could no longer fall, the stabbing jaw, the backwards right knee, the missing fingernails jammed into the door and floor.

He prayed and he prayed and he prayed, but nobody heard his prayers. Either that, or God didn't feel like those prayers were worth being answered. He could still hear his tía Nacia loudly declare in her Stockard-Channing-if-she-were-a-chicana voice, "God do not give us nothing more than we cannot handle, love," but even though her voice pounded his ears until they bled, the words were nothing but petulant lies swatting him long after he passed out from the exhaustion of survival he no longer wished his instincts insisted upon, hoping that the next time the door cracked open and blinded him it would be the last.

Could this be the day?

It was darker at the bottom of the cliff than Antonio ever imagined it could be. God definitely was joking about handling shit as he felt every bone in his body shatter, every muscle snap, every inch of his skin come undone at the seams as if he was nothing more than a poorly stitched muslin doll. And as much as he wanted to move, movement simply was not having any of it. Stubborn little bitch. Oh, how he wished he was a witch! Then he could heal himself the way that Song's End healed himself after he drained him so completely, emptying his reservoir father to replenish the wayward son.

"Grrraaawwwaaarrghhh!" Antonio screamed a guttural growl so wild he thought a wild beast had joined him in the valley of death.

It took an eternity for him to realize the beast was inside him all along.

The crystalline bones reassembled. The sinewy flesh restrung itself. The terra cotta skin tightened into marble. No, granite. No, quartz! And suddenly Antonio felt lighter than air. Good as new! But then he felt the emptiness in his chest and realized his heart was still stolen. Gone. Taken. What remained hidden in a jar by a boy so many years ago when his whole world fell apart in one perfect storm. He was not whole, and didn't know if he could fill his hole with Brendon now that he knew too much. He also had to somehow get out of the hole he'd fallen into.

At least the full moon was there to keep him company now that the darkness had passed.

Digging into the rock, one of dozens of layers stacked on top of one another from thousands of years of flows that make up this edge of the Columbia River Basalts, Antonio could feel the stone yield to his fingers, letting him slide his digits through its tightness. So, he pushed them in. It felt good. Natural. Raw. Just how he liked it. Then he climbed his way up the cliff wall, feeling the power it held penetrate through his fingertips into his soul, or at least the facsimile he assumed he must have somewhere buried deep inside the recesses of his not-quite-living carcass he still called a body. His body. His father, Song's End, had been here as well. He became what he is now here. This very spot, hundreds of years before, causing the earthquake that violently shook the region and the crater-like hole he continued digging himself out of. Antonio watched through newborn Song's End's eyes as his own father, Chief Ravenwood, namesake of the city he called home, buried him beneath heavy stones, crushing his infant body, before setting him ablaze in a fiery rage. Watched as the smoke cleared the next day. Watched the sky open as he rose up the canyon his metaphysical ascension created. Watched the destruction of the entire Oaxaciian tribe as Song's End's bloodlust ravaged the landscape, painting the world red. Watched as he spared the last living representation of that tribe, Chief Ravenwood, his father, who wept and begged for forgiveness Song's End could never give.

The moon laughed as he reached the top, followed by a wolf's piercing howl. Only it was no ordinary wolf. Fur? Check. Fangs? Check. Claws? Check. The voice of a twenty-something boy? Check.

"Brendon said I might find you here," the werewolf said, eyeing him up and down, though not so much checking him out as checking for signs of stability.

"Wayne?" Antonio asked, instinctually squinting for no logical reason.

"In the flesh," Wayne answered. "Wow, that was, um, sorry, I don't know why I answered like that."

The werewolf's diction eerily reminded Antonio of Brendon, which, given the friendship history he'd known of between the boy and this wolf boy, took the mystery away like spraying Febreeze in an avenue of stank. Still, that touch of familiar helped calm his nerves, which at the moment all stood on end like toy soldiers waiting to spring into battle. The way Wayne's bangs were jacked up to Jesus—"The higher the hair the closer to God!" his tía Guadalupe delightfully told him after a particularly grueling mass when he was eight—however, made him want to tell the boy that the early 1990s called and they want their hair back.

Antonio's lip curled up, imperceptible to the common man. But this werewolf was anything but common.

"Why were you looking for me?" Antonio asked, suspicion getting the better of him now that confusion was swept under the rug for the time being.

"Got a proposition for ya," Wayne said smugly, his grimace decidedly haunting.

Haunting and adorable all at once, like John Dall in the underrated *Gun Crazy*.

"Some stupid Supernaturals Only Club?" Antonio asked, chuckling at the thought.

Silence.

Standing mere feet away, Wayne suddenly let out his unease with Antonio's presence, or so he thought. Antonio watched as Wayne's pointed ears perked up, bending backwards. His also perked up as he heard the footsteps.

"We're not alone," Wayne said curtly.

"No shit, Sherlock," Antonio said.

"How Audrey II of you," Wayne said, rolling his eyes as he turned around. "And for the record, yes, it's a secret club. We want you."

"Oh Jesus, you're fucking with me, right?" Antonio asked, waiting for whoever was approaching to reveal himself as a terrible thought entered his mind, strangling his insides, suddenly wondering if this was the price of knowledge he sucked out of his father, momentarily regretting their brief yet devastatingly ecstatically erotic encounter. But could it be? Could his greed be his undoing? Didn't Song's End express that the truth would set him free? Or did he just assume as much as he drank his father's delectable bodily fluids until he'd sucked him completely dry?

"No. But what the hell is that?" Wayne asked.

"No clue, which is oddly comforting," Antonio said, the terrible thought slipping away just as quickly as she entered him, much to his amusement.

"So, you don't sense danger?" Wayne asked.

"None," Antonio said.

"Me neither," Wayne said, disappointment filling the air.

"Awesome," Antonio said quietly, smiling to the ground.

"Why awesome?" Wayne asked, noticing the sarcasm dripping from Antonio's mouth.

"Because that means we're both fucked," Antonio said, staring straight into Wayne's dark blue eyes surrounded by the cute fuzziness of fur that made him wish he had a puppy to snuggle with. He began laughing at his feet, eyes glazed as Donnie Darko's when he knows his end is eminent.

"Shit. I didn't want my first time to be a surprise encounter," Wayne said, suddenly springing into a Kung Fu stance as he clenched his ass cheeks, making his baseball player ass bubbleicious.

"What the hell is it with virgins in this town?" Antonio asked loudly, still unable to see the person slowly making their approach.

"Uh, when you've got a genetic disorder that has to be passed down in a pretty specific manner, you get a little picky in the selection process," Wayne revealed.

"Ah, so no girl finds your werewolf side a perk yet?" Antonio asked.

"Precisely," Wayne said, smiling through the sadness his heart pumped out, one sad, slow beat after another like teasing a limp dick in desperate need of Viagra into an erection.

"I know plenty of furries. Well, they all play for my team, but still…" Antonio said, cut off before finishing.

"Yeah, my brother's been trying to hook me up with one of them for years. Thinks it's a big joke. Ha ha," Wayne confided.

"But you aren't gay or even bi or even put off an air of bi-curiousness. Hell, I know some pans who aren't even into furries, and they're pretty much into anyone!" Antonio said, hoping to lighten the mood.

It failed.

The footsteps continued towards them.

Slowly.

Methodically.

Like the tick and tock of Crocodile's goddamned swallowed clock.

"Loosen up, kid," Antonio told Wayne. "I mean, at this rate whoever this asshole is won't be here until tomorrow."

"Sorry. I just really want you to join our club, and yes, I realize how childish that sounds, but think of it like a coven that actually understands you, not that fakeness the other vampires on our street convey, because, well, we already have all the other puzzle pieces that shouldn't fit together," Wayne revealed.

"Puzzle pieces?" Antonio asked, his mind taking every avenue to ascertain what the wolf boy meant by that particular phrase, twisting and turning like a drive on the Terwillegar Curves.

"Yes, puzzle pieces. Like a werewolf who was never bitten, a girl who didn't die but was pieced back together with other body parts, a ghost who never lived, a self-taught medium who had no idea most people didn't randomly get inhabited by dead people, a boy witch you know all too well, oh, and a magic genie I can't get rid of," Wayne said bluntly, his annoyance over the last one beyond obvious.

Waiting for a sign, anything that Wayne was just messing with him, Antonio searched and searched but came to the only illogical conclusion he could: Wayne was telling him the honest-to-God truth, and it was crazy as fuck. He was just a vampire, albeit maybe with a few alterations, but vampire nonetheless, so what would make him unfitting? And he knew of werewolves and mediums, a little about ghosts, but Frankensteined creatures and genies? And what was that whole thing about not being bit? All werewolves become such from bites, right? What does that mean for silver bullets and full moons and nards?

"No fairies though, right?" Antonio asked, not letting his confusion or bewilderment or disillusionment filter through his words.

"Gawd no! You ever met a fae? All talk and tricks and schtup," Wayne said. "Seriously, and I hate discrimination with every fiber of my being, but we can't allow fairies in until they show some level of being trustworthy."

There's always an Other. Even in the supernatural world.

"Why are you. Talking about. Fairies asshole?" a low voice asked, short and punctuated before high-pitched giggles pierced the cold night air, pushing with it a dusting of snow.

"Who the hell are you?" Antonio asked, slowly turning around even though his skin crawled off and ran into the forest to take cover from the fright. *Are my senses broken? What has Song's End done to me?*

"Anna. Sam says hi," the woman said, dressed like a plump snowman, a twinkle in her slanted eyes.

Antonio had never met anyone like her. I mean, yes, he'd met other people with Down Syndrome before, but not like Anna. She was calming while at the same time scary as shit. And the way she just casually name-dropped Sam? His Sam? Almost unforgiveable. Still, he knew he needed more. Needed to probe. To dig deeper. Hello was nice and all, but he had to know, deep down, whether his Sam was okay, even if it was all a lie.

"Can I talk to Sam?" Antonio asked, not wanting to let out how desperate he was to do so, but failing as his voice cracked under the pressure of wants and needs, wondering just what he would say to him, what he could say to him, what, if anything, would make the hurt he still clung to, not wanting to let go like the red maple leaf that only sacrificed himself to lead him to his current location to suck off his father and fall deep deep deep inside the devil's sphincter.

"Sorry. Sam's not here. Right now. Maybe later," Anna said bluntly.

Cold.

As.

Ice.

"Bitch," Antonio said quietly.

"Takes one to. Know one. Bitch," Anna said, bursting into giggles. "Now who's walking. Towards us?"

"Oh shit, Anna! I thought that was you?" Wayne said, suddenly shaking.

"You're the worst. Wolfman. Ever," Anna said. "And you? Vampire hotness? You make me. Moist but. Seriously? Use your senses. Daddy gave you."

If Antonio's jaw could literally hit the ground, it would have. Anna's bluntness was both jarring and refreshing like breakfast sangria. *Mmm… sweet sweet sangria like mama used to drink Sunday's as she got ready for church*, Antonio thought. But then Anna winked at him and he felt violated. Used. But then he felt a sudden resurgence of his old self, the assured self that knew he was hot, knew he made men and women beg for absolution, the one his mother had forsaken, and knew what to do. He winked at her and she fell into a metaphorical puddle of goo.

"Careful, Antonio. Anna's been known to publicly masturbate. She has no shame," Wayne told him.

"Same here," Antonio said, sly smile creeping over his mouth.

"Oh gawd. Why?" Wayne asked the universe who failed to answer back.

"Please say. You'll join our. Club!" Anna squealed, jumping up and down.

"It's not a masturbation club, is it?" Antonio joked, visualizing Wayne's anatomy changing into something more canine-like.

"No, we dismantled that after middle school. Brendon started it in the fourth grade," Wayne told him, eyes back to the approaching footsteps.

"You must tell me more about this," Antonio begged.

"Later. We've got more pressing matters and no Anna not your fingers against your crotch but actual possible bad guy crap we have to fight," Wayne said, his sharp canines prominently displayed as his snout curled back.

Disappointed at Wayne's decision, Antonio understood the tangent would only distract them like their previous one that led to Anna's arrival. He scanned the forest, laserly focusing on where the steps emanated from, but nothing registered.

The footsteps continued coming toward them—thumping and thudding—but still somewhere in the forest, behind the forest, hiding who they belonged to. Crunching the fallen leaves. Snapping the fallen twigs. Pressing the fallen needles into the frozen ground with impunity.

Crunching.

Snapping.

Pressing.

Annoying.

"This might be. Faster if. We ran towards. The bastard," Anna offered, looking at a hangnail and digging out the offensively dangling skin with her obscenely short, jagged, chewed nails.

She wasn't wrong.

Wayne sang, "Ah, it'll take a little time."

Without missing the cue, Antonio sang the next line, "Might take a little crime to come undone."

Anna finished with her choppy rendition. "Hey child. Stay wilder. Than the wind. And blow me. In to…."

"CRY!!!"

"Who the fuck are you?!" Wayne screamed, his voice so feverishly high-pitched Antonio found it comical; his furry hands karate chopping the frigid air only exacerbated the hilarity.

A heavy wind zipped by, stripping the clouds from the full moon, whose naked light revealed Brendon dressed in the PNW winter's finest: blue jeans, red and black checkered flannel, and a puffy navy vest. "Grandpa Jonathan told me I'd find you here," he said to Antonio, ignoring his friends in favor of his lover. "Said you might need my help, so I called in backup."

"My other dad is funny like that," Antonio said with a half-hearted chuckle even he found depressing.

"Yeah, your life is basically a shitty late eighties sitcom," Brendon said bluntly, rolling his eyes.

"That hurt."

"It should."

"Why are you so pissed at me now?"

"Why? WHY?!" Brendon shouted so loud it shook the ground, causing snow to plummet off Douglas firs hundreds of feet away.

"Yeah, so, this is awkward," Wayne said, tapping his fingers together as he avoided eye contact.

"I wish. I had. Popcorn," Anna said before busting out into a giggle fit so violent she looked like she was seizing.

The footsteps in the woods continued.

Slow.

Methodical.

Haunting.

"Oh, for fuck's sake, I thought those were yours, Brendon!" Wayne cried.

"And I thought I was following them to you," Brendon said.

"Well, shit," Antonio said before collapsing onto his back.

Brendon just stared at Antonio, followed by Wayne and Anna when they realized what he was doing.

"Are you seriously making a snow angel right now?" Brendon asked, watching Antonio's arms and legs wipe the snow into lined piles edging pressed wings and dress.

"Yep."

"Um, yeah, so, we should either be ready to fight or run for our lives from whatever that thing is in the forest," Wayne said matter-of-factly, bobbing his head for effect.

"Or die," Anna added, ever the optimist.

"Seriously?" Brendon pleaded. "Get up."

"Nope. Join me," Antonio demanded. "It's way more fun than I remember as a kid."

Brendon glared at Wayne who said, "Don't look at me, Bren. You're the one who's been gaga over this guy since middle school."

"And you were. Fat then," Anna added, her trademark laughter finishing the insult.

"Wow. We're all about to die, but hey, let's just make some funnies," Brendon said, his voice conflicted between laughing and crying tugging on him like toddlers at Target during Christmastime.

Antonio laughed. As he got up to admire his snow angel, the moon catching the edges and making the bevels glow, he still sensed no danger from the shadows, the footsteps in the woods. In all honesty, he didn't sense anything, good or bad, from the direction of the steps. They just kept ticking and tocking.

Tick.

Tock.

Tick.

Tock.

Crunch!

Crunch!

Crunch!

Snap!

"Well, I wanna live, so, uh, see ya? Maybe?" Wayne said quietly.

"I can't die," Antonio said nonchalantly, pulling Brendon in for a kiss.

CHAPTER 12

Wicked Game

"I don't want to fall in love."

"Too late, asshole," Brendon said, easing his way up from Antonio's crotch to kiss his mouth with cum-laden lips, making sure to share the load this time.

"Mmm…."

Brendon kissed Antonio again. "You taste so much more alive."

"I do, don't I?" Antonio said after swallowing the hefty gift. "I feel so much more alive as well."

"Good," Brendon said as he got on top of Antonio's dick and slid it into his ass, riding him like a cowboy into the goddamn sunset until they both burned with fiery heat and exhaustion in desperate need of a watering hole to quench their thirst and continue along the journey of multi-orgasmic bliss.

I never intended this to happen, Antonio thought, looking into Brendon's soul as he bounced.

Up.

Down.

Up.

Down.

I did, Brendon thought without missing a beat.

Methodical.

Tick.

Tock.

Like a clock.

Then out of nowhere he changed up the pace. Sped up. Slowed down. Flew into the event horizon abyss as eruptions showered inside and out.

Antonio didn't know if he would ever get used to loving someone who could hear his every fleeting thought without even trying, but here, now, in this moment while covered in milky ribbons, he didn't care. He wanted this. He may have never intended for this to happen, to be with someone again like this after losing Sam so many years ago, but Brendon made it easy. Home.

Sliding over to his side, Antonio could tell that Brendon wasn't completely finished, but needed a break. Wanted a slow dance after the heated electronica disco rave that twirled them like the glimmering flickering of a fucking mirror ball until the lights dimmed the twinkles. Hand on chest. Rubbing the mess. Fingering figure eights.

"I never dreamed that I'd meet somebody like you," Brendon whispered. "That is, until I did meet you when I was nine and you were 23."

"And now you're 23 and I'm still 23," Antonio whispered back with barely a hint—though more callous than he planned it to be, which made him wince with unease at his oftentimes lack of waiting to form words before fully untangling thoughts—of sarcastic assholery.

The asshole, however, was dripping with goo.

"When do we need to address the elephant in the room?" Brendon asked, hands stopped just over Antonio's right nipple.

"Which elephant? The vampire? The witch? The age difference yet similarity?" Antonio asked with a subtle smile Brendon could just barely perceive, a childish renewal he hadn't felt since ages past, but after recent events, his playfulness resurfaced, climbed the cliff onto a snow-covered plateau, and snuck its way back.

"Okay, so those are all elephants, too, I suppose," Brendon said with a slight head shake. "No, I'm talking about that one."

Following where Brendon's finger pointed, Antonio shot out of bed. "What in the actual fuck?!"

The elephant.

Sam's elephant.

The one Antonio won for him at the shitty winter carnival that popped up faster than a mole hill after paying thousands for weedless sod.

Antonio slowly relaxed. Brendon stood next to him and resumed swirling. Antonio stared at the elephant. Brendon had his back to it.

"I know it's Sam's. I just don't know why it's here. Last time I saw it was at Anni's…" Brendon started, but trailed as his fingers snaked off Antonio's chest and onto his own.

"Someone's playing wicked games." Antonio just stood, frozen in place but dripping like melting.

Nodding, Brendon said, "Kwirk, next door. He loves Chris Isaac."

The confusion Antonio wore lasted shorter than Danny DeVito, but then quickly shifted to laughter like Danny DeVito. "I stepped in that."

"You're stepping in a lot of that."

"Hush."

"Squish."

"I… I… I don't have any idea how or why."

"It could be a sign."

"From Sam?"

"From Sam."

"But how?"

"There are ways."

"There are?"

"There are."

Antonio shot a death glare. "AND YOU'RE JUST NOW TELLING ME THIS?!"

Brendon stayed calm and cool. "I am."

"Because?"

"You weren't ready."

"And I am now?"

"You are."

"How are you so certain?"

Brendon's eyes twinkled with that mischievous grin he had in his youth that Antonio found annoying, but now that he was a hunk, had added value and intrigue and sexiness. "Because you sucked off your dad."

"You went there."

"I went there."

Brendon grabbed his erect dick.

"And I'll tell you how while you suck me off."

Hoover vacuums? Nothing beats the sucking power of a vampire intent on information. Antonio sucked. Brendon told. Breaths heaved. Climax.

"Thank you."

"Thank you. Now give it back," Brendon demanded, grabbing Antonio by the hair and pulling him in for a kiss to reclaim his seed.

Something about Brendon's greediness made Antonio spontaneously ejaculate onto Brendon's sweaty torso and legs.

"Clean it up. I want that too."

Antonio obeyed.

What else could he do but obey what his witch commanded? After all, Antonio had hundreds, thousands of sexual experiences. Brendon just started. Saved himself. For him. For an otherly othered Other.

"Stop. I know what I'm doing."

Antonio snapped back into place like the puzzle he was. Licking and gulping and slurping without swallowing before plunging his cum-filled tongue into Brendon's eager mouth. His boy looked satisfied. Teacher's pet. A+.

"I haven't even started applying for any teaching positions," Brendon said after the taste dissipated.

"What's the rush?"

"Schools are already starting to hire for next school year?"

"I meant with life."

"It's short."

"Doesn't have to be."

"Short for now."

"Really?"

"I'm thinking about it more than I should, but, you know I'm not ready, but maybe that whole ten-year thing might be too long."

"Ten? What happened to seven?"

"We talked about this."

"We did?"

"We did."

"I know it's too long either way."

"Not for me."

"For me."

"Don't rush it."

"Why not?"

"You can't take it back. No return policy."

"Speaking of returning."

"Again?"

"Sorry. I know it's more than you're probably used to. Lots of one and dones. Guess I'm just different. Defective."

"Not defective."

"No?"

"No."

"Then what am I?"

"Wicked."

For the first time in a very long time, Antonio hopped onto a dick and rode it like tomorrow'd never come. Not that he never considered himself vers, it's just that most wanted him to top. Assumed he was a top. He had to admit that there was pain involved last time he bottomed… at first. But not now. Not with Brendon. Brendon didn't miss a beat, pumping in and out before flipping Antonio over and getting onto his knees to fuck him doggy style while jerking him.

But like everything else in this world, it ended too soon.

A quiet moan of ecstasy as they came together.

And Brendon just stayed there inside Antonio while he caught his breath.

And Antonio watched the stars dance and twinkle and flutter about all around him.

And the night faded into morning faster than either of them thought it would.

Brendon pulled out slowly and Antonio was about to turn around when Brendon pushed his back down before spreading his ass cheeks to eat him out. "Give. It. Back," he said between licks.

Antonio instinctually clenched.

The last time someone rimmed him, it was disastrous. He was sixteen. The guy rimming him was some thirty-year-old married closet case who sold insurance and smelled of shitty knock off cologne and too much of it at that. Unfortunately, like most teenage boys, he had an affinity for a certain fast food taco joint with a reputation for anal destruction.

But this wasn't like last time. This was different. Superior. Softer. Safer. And he had far more bodily control than he did back then when he was still human and still figuring out things. Of course, he was still figuring out things. Lots of things. And navigating this new thing with this newish person was quickly becoming a challenge to keep up, something he never in his life anticipated could be possible, but possibilities suddenly seemed endless and achievable and magical.

Antonio eventually loosened.

Brendon lapped his man juice back into his body before getting out of bed.

"Stay."

"I can't."

"You can."

"My dad's expecting me first thing, and it's first thing."

"You haven't slept yet."

"I'm young. Sleep is for the weak."

"You're human. Sleep is necessary."

"I'm a witch. Sleep is a construct meant to deter full potential of humanity."

"Liar."

Brendon yawned. "True, I lie."

"I love you."

Brendon froze. He didn't want to leave. Didn't want to be responsible. Didn't want to break promises either. "I love you."

"When will you be back?" Antonio asked, feeling desperation slither through his body like a disease, infecting his veins that used to flow with life.

"Soon. After I take care of… this thing with my dad," Brendon said.

"Secretive much?"

"It's complicated and I will fill you in when I can. Just, not now," Brendon told him.

Antonio saw the hurt and pain behind his words, pulled himself off the bed, grabbed Brendon's head, and brought him in for a kiss. "I know. And if you don't, that's okay too, so long as you come back to me."

"I will."

"Because we still haven't talked about what happened at the cliff."

"I know."

Kiss.

Within a minute, Brendon was out the door and walking home. Only he wanted home to be his home. His bed. His arms. His. He wanted Brendon to be all his, and hated himself for even thinking a wicked thought like that. Another baseless cry of selfish manipulation like his parents pulled on him until he was older and wiser and realized just how unloving such acts really were. Still, the hurt was there, beating his empty cavernous chest like a drum. Even without a heart he knew heartache. Would it be even worse if it was still inside him?

One day he'd ask for it back.

One day when these wicked games were over.

One day.

Just not today.

CHAPTER 13

Communion of the Cursed

"So, what's your superpower, Red?" Antonio asked Wayne's twin brother who, had it not been for the different hair color, would be identical, as he walked into their house that was really their parents' house neither had moved out of yet for reasons unknown or known and not readily available to decipher.

"I'm a ginger," Kwirk retorted.

"That's not a superpower."

"Gingers are soulless. A soul is required for paranorms to manipulate. I cannot be manipulated."

There was silence.

For about three seconds.

Then the shit really hit the fan when the whole room exploded with laughter so loud deaf Aunt Betsy at the far end of the street where it turns into Main fell out of her rocking chair and squished her cat. A Siamese. Named Charlotte.

"So, you're the guy who killed my brother," Anni said with a creepy smile reminiscent of dolls from decades past, left in landfills and haunted houses and places where you least expect them, like Grandma's guest bed.

Antonio stared dumbstruck. Sam's sister. His dead Sam's sister. Words swirled like vanilla ice cream with caramel. Frozen, stuck, sticky.

The world spun like cotton candy onto a stick at the fair, silky hairs flinging around the base and onto anything they could find, attaching themselves to the most improbable places in search of new homes. Sam's face at the center. Red hair. Freckles. His sister looked almost exactly like him. Anni. Born with male parts that never fit her. Sam born with female parts that never fit him. God's cruel joke on humanity to make us all feel broken and less than and always in search of how to fit into a world that is built to keep you trying until you run out of could.

And as the spinning continued save for the focused face of his former love, that he knew was not his face but didn't matter at the moment, he wanted to reach out, find Sam, bring him back to the world of the living even if only for a day. But he wasn't there. Never was. All an illusion. He knew this to be true, but didn't want to know. Refused to believe. Wanted the guilt to overtake his body and mind since it already had his soul. How many Hail Marys? How many Our Fathers? How many times did he need to beg and plead for his past mistakes to stop haunting him?

The swirls faded as he felt a hand on his back. Calm. Cool. Collected. Brendon.

Antonio turned around to weep into Brendon's arms.

Nothing else mattered.

Not even Sam in this moment.

The only thing that mattered was Brendon. His warmth. His touch. His scent. His neck. His blood. Wayne nearly pounced as he saw Antonio's fangs grow out of his mouth, but Brendon held his hand up to stop him.

"You can't hurt me, but you can drink me," Brendon whispered so softly as he held his head and pulled him in closer to the spot on his neck he knew Antonio was coveting.

Brendon let out a quiet moan as Antonio sunk his teeth into the right side of his neck. It felt like a violation to be so exhibitionistic as the voyeurs gazed. He also felt the thrill of it all, and had to quiet the demon inside his pants.

Sucking and sucking and sucking, Antonio wondered just how much Brendon could give before passing out, but he never let on that there was a problem. He just allowed his mouth to Hoover the blood from his neck for eternity. *How is this possible? How can he still have so much to give after giving more than three people before dying? How can he continue to pump and flow and pump and flow and pump and flow?*

Antonio knew he needed to stop, but the comfort told him to continue. Why was he so distraught? Sam's sister? Or was it something else? Something he needed to do to prepare for the coming fight they all needed to discuss, even though everyone felt completely clueless.

Let go, Antonio thought, forcing himself to stop feeding on the man he loved.

Then he did.

"Hey, Brendon, catch," Wayne said before tossing him a Snickers that Brendon immediately devoured like a chocolate dick.

Just like sex, Brendon was insatiable and always had more. Moments later, he was back to his old self again. Shiny.

"I'd say it's a witch thing, but really I think it's just a me thing," Brendon told Antonio before he could even ask.

"Or both, my dear friend Brendon," a green man with no legs said from out of nowhere.

"What the shit!" Antonio squealed so high pitched it tore a hole in Wayne's inner ear that would require healing that Wayne finally managed to figure out how to do himself.

"Art!" Brendon said gleefully, rushing toward the green person with no legs and hugging him tightly before introducing the guy to Antonio. "This is Art, he's an interdimensional being. A Zeta Reticulan."

"And he looks like a magic genie because…?" Antonio asked.

"The bastard tricked me," Wayne said, shooting a glare at Art, who turned away to stare at a small house spider on the wall.

"It's true. I was there," Anni said, causing Antonio to tremble slightly.

"Me too," Kwirk said.

"The writing was literally on the walls!" Art said, telling no lies. "You chose to ignore the warnings and free me, Master Wayne. Don't deny it. Besides, you love me now, and you know it."

Taking inventory, he found the oddities in the room to feel comfortable. Maybe it was the refreshing meal Brendon provided. Maybe it was the assortment of oddities in this middle-class living room next door to his own home. Maybe it was…

"Oh good. Vampire hotness. Is here," the unmistakable voice of Anna the medium quipped from behind Antonio without warning.

"How do you do that?" Antonio asked, checking to make sure he didn't piss himself even though such things had never happened since he turned.

"I'm a sneaky. Bitch." She smiled her creepy smile that really wasn't creepy until you looked into her eyes and knew damn well she did it on purpose to freak people out. "So, everyone is here?"

"I guess this makes me part of the Monster Squad Rejects Club now, doesn't it?" Antonio asked.

"No. We rescind our offer," Wayne said coldly, no hint of sarcasm.

"Yes," Anni said before mentioning, "I'm the Frankenstein's monster of the group. Dad's always fixing me because I keep falling apart, and sometimes my parts don't stay on anymore, so Dad replaces them with new parts he gets…"

"At the morgue?" Antonio asked, and Anni confirmed. "No short supply of those here in Ravenwood."

"True dat," Kwirk said.

"So, can we get back to the genie?" Antonio asked quietly, curious as a kitty cat.

"I thought you'd never ask!" Art squealed with delight. "So, about 10,000 years ago or so I…"

"Yeah, we don't have time for your backstory," Wayne said, cutting Art off. "We have to talk about what we're all sensing is on its way."

Darryl leaned in super close to Brendon and said as loudly quiet as he could manage over the blaring nightclub speakers forcing Kylie Minogue into everyone's ears within a three-block radius, "I'm in love."

"That's awesome!" Brendon said, eyes lighting up as he reached over and hugged his friend

Antonio tried to be cool. Tried not to bite the black boy his lover embraced. Tried to let the jealousy out the back door since he knew deep down in that damn jar where his heart lay the two were only friends and nothing more, even if his brain continued to suspect something else, although that was preposterous as he'd known them as childhood friends, but known is probably not the right word, rather seen them as children playing next door at the Werewolf house more times than he could count, which was a lie, as he did keep count. 713 times from 1999 until late 2010 when everyone in that group started drifting apart, even though they all said it would never, could never happen. It happened. And now, a little over three years later, the gang was gathering once again, all except the Asian kid—what was his name again? Ah yes, Chuck—who was busy teaching English in Vietnam where his mother grew up before his French father snatched her away to America for the dream.

Antonio forced a smile, but Darryl caught the discomfort like a shiny penny in a sea of spent wishes. Sitting. Mocking. Laughing at the misfortune of the other pennies who lost their luster and thus their ability to capture the attention of bystanders and onlookers alike.

"At some point you're going to have to trust me, old man," Darryl said so nonchalantly to Antonio that the vampire was almost taken aback at his forwardness, no doubt a trait he picked up from his older sister. Brendon looked hurt, maybe even a little confused. Antonio wanted to make it all go away, make the hurt stop, pretend like the elephant was merely a white cloud, but that was impossible. There it was, squishing his whole being like he was nothing but a down and dirty rat waiting for a train that would never come.

"No, you're right, Darryl. I need to figure out how to keep my bat-senses at bay. Or at the very least, my incredibly active imagination." Antonio put on a genuine half smile.

"Wow, Antonio. So brave," Brendon said, rolling his eyes.

"It was, actually," Darryl said. "Thank you. I know you've always suspected more than friendship between Brendon and I, but—"

"What?! Seriously?" Brendon interrupted.

"Dude, for a witch with the ability to read thoughts, you seem to suddenly be immune to his," Darryl said.

"Because I am," Brendon said.

"You are?" Antonio asked.

"Yep," Brendon responded quietly.

"Oh, well, that's awkward…" Darryl trailed off, searching for something, anything to focus on other than the two he was sitting with at a table by the stage.

"Not awkward at all for you, but really a massive amount of awkwardness for me, so, please, Darryl, continue even though I have a feeling I know where you are going," Antonio urged, telling himself he must remember to ask Brendon when, how, why.

"I haven't felt that way about Brendon since we were nine," Darryl admitted, darting his eyes away from his best friend.

"You? In fourth grade? Me?" Brendon asked.

"Yes, dummy! Seriously, you were so adorable that first day of school. And then you handed me those issues of *Super Samurai Slugs* and I was over the moon!"

"Because he lent you comic books?" Antonio asked.

"Because he was genuinely sweet. Not to his sister, obviously," Darryl said.

"Obviously," Brendon reiterated.

"But to me and Kwirk? Instant besties," Darryl said with that nostalgic twinkle in his eye many a cinematographer has tried and failed to capture just right, but when they do, pure magic.

Antonio felt the guilt rack up inside his not so living shell that felt more alive with each passing second the longer his father's bodily fluids coursed through his veins in ways he never felt possible before sucking the old man dry. What a kiss.

"You never told me," Brendon said, dripping with sadness and heartache.

"I never told anyone. Not a goddamn soul, till now," Darryl confessed.

"Why now?" Brendon asked.

"Cuz yo boy over there needs to hear it. I can sense that jealousy oozing outta him from miles away. Stench is nauseatingly unescapable," Darryl told Brendon while looking Antonio dead in the eyes.

"Thank you, Darryl. I can already feel it slipping away," Antonio said without any hint of sarcasm.

Darryl sniffed. "Finally!"

Brendon hugged Darryl again, and Antonio found himself shocked to shit that the urge to kill the black boy was missing from his reactionary state of being. He let out a long and lifeless breath out of pure habit. A small part of him waited for the inevitable that never came.

"Okay, so what's their name? What are they like? Where did you meet? Is it a man? Woman? Why aren't you answering me?!" Brendon rapid-fired.

"Damn, you been hanging with Courtney too long," Darryl said before laughing.

"Sister-in-law-ish may have rubbed off some of her linguistics," Brendon said.

"Sister has that effect. Thinks it's hilarious when white folks try to imitate her."

"You're dodging."

"I'm building suspense."

"Bullshit."

"You remember Tommy?"

"No! Not Tommy!"

"Please tell me you're not dating Tommy Fucking Gufflebacht!"

Antonio shouted so loud the glasses on the mirrored bar on the opposite side of them shook.

"Ew, no, not Tommy. Gross. His brother, or sister, Alex," Darryl said.

"Whew! So, Alex finally transitioned. So happy for her," Brendon said.

"Well, kind of. Alex has the tits and can totally pass as a woman, but they've got dick for days!" Darryl said with a boisterous laugh complete with a table slap.

"So, like our mayor? Chick with a dick?" Brendon asked.

"Best of both worlds as far as I'm concerned," Darryl said. "But more than that, they're just, wow, incredible. Never thought I'd meet someone like them, and to find it in someone I grew up with? Total shocker."

"How's Gufflebacht taking it?" Antonio asked before Brendon could, beating him to the punch before Brendon playfully punched him and turned the metaphor literal.

"In typical Tommy fashion with a side of supportive grossness," Darryl said.

"Wow. Alex, huh?" Brendon said.

"Yeah, Alex," Darryl said. "Started catching up about how we barely knew each other even though we lived next door to each other and are only a year apart age-wise. Found out we both have a love of *Star Trek* and *Super Samurai Slugs* and, I shit you not, Kokopelli."

"Nobody loves Kokopelli as much as this guy," Brendon told Antonio, pointing his thumb towards Darryl like an arrow.

"Well, Alex does. They confessed I influenced them. Saw me on the playground wearing one of my Kokopelli shirts and started looking into it."

"Fertility gods have that effect," Antonio said.

"True, but more than that, Kokopelli represents pure and unadulterated joy," Darryl said, smiling white teeth pushing into his cheeks.

"I'm happy for you, Darryl. Truly," Brendon told him.

"Thanks, man. I knew it was the real deal when we went on our first date, and please don't mock me, but it was that mess of a movie *Star Trek: Into Darkness*, and they turned to me when it was over and said, 'I've seen worse. Seen much better, but still doesn't make me hate the franchise' and I was like, oh my gawd! Someone who gets me!" Darryl said, leaning back and throwing his hands in the air.

"That's awesome! Not that I want to minimize your joy, but…" Brendon started.

"Why didn't Alex fully transition?" Darryl finished, knowing exactly where his friend's mind was stuck.

"If it's too personal, just let me know. I'm just genuinely curious," Brendon said, his innocence and inquisitiveness still intact after so much trauma.

"Honestly, I asked the same thing. Alex brought up the dick thing and said they'd understand if I wanted to back out and not pursue this relationship. And, I don't know, the thought got me incredibly excited. Like, my whole life I thought I'd have to choose between a man or a woman or have an open relationship so I could satisfy both sides of my sexuality. Not that I couldn't commit once I found the so-called one. I can. And I'm not saying I think this is a forever kinda deal with Alex, but it sure feels right. And after they told me about the penis thing, I asked why too, and, I mean, we get this, right? Alex said they were too attached to their dick to get that part of the transition surgeries. Said they never felt like they were all male or all female, but rather loved looking like a woman and loved having a cock to fuck with. I'm telling you, I'm the luckiest bi guy in the sack, but more than that, I'm just the luckiest guy to have found Alex. Seriously the best. We connect so well," Darryl leaned forward, elbows on the table, resting his face in his hands as hearts blocked his vision.

"So, nothing like Tommy?" Brendon asked.

"Nope." Darryl slightly shook his head.

"Good," Antonio said as Tommy Fucking Gufflebacht walked into the bar.

"And now things get awkward. Seriously, what the hell is he doing in a gay bar?" Brendon asked.

"Well…" Darryl poured out like thick molasses.

"No…" Brendon said, eyes wider than Dolly Parton's tits.

"Darryl!" Tommy said with a wave, all smiles and walking towards their table.

They bro hugged like fucking straights. Antonio noticed a fire burning inside Brendon and he understood that anger and where it stemmed from. Surprisingly, it was as short-lived as a poorly acted political sitcom from the early 90s.

"You remember…" Darryl started.

"Brendon! Wow, adulthood looks good on you! Like, really good. Must be your daddy's genes," Tommy gushed.

What. The. Fuck.

"You finally got my name right," Brendon said, teetering on getting up or staying seated.

"Only took thirteen years," Tommy said.

"Fourteen," Brendon corrected.

"Shit, yeah, has been that long since you moved here, huh?" Tommy said, doing that cute thing with his face that made him everyone's ogle object in school. Time only improved his accidental charm. "So good to see you again."

"Really? You barely acknowledged my existence as a kid unless it was convenient for you," Brendon said, squeezing Antonio's hand so hard that, had he not been a fairly invincible vampire would, have cried mercy over crushed bones and torn flesh.

Tommy sidestepped, did the shy guy head tilt thing, and said, "I was kind of a dick. Scratch that, I was a total asshole. Like unwiped with crusties. In short, I was gross."

There was that word again. That goddamn word Tommy was famous for saying and making everyone in the room feel like shit. Gross. Like the fact that every other person was somehow disgusting and he was the only clean one. The shining pillar on the hill. The one everyone envied, mostly because of his devilishly handsome looks and smile that could melt the mythical Ice Queen and dimples that make you want to go swimming in them. Ahhhh... Tommy the dreamboat.

"But why?" Brendon asked, holding back tears that weren't angry tears but sad and hurting and questioning tears.

"Truth be told, had a lot of hate for myself. Bullying was a coping mechanism to survive my childhood. Not an excuse for my behavior by any means. No amount of apologizing can ever make up for that." Tommy sounded genuinely sorry, like, actually felt bad for his past dickhood.

"Hear him out, Bren," Darryl said quietly, hand on Brendon's upper arm.

"I'm listening," Brendon said.

"We all are," Antonio said sternly and causing Tommy to tremble at the iciness.

"And you are...?" Tommy asked, hand gestured out and immediately regretting both the tone and the action. "I don't think we've been introduced yet, but I could be wrong."

"My boyfriend," Brendon said before Antonio said anything or did anything rash and end up in a puddle of blood and regret.

"Boyfriend got a name?" Tommy asked, slipping back into that schoolboy charm.

"Antonio," Antonio said, calm as a summer morning.

"You must be feisty to keep up with that witch," Tommy said with a twinkle.

"You… know?" Brendon asked, suddenly taken back to fourth grade vulnerability when he was just another fat boy getting teased on the playground for trying to keep up with all the athletic boys.

"I recognize a curse when I see one, like that stunt you pulled in fifth grade when I was teasing you about being a faggot," Tommy admitted. "I'm not going to mince my own words to make them sound softer. And for what it's worth, I deserved the rash."

"But, and I only told a few people, all of whom hate you," Brendon said matter-of-factly, even though the fact of the matter lay in question.

"Like I said, I recognized it," Tommy said, twisting his fingers and twirling a ball of fire in his hands like it was a baseball.

What.

The.

Actual.

Fuck.

Darryl didn't look surprised, but Brendon and Antonio wore it like a comfortable sweater. They watched the ball of fire twirl and twist and slowly extinguish leaving behind a whiff of smoke that dissipated into the ether.

"Also, like I said, there are things I hated about myself when I was younger. Being a witch was one," Tommy said.

"And the other?" Brendon asked.

"Being a friend of Dorothy?" Tommy said, scrunching his lips.

"Wow, really?" a voice from behind them said, causing Tommy to nervously jump out of his skin for a brief moment.

"Kwirk!" Tommy shouted enthusiastically before pulling Kwirk in for a hug.

Kwirk was, to say it bluntly, taken aback. The school bully who caused so much drama was standing in a gay bar hugging him. Hugging him for a long time. Like, a really long time for what most would consider normal.

"I am so sorry, Kwirk. You have no idea," Tommy said, crying tears he couldn't hold back even if he wanted to.

"Gonna take some time for me to accept that apology. There's a lot of damage in here still," Kwirk told him, but deciding to take a step into the acceptance stage light and slightly tightening his grip on Tommy's back.

"I know. And it's okay if it never happens, I just wanted you to know that, for what it's worth, it was you who made me realize something about myself that my old man railed against since before time. I couldn't let him find out I was one of those sissy faggots he wanted to all die of AIDS," Tommy said quietly, barely a whisper as he whimpered it out into Kwirk's shoulders along with a few tears wetting his sleeve.

"I knew you couldn't just be so mean for no reason," Kwirk said. "Didn't I tell you that I suspected that, Brendon and Darryl?"

"Yep."

"Mm hmm."

Tommy let go, wiped his eyes, and said, "Yeah, well, this wasn't supposed to be about me. I just got overwhelmed with everything I've had bottled up so long…"

"That it burst open like your ass after Taco Bell?" Kwirk said, chuckling.

"Something like that," Tommy admitted, chuckling.

"So, where's Alex?" Kwirk asked, searching around to see if he missed his friend's lover in a fit of rage over finding out his childhood tormentor was secretly gay all along.

"Yes! I have so many questions I need to ask them!" Brendon said, suddenly excited.

"You didn't tell them?" Tommy asked Darryl, one eyebrow cocked.

The stage lights turned on, house lights dimmed slightly, and a single note belted out of the speakers so loudly Antonio thought his ear drums might burst into an explosion of Hollywood proportions. Perfect pitch. Steady and strong and simultaneously vulnerable. And then, ***BOOM!*** drums, guitar, and keyboard blasted in.

"Alex is the lead singer in the band," Darryl said.

And that they were.

CHAPTER 14

Back Alley Dream Street Song

Shuffling into the dark recesses of Antonio's living room and pushing aside the armchair and kicking up the rug, Brendon said as he moved the coffee table that was used for practically everything but coffee, "I'm gonna need crow's blood, kosher salt, five candles, and vodka."

"This spell requires vodka?" Antonio asked, an eyebrow raised as to the validity of Brendon's request.

"Vodka's for me. Gotta make myself feel better about ripping a hole in the universe," Brendon said calmly holding the antique brass lamp Antonio refused to get rid of even though it went with nothing he owned.

The lamp caused Antonio to pause and reflect, recalling the day he bought it at Goodwill all those years ago when his life was renewed and he had to start all over. Again. Not like he did when his papa lost the job at the mill when it closed or when his abuela died and his doting grandfather moved into his room and he had to move into his brother's room. The brother, the family he'd never be able to see again because of some ridiculous vampiric law he never asked for or consented to. A rule he debated over breaking (especially knowing that those rules didn't apply to him) because he ached to see his grandfather one last time, or more accurately, to speak with him one last time before he succumbed to that damned thing called death he'd never be blessed with. But that damned lamp he found thirteen years ago at a Goodwill in the neighboring city of Vancouver on a street called Fourth Plain Boulevard wanted him to take it home, to love it, cherish it, wipe it clean of all the filth and tarnish its advanced years had accumulated. The sun had just set and the store was about to close, so he felt the need to rush through the haphazardly crammed aisles for essentials, the least of which was a lamp but ended up being the only thing he bought that trip. Inspecting the bottom confirmed his suspicion that this very lamp was the same his grandfather owned with his abuela until he moved in after she died, purging his belongings like a snake shedding its skin. Renewal. Rebirth. Out with the old, in with the new, even if the new was a kid's twin mattress and painted dresser and twelve-inch black and white television with foil-wrapped rabbit ears, all of which stayed in the bedroom Antonio once occupied. He never asked, but now that he was older and wiser and undead, he had more time than he cared to admit left to ponder life's unanswerable questions, like why his grandfather got rid of practically everything he owned, including his house. The only thing he could come up with was medical costs. Cancer ain't cheap. And cancer in the 1980s? Might as well just hurry up and die.

"Where do you want this?" Brendon asked, cradling the lamp like a toddler.

"I'll get it out of the way," Antonio said, carefully taking it out of Brendon's arms, walking into his bedroom, placing it on his nightstand after using his feet to kick off the lamp that once graced its presence.

The shatter startled Brendon. "You okay? Your lamp okay?"

"The one that matters is," Antonio said, staring at the broken pieces of his expensive design tastes scattered across the bedroom floor he'd have to wait to sweep up later.

"Crow's blood. Kosher salt. Candles. Vodka. Stat."

"Okay, so why are we doing this at my house anyway? You know I don't keep ingredients here?" Antonio asked before adding, "Or vodka."

"Mom and Dad can't know what I'm doing or they'll send my sister over to stop me because, well, this is some pretty dark shit and then we'll have the talk about dark shit and I don't wanna deal with shit so just help me out. Please."

"I'll see what I can do about the kosher salt and vodka. Candles are in the pantry. Hundreds of them. One of the coven chicks hosted a PartyLite party years ago and I went a little crazy with the smells."

"Wow."

"Yeah, my senses were a little out of whack back when things were new."

"Yeah."

"Intoxicating."

"Uh huh."

"I'll go get your shit."

"Thanks."

"You could use your witchy powers to teleport them all here."

"I could but then I wouldn't be able to do this spell. Everything has to be magickless. And I need every bit of my power just to possibly pull this off."

"Got it. Be right back. Know where I can get crow's blood at a time like this?"

"Your backyard."

"And does it have to be kosher salt? Couldn't you just use table salt?"

"Are you kidding me? Table salt is disgusting."

"You don't have to eat it."

Brendon just stared blankly.

"Brendon, you don't have to eat it do you?"

More staring.

"Fuck."

"Yeah, maybe after this is all done we can do that, but first let's rip a whole in the universe and possibly disrupt the whole space time continuum and all life that ever existed and ever will exist in the process. Don't forget the vodka. The good shit too, none of that bottom shelf stuff your mom drinks."

"Hey, how do you know my mom drinks the bottom shelf stuff?"

Brendon just gave him his resting bitch face.

"Right, man-witch," Antonio said before realizing just how horrifyingly degrading that was and instead of waiting for Brendon to answer in offense or defense or any other fense, he pressed his lips to Brendon's, forcefully kissing him. *What the hell is wrong with you? This is just making it worse! Silencing him to prevent him from defending himself? You are a sick monster. A monster!*

"Thanks, I needed that," Brendon said as he pulled away, connecting forehead to forehead as he held Antonio's hands in his.

"I didn't mean to call you a man-witch."

"I am. Used to be called a boy-witch so I suppose that's an upgrade."

A nervous chuckle escaped Antonio's lips unexpectedly, fresh with the taste of Brendon clinging to them. The boy who loved him sometimes caused him to lose his sense of self and sense of control and sometimes all his senses at once. But it quickly left. Sam entered the room and he couldn't tell if there was happiness or sadness on the stoic face his once lover held. Standing in the center of the emptiness of his living room. Once fierce green eyes tired and weary. Fiery hair fading like dying embers. Milky skin whiter than ever. Freckles faded to oblivion.

"Sam's here, isn't he?" Brendon asked, knowing the answer.

"Of course he is. Bastard. He just keeps. Barging in. Like a creeper," Anna said from behind Antonio before breaking out into giggles.

"Speaking of creepers, is the gang all here?" Brendon asked, eyes still closed, refusing to let go of Antonio's hands or disconnecting foreheads.

"Yep," Wayne said.

"Brought the salt," Anni said, dropping it onto the counter. "Don't worry, it's kosher. Only thing the Werewolfs have because, you know, their Jewish."

"Thanks," Brendon said.

"That's Mom's?" Wayne asked nervously, looking at the box, but Anni didn't answer.

"And the vodka," Kayla said from the front door. "The good shit. Stole it from Mom's stash."

Brendon's eyes shot open. His sister. The sister he explicitly did not want to be a part of this. The sister who'd assuredly stop him at all costs from performing what he knew in his heart he had no choice but to commit to. The spell. The very dangerous spell that might cause the universe to cease to exist. "What are you doing here? Please don't say it's to stop me because that's not gonna happen."

"Don't worry, baby brother. I'm here to make sure you don't fuck it up," Kayla said, handing Brendon the bottle and winking at Antonio.

Kayla's wink made Antonio feel uneasy, and while he knew that she was the cause of the accident that nearly killed him and her great-great-great-grandfather is the direct reason he was cursed with everlasting life, she was and always will be family. Still, he couldn't help but wonder if something more malicious was behind her intent. Or was it just a wink? A reassuring wink to let him know that shit's about to get real but it'll all work out in the end? All he wanted to do was leave. Leave with Brendon. Just the two of them. Never look back. Leave it all behind and let his past stay where it should instead of dragging it back from the grave. But Sam still stared blankly, awaiting what comes next, and he knew he had no choice but to get that damned crow.

A dead crow plopped onto the kitchen counter, splattering a bit of blood from its mouth. Kwirk wiped his hands with one of the good towels.

"Awesome. The Supernatural. Club is all. Here now. We can get. Started," Anna said, smiling gleefully at the ghost of Sam.

"Happy birthday to me," Brendon said before he chugged the salt and washed it down with vodka.

Antonio realized the day, put two and two together, and hated the math.

Antonio burned with hellfire, waiting for the flames that licked him to engulf his skin, muscles, bones. But no burning today, just another fucking unexpected Pacific Northwest heat wave in the middle of March trying to kill anyone and everyone, including the dead and the damned. Yet, as he looked into the waves radiating from the asphalt and colliding with his eyes in ripples, he sensed something else, something sinister, something not right about the situation and came to the only logical conclusion one could conjure in times like these: fairies.

Ever since that chance encounter with short big-dicked Sam in the back alley, ever since tasting the sweet chocolate syrupy nectar of his blood, he knew there would be another encounter, and another and another and another until they finally resolved the issues that, surface-wise, seemed so easy to identify and quantify, but below, deep inside the recesses of pleasure cavities of pure chaos magic held the truth. What truth? What was it that Sam had that Antonio needed? Any why him? The vulgar Sam? The ugly Sam? The bad Sam? The one who can't be turned, can't be killed, and can't be anything but what nature chose to deal in his deck of cards called life? And yet, what life? A life of constant fear and constant disappointment and constantly craving what he cannot ever have and never having the absolution of satisfaction?

Half a life at best.

But the scent was there in the heat waves and radiation swirls. Like swimming without water. In other words, trekking through Disney World in August. Antonio followed the scent, not of freshly baked chocolate chip cookies, but fairy musk one can never forget once inhaled, following it into Alice's rabbit hole, channeling the streams of Small World, pensioning for just one nibble, one lick, one more chance to discover the connections through Neverland that felt so innately disconnected.

Over the river.

Through the woods.

Only this wasn't grandma's house.

"Puta," a voice greeted Antonio in barely a decibel.

"Fucker," Antonio responded.

"You wish you could have this," Sam said, grabbing his dick through his jeans that still looked and smelled the same as they did so many months ago.

Antonio shook his head no, but he couldn't deny the part of him, the strong desire, to completely engulf the short man's giant member of a slim society. And yet, even through the disgust and shame he undoubtedly would feel afterwards for doing this to Brendon even if he never told him and kept the secret his eternally damned life, he couldn't shake the feeling that he wanted to risk it all for just one taste. Brendon would do the same, wouldn't he?

No.

No, he wouldn't.

"I see you sucked your daddy off and now you all even more sensitive to my blood, huh?" Sam said, his gravelly voice piercing.

"Word travels fast."

"Word travels, but I don't know about fast."

"Why the heat?"

"To get your attention."

"What do you need my attention for?"

"The coming darkness."

Antonio laughed. "You sense that too?"

"More than I've ever felt a presence in the last five-hundred and twenty-three years."

For some reason, Sam revealing his age made Antonio suddenly uncomfortable. Sam was old. Like, really old. Older than Song's End. Older than…

"I know what you're thinking: 'Damn! That asshole look good for his age! Now I really wanna fuck him!' No?"

"No."

"Lies."

"Truth."

"You know as much as I do about this shit."

"Then why the message to find you?"

"To warn you if you don't already know? To make peace so we can fight this thing together and have a goddamn chance of coming out alive or whatever shit we wanna call our situations? To try to be better than mi madre who fuckin' up and went into hiding once she caught onto whatever's headin' our way. To… sides, you called me. I'm just calling back."

It was true, Brendon had to work his magic to make this happen, even if it took almost a month to get a response. Fucking fairies. And now, here, with the very person he didn't want to see, but knew he had to see, opened a doorway into the unseen to… to what? Help?

"Fine."

"Damn, you eager?"

"Nobody knows how to fight this or even what this is, but everyone sensitive to the shifts know it's coming. I can't believe I'm actually agreeing to let a fucking fae into the group."

"Shuh, your group won't accept me. Gotta be peripheral and shit, y'know?"

"Why?"

"Like they say, can't trust a fairy." Sam's voice hinted at sadness and disappointment, like drinking a LaCroix.

Silence.

A light breeze shuffled between them, but brought no comfort. If anything, it made the world around them hotter. And then the air stopped, the breeze gone, the leaves just barely starting to emerge from winter dormancy froze in the unbearable heat.

"Shit," Antonio muttered, closing his eyes for the oncoming wrath that surely would come.

"Shit right, man. You didn't tell me you an' the Hollins boy were a thing," Sam said after sniffing the air, eyes wide with intrigue and jealousy.

"Shit, Antonio," Brendon said as he eased up from behind before taking his hand. "Sam."

"Bren."

Antonio shook out of the shame and shouted, "Wait, you know each other?"

"Uh, yeah," Brendon said.

"Go way back," Sam said.

"The hell?!" Antonio said.

"Remember when I said you can never trust a fae?" Brendon asked.

"Of course."

"Sam is the reason. Well, not just Sam, but like the whole lot of them."

"Racist much?"

"Specist not racist, but for good reason."

"Kid's right," Sam said. "You trust a fairy, and we can no longer protect you. I mean, once we earn your trust we can also kill you pretty easy, even the so-called immortals and shit. So, yeah, good reason."

Heat radiated in the stillness.

The stiff air pierced through his skin, cutting the impenetrable flesh like it was nothing more than crepe paper husk.

Why did Brendon hide this from him?

What else was he hiding?

Did he lie about being a virgin too?

Why would that matter?

Heat.

Stiff.

Questions.

"But, you know each other?" Antonio asked, suddenly hurting in places he didn't understand, wanting the reason to be mundane and innocent, but a nagging part of him couldn't shake the nefariousness of it all.

Shaking his head, Brendon said, "Funny story."

"Funny? Funny?" Antonio fumed.

"You can calm down now, mostly because you'll probably be even more furious after I explain."

"Calming down. Now."

Sam snickered as he took a cautious step backwards.

"Listen to everything I say before reacting, okay."

"Okay."

"Promise."

"Promise."

"The night I stole your heart, I wasn't the only one there. I thought I could heal you after the branch pierced your chest, but nothing I tried was working. And it tore me apart, because, and I can't explain it all that well, but I've always known that one day I would be yours. So, seeing you looking so lifeless next to…" Brendon gulped, searching for his next words carefully before deciding to just say what he was originally going to say, "…Sam, my good friend's older brother, and you both were dead, was a lot. And I tried and tried and tried to save him! But he was gone, lost, and not by some supernatural magic shit, but a fucking brain aneurism at the most inconvenient time. Seconds. Just seconds more, and another vampire could have been there to turn him, save him. But I was too late. Then Sam," Brendon pointed to clarify, "this Sam, was by my side, offering me whatever I most desired for the heart—your heart— in my hand. What I most wanted was for you to still be here, so…"

"You didn't," Antonio said, eyes wide.

"Of course not!" Brendon said. "You started moving, even without your heart, and I watched as the hole inside your chest began to heal. Sam told me that a vampire heart was useless to a human, even a witch, but it isn't. The heart, your heart, was mine and mine alone. Not to be tampered with or used, but to be kept safe from harm."

"In a mason jar in your basement?" Antonio asked.

"You ever been to that basement?" Sam asked. "Deep dark magic up in that bitch."

"You do know Jessica is gone, right?" Brendon asked Sam, casually first name-dropping his great-great-great grandmother.

"You witches keep sayin' that, but I was there in 1901 when they cast her out and killed her the first time. I was there in 2000 when they killed her again, same day this puta crashed into a tree cuz your sister screamed and Jessica screamed and your great-great-great granddaddy's vampire-witch lover turned him into a vampire with the kiss I so crave so you two could be together right here right now. So, forgive me when I say I can't trust dead witches," Sam told them.

"The house doesn't have her presence anymore. If it did, her portrait would still find your eyes to lock onto," Brendon said.

"You keep a picture of that bitch in the house?!"

"As evidence. Just in case."

"And that dark magic?"

"Song's End's magic."

Sam nodded. "Okay, okay, okay, that makes sense."

"Can I continue?" Brendon asked Sam.

"There's more?" Antonio asked, still trying to take in all that his ears were hearing.

"There's more," Brendon said quietly.

"Oh shit, there's more!" Sam said excitedly.

Anticipation permeated the frozen hot air. Antonio felt his knees start to give as it sunk in that his own creator, his father, the one who turned him all those years ago then allowed a fuller experience just a few short months ago, was part of keeping his ripped-out heart safe. Safe for what? Safe from what? Why keep it at all? Useless lump of dead cells he so wanted to smash into a million pieces.

"Don't get mad at Sam, but he wanted your heart so he could try to become a vampire himself. He knew he couldn't be turned since he's a fairy, but thought that maybe eating your heart would give him some of your vampire abilities, even if only for a short time. Something about legends and myths from thousands of years ago where white people lived and made stuff up," Brendon said, staring straight at Sam to emphasize the ridiculous notion, or so Antonio and Sam thought. "The problem is that he was right, and I knew it, and Song's End knew it."

"Mother fucker," Sam spat.

"You wanted to eat my heart?" Antonio asked, almost humored by this revelation.

"And you wanted to eat my dick," Sam said with a slight grin.

"But why keep it? Why not destroy it?" Antonio asked Brendon.

"Because… Because…"

"Because it is the only way for you to fully ascend to who you were always meant to be," a soft-yet-powerful voice said from behind Antonio.

"Dad? Is it safe for you to be out here in the open," Antonio asked, shocked he called Song's End 'Dad' and even more shocked to see him in the sunlight.

"The world has stopped between tick and tock, so to speak," Song's End said, winking at Brendon. "So, the only ones who can see me are the ones I wish to. Besides, we are quite hidden through the works of Sam, correct?"

"Ascend?" Antonio asked, still trying to understand it all, which frustrated him to no end as he felt he should be able to comprehend the facts told to him so plainly.

"Ascend. Inside your heart is the key to unlock your full potential. To become more than you are. You are powerful, true. You are strong, true. But you are not whole. When you drank from me a second time at the place of my death-birth, you took in everything you need to lock in your potential. Your body is the lock. Your heart is the key. And your…"

"What if I don't want it? My heart? So much pain and suffering and ache!" Antonio screamed.

"And so much love and compassion and magic," Song's End told him.

"Magic?" Antonio asked, wearing confusion like the age-old last year's Versace.

"Magic," Brendon confirmed.

"Holy shit! Slap me so I know I'm not dreaming!" Antonio screamed like a child on Christmas morning after realizing Santa brought the coveted Nintendo Entertainment System from the North Pole that year. Picture it: Ravenwood, 1986…

"I'm not slapping you," Brendon said, rolling his eyes.

"I will," Sam offered, taking an inch.

"Say I believe you, does that mean I'll be a vampire witch?" Antonio asked, shocked to shit.

"Such small words for such grand power. But, essentially, yes," Song's End confirmed.

"Then what are we waiting for?" Antonio asked excitedly. "Let's jumpstart that bitch!"

But the other three men did not share his enthusiasm. Nor did they look willing to explain why their apprehension was prevalent. But why? Why tell him that he was destined to be more than he was? Why explain why Sam wanted to eat his heart, why Brendon saved it, why Song's End protected it all these years if not to finally put it to use? What reason could they have for delaying something that would undoubtedly be in their favor against the coming darkness that hovered closer and closer?

"Remember that night at the cliff? The night you rose after drinking me again?" Song's End asked.

"Of course." Antonio seemed disturbed that anyone could possibly believe he would forget this life-altering event, but he realized so many things he'd forgotten had happened, been told, explained, and he didn't know why, but figured the refreshers were just in case this one, like so many others, slipped through the cracks, the sinews, the crevices of the wrinkled fatty blob.

"That sound we heard?" Brendon said.

"The one we never figured out the source?" Antonio said.

"It was the thumping of your jump-started heart in the jar in my basement."

CHAPTER 15

Red Leaf

Dancing, the red leaf glided gracefully through the stillness. No wind. No rain. But there it was, fluttering through the air in front of Antonio's bedroom window, begging him to join.

"Leave me alone," Antonio grumbled.

But something kept drawing him to the red leaf. Something kept pulling his attention away from the work he was trying to do and back onto the leaf that shouldn't even be there. It was April, and the new leaves were pushing through the maple the red leaf once called himself green. All the other leaves had decayed and crumbled through the winter rains and recent heatwave that burned them all to a crisp before a swift wind carried them off to scatter amongst the nearby gravestones and provide cover for potato bugs, earth worms, and field mice.

All but one.

One goddamn red leaf that refused to leave.

Only it did leave. Once. Left and carried him through the forest, to the cliff, to meet his maker. His father. But where did it go after that? Back onto the tree? Again? It couldn't be true, but there it was. Continued to cling to the branch like a squatter in a slumlord's rental long past the eviction notice should have sent it packing. He swore it guided him to the cliff, to the edge of the forest where he was reborn yet again after swallowing nearly every drop his father offered with abandon, but when he returned home, it was back, taunting him.

"I'm not leaving until you acknowledge me," the red leaf said.

"Just leave me alone already," Antonio said.

"I may not be what I once was, but I'm still here."

"Why?"

"To make sure you will be alright."

"Me? I'm fine."

"Right now, but what about the darkness?"

"You know about the darkness?"

"I fear I might be the cause."

"You? You're just a leaf! A leaf that isn't even real! I'm just talking to myself."

The red leaf snatched away from the branch, grew arms and legs and a face and walked right into Antonio's bedroom, standing before him as not necessarily a corporeal being, but some cheap facsimile of one. A ghost?

"Sam?"

"Yes."

"You're… you!" Antonio cried, pulling his past love in for a hug but failing to connect to where the body should be. Just pushed through air before his hands found each other to cradle into grief.

The unmistakable body of a man that Sam never had in life was here in death. And without Anna here to both creep him out and help communicate, he couldn't understand how Sam was here, now, in his bedroom, standing before him. What magic was this? What force behind the curtain pulling all the levers and pressing all the buttons? What could possibly explain the unexplainable?

"I'm just passing through," Sam said, putting a hand on Antonio's shoulder that he could feel the presence of, but when he reached out to touch it, felt nothing but his own shoulder.

One way, and no way to reciprocate.

Just as it was during Sam's life.

And as Antonio beat himself up for his past selfishness that he had to reconcile never changed, even with Brendon, even with Song's End's glorious gift, Sam sensed the torture and pressed his finger onto Antonio's lips.

"Stop it."

"I can't."

"You have to."

"Why?"

"Because it's almost time, and I will be long gone before the darkness comes, but I have to know that you are ready."

"Gone?"

"This is temporary."

"Being gone?"

"Being here."

The Band-Aid ripped off yet again, pretending to be Velcro, but each time it reattached, it held on a little bit looser and looser as lint clung to the hooks. Losing effectiveness even though the wound never healed. Losing its grasp on life.

Losing.

Losing.

Lost.

And now Antonio was on his knees weeping like a fucking baby on a crowded airplane, teething and refusing to suckle on her mama's titties. Only Sam no longer had his tits, and the only thing worth sucking was his dick, neither of which made much use in death. He was who he was always supposed to be in life, but cruel Nature wanted a laugh.

His Sam.

His beautiful Sam.

"Look at me," Sam commanded. Antonio obeyed. "If you take your heart back before defeating the darkness, nobody is going to make it."

"But it's mine."

"It's Brendon's now," Sam said, a hint of sadness before a chuckle and smile crept up. "It's always been Brendon's. You gave me what I needed in life, but Brendon is here to give you what I never could. I'm at peace, and want you to be a peace too."

"But, how can I? Knowing that you died so close to having eternal life?"

"You know you never could have given me life. Not yet."

"I know, but another!"

"Dwelling on what could have been is empty."

Emptiness enveloped Antonio like the plague, filling every cavity, every crevice, every hole. All-consuming emptiness. Nothingness. The Nothing. Crushing him. Sweeping him up. Wondering if his Moon Child could save the world.

"All I have is emptiness."

Sam smiled. "You have people, friends."

"I have pain."

"You have love."

"I have nothing."

"Then let me offer you hope."

"Hope that I make it out alive? That all of us make it out alive? What can you promise?"

"I promise nothing, but I know that if you let others help, you will succeed."

Going over scenario after scenario in his head, Antonio tried to understand how the Island of Misfit Toys could possibly be the solution to whatever evil, whatever darkness was coming to destroy them all. And nothing made sense. The darkness didn't make sense either, but utilizing the B-cast seemed preposterous at best and disastrous at worst, yet here they were, at the crossroads and the A-Team didn't show, probably doesn't even know, what to do or where the fight is. And it gnawed at him like a lion chewing a gazelle's femur with feverous passion while the onlooking hyenas cried and howled in painful laughter.

But here the red leaf was holding up the white flag, not as surrender, but as comfort. Sam begged Antonio to align fully with the group. To align with Vulgar Sam and Tommy Fucking Gufflebacht. To take his father's warnings and Brendon's concerns to heart. To listen to him.

"I am listening to you," Antonio said angrily.

"But are you hearing me?" Sam asked.

"I feel like a child who's being told no without reason."

So, Sam explained it once more as if he were a child because using adult words wasn't working. Antonio listened to hear this time, but only out of spite. He still felt like it would be better if he were more powerful, as powerful if not more so than Song's End. But the planets weren't aligned quite yet, which was why he needed to align with friends and foes alike.

Shit excuse.

Not knowing whether to take his word at face value or devalue it through the skeptical lens of doubt and fear broadcast to the masses as truth and justice and the American way, Antonio waded through the shit and found that Sam was right. It really was the only logical conclusion. He wasn't ready for the power he was destined to receive.

"I hate myself because of you." Antonio wept, staining his cheeks, shirt, and floor red.

"I loved myself because of you," Sam said, his smile finally masculine as it always should have been.

"But you had so much life to live and I stole that from you. So young. Too young. I should've known. Should've been more careful. Shouldn't have taken advantage of a child."

"I was no child."

"Seventeen."

"Mere days away from eighteen when we met, and old enough to consent. Old enough to know what I was getting myself into. Old enough to wait until I was an adult before deciding what I wanted even though I knew who I wanted."

"A baby."

"Not a baby. You made me feel like a man. You made me feel loved. You made me feel whole. Don't let anyone take that away."

"I wish there was more time. I want you to tell me again what I have to do."

"You don't need me to. You know. It's time."

With a subtle nod, Antonio agreed. Sam smiled, gave him a kiss, and faded away.

"Sam?"

Nothing.

"Sam?"

But there would never be an answer.

Looking out the bedroom window, the red leaf was gone.

"Sam."

CHAPTER 16

¿Por Qué Te Tengo Que Olvidar?

"I don't want to forget you," Antonio quivered.

But there was no answer, only silence and heartache and pain and the thoughts of tearing oneself apart just to feel something other than loss. Strip away the flesh. Cut away the meat from the bone. Be one with calcium sans the meat puppet so many found desirable.

So many.

Countless many.

Even with superior intellect, trying to number the boys and men of his youth and adulthood and vampire prowess was intangible. What counted? What didn't? What about the times he was so high he didn't know? What about the blurred lines? True, he tried and tried and tried and failed to reign in his consumption, tried holding off on random hookups and human blood for celibacy and pigs, but the temptation was always there, eating away at him like a parasite, nibbling and nibbling and nibbling until he gave in.

And now, just a year after Sam—his Sam—was taken after he went too far, consumed too much, gave into the temptation, the bloodlust, the all-encompassing desire to feed as only a heartless bastard could, for his heart was gone, justifiably removed after taking his innocent lover's life, he found himself standing at the very place he stole Sam's life and life stole his heart only to find a child waving at him.

"Shouldn't you be in bed, young man," Antonio mustered the courage to say in what he hoped would come across as stern, but being the twenty-three-year-old looking vampire he was, came across as threatening.

The plump child didn't say anything as he lowered his hand.

"Brendon, I'm sorry."

"Don't be. I'm just waiting for my friends. We're taking a midnight walk through the woods, but apparently I'm the only one who can tell time," Brendon said, a short but punctuated giggle after that was tainted with nervousness and frustration.

"A bit dangerous at your age, isn't it?" Antonio asked.

"I turned fourteen today, we'll be fine," Brendon assured in the confidence of an eighth-grade kid most wish they still possessed.

Taking one last look at the child, seeing the broken branch that stole his heart healing itself despite the massive missing piece, Antonio told him to have fun and be safe before he walked downtown to Communion for absolution and distraction and to forget even though he never wanted to forget, but forgetting was the best he could do to alleviate the suffering, and if there was one thing he was tired of feeling, it was suffering. So much suffering.

And so, he fucked the night away, trying to forget his Sam. But every guy looked like Sam, smelled like Sam, moaned like Sam, tasted like Sam. One guy after another after another to no avail. His stomach and ass were filled with so much cum that if someone were to pop him like a balloon, nothing but creamy white goo would be seen for miles and miles and miles. A river of spooge snaking its way to an outlet.

When the night was nearly dawn and his Catholic shame kicked into overdrive, he sought the comfort of one of his only true friends he'd ever really had. They grew up together, went to senior prom platonically together, shared each other's secrets. When he turned, she was the first to know. When she decided to become a prostitute, he was the first person she told. They shared so much, including a love of sex, just not with each other.

Their junior year, they challenged each other to a blow off during school, and despite all efforts, ended up tying with fifteen each. Then on Sundays as they took communion together during mass they both enjoyed giving the most seductive look they could manage as they awaited the wafer and wine and "And also with you"s just to get a rise out of the clergy. Confession was their favorite way to toy with the priest, making sure they went back-to-back for the most effective way of ensuring his dreams were vivid and impure.

Walking out of Communion towards the corner he knew she'd be about to walk back home from, Stacy spotted Antonio filled with hurt and pain and suffering and shame and guilt and recognized the gait of a cum-filled ass trying to make it to safety. It was a familiar formula and she knew the solution. Stacy made her way towards Antonio, opened her arms. He fell to the ground. She cradled him in front of a pawn shop that catered to the lowest common denominator, which was great for business but bad for the Brads and Chads that frequented it for a quick buck or a cheap wedding ring before getting shipped off to boot camp.

"Cry it out, hon," Stacy said as she held his head.

"I just want to let it all go," Antonio told her.

She laughed. "Not here. Dan'll be pissed having to clean up what's probably a majority of his customer's DNA splattered all over the windows and doors."

Antonio wanted to laugh, knew it would help, desired nothing more than to feel like his old self again, but he held it in. Held it all in. Absorbed it into his being, his essence, feeding his psychosis. Stacy, his best friend. The only person left in the whole world who truly knew him.

"Let's go back to my place so you can get cleaned up," Stacy said.

Antonio agreed. They walked up Main street, past the shops and the outlet mall and the dairy farm where the farmer's son was fine as fuck, and were about to turn onto Baker Street when Antonio spotted the child again. The Hollins boy. Brendon. He looked tired and as if he'd had a blast hanging out all night in the woods with his friends. Stacy spotted the kid as he waved towards them. This time, Antonio smiled and waved back. He didn't know why. He didn't even want to wave or see anyone except Stacy, but somehow seeing the boy made him realize he didn't need to forget, but had to stop living like he was dying.

"You know that kid? Seems young," Stacy said with just a tad of judgment sprinkled into her tone for good measure.

"Gross. He's a kid. One of my neighbors. Frank Hollins's kid," Antonio said.

"Frank's kid? Holy fuck, what I would do to that man!" Stacy said as they crossed Main.

"You and I both," Antonio said.

"You're a bit squishy since you stopped using condoms after getting bit," Stacy scoffed.

"Maybe he likes it squishy," Antonio said, forcing a short-lived giggle before sadness slapped him back into the reality of his self-imposed hell.

And then Stacy realized something. The spot where the boy stood. That spot. That very spot. The place where her friend tried and failed. "Oh shit! Oh shit oh shit oh shit! It was a year yesterday and I didn't take a fucking day off to be with you!"

"I mourned without you," Antonio said, feeling the swimmers in his full stomach start to push their way either up or down. "But if Frank's down, I can keep on mourning."

"Whore," Stacy said, shaking her head.

"I don't ask for money, you do," Antonio said.

"Whatever, let's get you cleaned up."

Brendon watched them disappear into the sea of houses that lined Baker Street before heading home for sleep that would not come for days as his brain raced through the thousand ways or more he wanted to help make Antonio's pain go away, to help him forget, move on, get back to himself again, but couldn't. This was an unsolvable problem, one of many he would find in the coming years.

It's easier to forgive than to forget, but both come at a price nobody is truly willing to pay.

CHAPTER 17

Tell Me

"Hey, Antonio, we need to talk," Brendon's voice said calmly.

"Currently I'm fucking busy, and unfortunately it's not the other way around," Antonio said back as a fist connected with his lower jaw, cracking, nearly knocking his phone out of his hand.

"Yeah, um, I don't care what you're busy doing. This is serious," Brendon's voice said, lacking anything resembling patience and calm and all that lovey-dovey cliché shit.

"Fuck! That hurt asshole!" Antonio shouted, kicking his assailant in the chest as another fired up a flamethrower.

"Dammit, Antonio!"

"Dammit, Brendon! I'm about to get set on fire after fighting off like eight abnormally strong assholes. What part of 'I'm fucking busy' do you not understand?"

"Oh, for fuck's sake," Brendon's said with more annoyance than a desperate housewife whose husband's still out with the boys while she's been trapped at home with the kids he insisted they have and she never wanted and wished she'd taken her mother's advice. But this was

Brendon. His mother gave terrible advice. And thank fucking baby Jesus there ain't no kids, because fuck that shit. Transporting straight to the danger, Brendon appeared right in front of the flamethrower as fire swallowed him up.

"No!" Antonio screamed, falling to the ground, knees digging into the soft grassy loam made moist by recent rains, dropping his phone still clinging to the line that so plainly no longer exists.

The flame subsided. The boy appeared unburnt. Antonio thanked every god he knew by name. Just as he was about to rush towards Brendon, who remained frightfully still as a marble statue, an animal-like guttural howl escaped Brendon's mouth as an immense fireball flew out of him, turning night to day for a split second, incinerating the flamethrower and its user to ash.

"Well shit, I had a question for that guy," Antonio said nonchalantly, brushing off the mud from his black jeans as best he could, but stains remained.

"Should've worn leather," Brendon told him as he turned around, wearing a smile despite the tear sliding down his cheek, puddling into the goddamned dimple Antonio loved.

"Yeah, I should have," Antonio said, walking towards Brendon with ease.

A sudden movement struck them both as one of the assailants cocked his Glock and said, "Adios mother...."

But he never finished his sentence. Brendon finger-banged him to death. "...fucker."

"I don't know how I feel about you killing with such, uh, how do I put this? Efficiency?" Antonio said.

"Those aren't the first people I've killed," Brendon confessed to Antonio. "Besides, it's not like they were really people."

"But they were people?"

"Nazis aren't people."

"Those guys were Nazis?"

"Oh, good night! Before the flamer went up, I caught the info we need. Well, part of it. He didn't have the whole story, just fragments he gathered from other conspiracy theorists."

"And…?"

"Let's just say it's a politician. High profile one, too. Now we need to figure out who it is and…"

"Bush."

"It's not Bush."

"But he's the President."

"No, he isn't."

"He's not? Still him."

"It's not Bush. The details are vague, but sounds like maybe a contender or someone who's always bragging about being something he's not. Someone who makes a lot of promises he never keeps and accusations he never backs up. Word on the street that I gathered before having to come here and rescue you is that he made a deal with the devil. Not the actual devil since Lucifer is really not such a bad guy, just has a bad rep, but some underworld demon willing to grant him the power to unleash Hell on Earth. Literally."

"Must be Tuesday."

"Must be Tuesday."

For the record, it actually was Tuesday, so even though they were quoting one of the best goddamn television shows of all time, alas, the stars aligned for layers of meaning. So meta. Praise be to Buffy. Fuck Joss, though.

Staring at the tear stain still streaking Brendon's cheek, Antonio couldn't help but wonder if the tear was for him or for something else, someone else, somehow not even considering it could just be personal and have nothing to do with anything outside Brendon himself. He cursed his heart-hole, thrashing and bashing away at the innards, the demons, the very depth of Hell this up and coming politician might release should even more power and clout come his way. Or hers. Gender never was mentioned, now that Antonio was starting to think more clearly, now that Brendon was not harmed, or worse, killed by Flaming Nazis. Shit's getting weird, and it's about to become diarrhea with no toilet in sight.

But the stain. The streak. The single tear. Lonely. Sad. Antonio couldn't shake its meaning. But worse, he feared it was something he wouldn't be able to heal. Wouldn't be able to wipe away with a kiss, a suck, a good long fuck.

Not that he wouldn't try those things. May not help in the long run, but distraction's distraction, and well, life's too short for the mortals to miss out on the small pleasures they get so rarely.

The shaking hand clued Antonio in that it was bad. Really bad. Like something one doesn't actually fully recover from.

Was it the werewolf? The redhead? The freaky Frankengirl? The black boy he had an irrational jealousy for the longest time despite knowing they've always only been friends? That goddamn Gufflebacht who tortured his Brendon so much in his childhood only to come clean he was also a fucking faggot and a fucking witch or warlock or whatever he called himself? What happened.

"My dogs died," Brendon blurted.

"Both Rex and Deschutes? At the same time?"

"Yes."

Antonio didn't know whether to be relieved it wasn't one of the people or scared because he knew how much those pups meant to his Brendon. But he couldn't shake that there was more. Much more Brendon wasn't telling him. Like he was sparing him details, needed details, to make sense of what has been happening as of late. However, it didn't matter as he squeezed.

It may have been a bit tight, but he knew Brendon could handle it.

"I'm sorry."

"I know."

"They had a good life. You gave them a good life."

"They gave me a good life. But they also gave me more than that."

"Dogs do."

"No, I mean, they protected me."

"Rex and Deschutes were very protective of you."

"It's more than just dog protection. They protected me from so much more than that."

"I don't want to let go, but I don't understand."

Brendon gave one last squeeze before pulling away, peeling off slowly like sticky plastic on a warm Jolly Rancher sitting in your pocket all day. He took Antonio's hands in his. Shaking. Still.

Antonio had hoped the hug would help, but it seemed to have only made things worse. Because that's what he does: ruin everything. That's all he'd done his entire life, especially purposefully revving his motorcycle engine as he passed the Werewolf house to irritate the matriarch, which made him laugh and try to one up himself each day. For what? Because he could? No. Worse than that, because he wanted to.

But Brendon continued shaking and Antonio continued pondering his past assholery and eternity passed before he got an answer.

"Not long after they came into my life, they licked my infected snot," Brendon said so seriously that Antonio wasn't sure whether to laugh at the dry humor, which Brendon sensed, well, not so much sensed as witnessed the chuckle being forced down to the quiet place. "It's kind of the same reason that Sheree can see you in daylight."

Confusion. Chaos. Ew?

"So, Sheree also licked your snot?" Antonio asked, trying hard not to vomit the last thing he ate, which, now that he thought about it, was also Brendon's bodily fluids.

"Actually, I spit down her throat," Brendon said casually. "Because it was the only way she could kill your stepdad's wife."

"Of course."

"No, really. It was. Because of my magic. My specific healing magic."

"Wait, so, your sister also protects you then? I mean, she can be a bitch, but…"

"Kind of? It's too complicated and honestly I'm still distraught and don't feel like explaining everything to you right now because it's all still a lot to process, but, um, Rex and Deschutes, they… they…"

"You don't have to tell me."

"I do."

"Okay. I have all the time in the world."

"Because you're immortal."

"Bitch."

Brendon smirked. It was short, but broke the tension more than Antonio intended. Yet the tear streak remained, undried and still looking fresh as new.

"I thought I'd have more time with them, which is why I've been keeping you at a distance."

"Wow, you have some funny way of showing your distance while we're…"

"Yeah, well, the sex thing is very much new and exciting, and don't get me wrong, fun as hell, but I haven't been giving you my all."

Antonio felt the sudden need to sit. Brendon was, by far, the most insatiable partner he'd ever had. To the point that he felt the need to take a break from one of their all night fuckathons. To hear he was holding back? He wasn't giving his all? How much more could there possibly be?

"It's the same reason I am not ready to make a decision to join you, you know, as a vampire."

"Because you may lose your powers?"

"Because I may lose my life."

This time, Antonio sat on the moist grass. Fell flat on his ass.

"Rex and Deschutes protected me from mortal danger. So long as they lived, I couldn't die. I couldn't be tricked or glamoured. I was safe. Ish. I'm no longer safe."

"I know how much they mean to you, but…"

"You don't fucking understand, do you? They licked my gross snotty nose! They were, in one sense, unmagicked and yet somehow also formed a protective magical shield wherever I went whether they were with me or not! I don't know how and no other witch has been able to explain it to me, but without their protection, I'm no longer the hunter, I'm prey."

"From who?"

"Others like you."

"Like me?"

"Well, not exactly like you. Vampires. I mean, I still have to keep up my own protection spell to stave off other vampires from my scent after you fucked me in the woods. But with them gone… it isn't… enough. They want me."

"You are the hottest commodity."

Brendon's head tilted in a way that reminded him of those recently deceased dogs. Eerily so. He did not look amused. But then again, here he was, spilling his guts and Antonio had to go and make another fucking joke to lighten the mood because darkness made him uncomfortable despite shadows being his best friends as a child while he was locked away and tortured and molested and raped.

After letting out the loudest sigh of a breath, Brendon said, "It's kind of like Sam."

Gut. Punch.

"Not your Sam. Fairy Sam."

Uppercut.

"Blood."

"Blood?"

"Blood."

Debating whether to get off the wet grass or stay there because it felt like the comfortable friend he missed, like the shadows, Antonio decided not to move. No budging. Stick this one out. See it through instead of hiding away. It was time to face an uncomfortable truth. Brendon crouched so they could see eye to eye.

"My family has a history, and that history is, to put it bluntly, tasty."

"You're tasty. I bet your dad is…"

"Stop. Probably. Mom says so. So did Amanda one time while she was over when I was a kid."

"Chad's mom?"

"Yes. And my parent's former throuple partner."

"Kinky."

"Yes, yes, all sorts of kink. Anyway, my mom's side of the family is the source, not Dad's."

"Interesting."

"Because of the witch gene."

"I'd say obviously, but I've tasted witches before, but now that I think of it, none taste like you."

"Because it's more than just witch in me."

"Fairy?"

"Oh, gawd no!"

"No offense, I just don't understand."

It looked as though someone was holding Brendon's tongue in a chokehold. No matter how hard he tried to get the words out, he couldn't. Stuck. Unable to breathe. Unable to form the muscles to bend to his whims. Over and over, he tried to vocalize what he so desperately wanted to tell Antonio, what he needed to tell him, but the words were silent as his lips tried to move.

"I'm a direct descendent of Lilith!" Brendon forced out so hard it knocked over several nearby trees and an abandoned car, reminding Antonio of the day his motorcycle flew off the road, crashed into a giant tree, and left him mangled and dying before a silver fox being carried by the most powerful vampire witch in existence told him to stop and save the victim.

Dumbfounded, Antonio didn't know what to think. Growing up Catholic, he knew the story of Lilith. Or so he thought. Now as a recovering Catholic vampire with the strength of Song's End himself, and knowledge beyond thousands, he knew he knew even less.

"She's the mother of both witches and vampires. She's the reason both of us exist. She's the reason my great-great-great-grandfather, Song's End's lover, can be both a witch and a vampire. It means I carry part of her in me, which makes me a target. A target that I was protected from until just an hour ago when my sweet puppies gave out their last breath in my arms."

The lone tear was lonely no more as brothers and sisters and extended family started running down the cheeks of the man Antonio loved beyond measure even if he too had to admit that he'd been holding back, preventing a huge part of himself from letting another see inside, take a peek, glance at the shitshow and smile or laugh or wipe away and flush. And as much as he tried to pick himself up off the ground, to move closer, to hold his boy, his man, his everything that mattered to him not only in this moment, but every moment that led up to this, prepared him for this, this love, this pain, this life he never thought possible as a member of the society of the damned. But move he managed. Wrapping himself around Brendon, he was shocked by how tightly Brendon squeezed back, the tears wetting his ears and shoulder, dripping down his back like rain.

"I'm ready to let you in."

"What do you need?"

Slow as Sunday morning, Brendon pulled away to look Antonio dead in the eyes and said, "Tell me I'm yours."

"What?"

"Tell me I'm yours."

"I don't understand? I don't want to possess you like some object."

"We've talked about this."

"You talked about it and dropped it," Antonio said, glad he remembered something.

"It's the only way for me to be safe."

"From other vampires? I will always protect you!"

"You can't be everywhere."

"I can be wherever you are."

"Not always. I can't live like that."

"In a relationship?" Antonio asked, wondering where the hurt and anger and fear he felt growing inside stemmed from. Brendon was asking for a commitment, and as much as Antonio wanted that commitment from Brendon, he suddenly had doubts. Was it really what he wanted? What about him made Brendon want this so much? Because he had his heart in a jar in his basement after plucking it out of a tree branch when he was thirteen? Is that love? Is that obsession? Is that reason to deny or give into the temptation of love-lust-hate?

Then Brendon's lips formed a slight smile and all the doubt lifted away as quickly as summer fog.

"For us. If you tell me I'm yours, others have to respect that. Not just, like, by law or anything, but bound by nature."

"There is so much I don't understand."

"Because your maker never stayed to teach you, but you know now why, right?"

"Why Song's End couldn't stay? Yes, of course."

"It's the same reason I'm at risk unless you claim me. Please, tell me."

Antonio couldn't understand the struggle he was having over this. Isn't this what he wanted? No, he wanted Brendon to join him as a vampire so they could live for eternity and rule the world together. Sort of. Not quite. He wanted Brendon because of his selfishness. His desire to be the powerful one in the relationship. And Brendon was a threat to that power because of his own power he could never possess. But could he? Could he possess the power? The power of Lilith given the opportunity, the chance to take everything? For what? For a little satisfaction at the cost of his soul should it even exist any longer?

Pushing through the thoughts poisoning his mind, Antonio clawed his way out. He forced Brendon to stare straight into his eyes as he pricked his finger with one of his sharp fangs and said quiet as a dormouse as he shoved his bleeding finger into Brendon's mouth, "You're mine forever and always."

Sucking on Antonio's finger like it was a goddamn baby dick, Brendon only stopped after the blood stopped flowing. "I'm yours."

CHAPTER 18

Owner of a Lonely Heart

"I'd take a bullet for you, you know that," Antonio said, sweeping his face with syrupy seriousness.

"You're immortal, and I'm going to kill you if you keep saying that," Brendon told him, punching his arm.

The walk back to Brendon's family home, his home, the place he grew up after moving to Ravenwood back in the summer of 1999 after knowing nothing but the hustle and bustle of what he thought was the big city of West Seattle off Alki Beach, was filled with empty banter. But that emptiness was fulfilling, at least to Brendon, who here, now, belonged after so much loneliness and loss and pain and suffering. Not that he didn't feel loved and wanted and nurtured, but that worry of wondering if when how had finally turned into now.

The slight windings and curvings of Song's End Road made for lackadaisical meanderings, swaying into one another with ease and impishness children often exude without thought. Gentle amber glows from streetlamps guided them down the empty street, quiet of cars at the late hour or early hour depending on your particular inclinations.

The closest thing to sound came from leaves beginning to sprout from the oaks and maples and ashes that filled the yards as they carried the impressions of the breeze that came and went of its own accord.

Slipping his hand into Brendon's, Antonio couldn't help but wonder just what exactly he got himself into with this whole situation of owning another goddamn person. Like a slave? Love slave? Does that make it any better? He couldn't help but get back into the deep recesses of his mind where the bad thoughts huddled in shadow and urged him to play. But Antonio fought through the shadows, the demons, the bad, and found light again. It may have just been another streetlamp closer to home, but it was light and he was going to take all the light he could right now. The darkness could wait. His boy needed him present.

"I have something to show you," Brendon said with a gentle squeeze, sending an electric wave up Antonio's left arm, through his torso, and down down down to the place he cherished most on his entire body where the sensation intensified, multiplied, defied logic.

Without even realizing it, Antonio found himself at the Hollins's front door. Brendon turned the knob. Like everyone else on the street it seemed, locking doors was an afterthought. Kind of odd considering the sheer number of unexplained deaths the town was famous for, but also part of the charm of small-town life that, now in 2014, wasn't so small anymore. It still hovered in the 3000s, but was inching upward toward the next big number with new families moving in, old children moving back home, the dead being replaced by cheap mortgages.

Antonio had lived on Song's End since moving out of his parent's house after graduation. He rented the place he now owned with a couple roommates who were never home but always paid their share on time until one day they didn't, so he went for a ride to visit his grandfather and never came back the same. His last human conversation. His abuelo. He was still flying high off his grandfather's gift and advice and love he wished the rest of his family had even a fraction of toward him when his bike flew into the tree and crushed more than just his dreams. And when he came back home, confused, cursing the cursed life he'd been granted, thrashing the street he called home, wondering what could possibly come from being the living dead, he paused toward the Hollins house. The family had only been there a year, but after feeling like an abandoned mess for years before where every once in a blue moon someone would come in, dust, clean out the rat traps, then lock it back up until next time, he felt a sense of calm so unexpectedly he crumbled to the concrete sidewalk just outside that old brown house whose living room lights softly spread onto the pristine lawn devoid of anything but pure green grass, and wept. This was the home, the life, the dream he had always wanted for himself despite being a cum whore in the back alleys, rest stops, anywhere desperate men wanted to feel a little less lonely in life. And he couldn't make sense of it all, the life part. It had only been a short time—what, an hour at most?—since the stranger turned him into the thing he was now, but in that time he knew that any chance of settling down and having any semblance of a family was not only off the table, but there was no table, no communion, no vows for La Padre to have him recite verbatim. No more. Not now. But thirteen years and some odd months later? A chance? How?

The Hollins house had always felt like the home Antonio wished he had growing up. Loving parents. Loving siblings. Sure, they also had the haunted ghost of the original owner of the house trying to kill some of them, but hey, isn't that the price one pays for the American Dream?

And here Antonio was, at the door of that great big piece of American pie, being led in by one of the Hollins kids, the boy… well, the boy with the last name Hollins since there was a half-brother a couple doors down, Chad, but he didn't live there anymore. Antonio made sure the door latched behind him as quietly as possible so as to not wake the living. Sheree had moved back just a short time ago, not long before Brendon. Kayla moved out to live with Courtney right after high school. He could hear Beth snoring and Frank moving a pillow, neither of which indicated they'd woken.

They stopped in front of the basement door. Brendon's free hand shook ever so slightly, but enough to garner concern.

"We don't have to do this now."

"Yes, we do. I'm yours now. And I need you to be you. All of you. Whole."

Brendon quickly opened the basement door. They were greeted with blackness so thick it crept into the living room light and drowned it out. The musty dankness overwhelmed Antonio's senses for a moment. It was so black! Antonio couldn't help but feel the fascination with seeing so much nothing. No matter how much he tried to tune his night vision eyes, he couldn't penetrate the darkness.

"Just warning you, that living room lamp has the smallest watt bulb in the entire house," Brendon said as he pulled a chain, flooding the basement in white that spilled into the kitchen, living room, den, back mudroom, laundry room, every crevice of the lower floor somehow couldn't escape the brightness that nearly knocked Antonio to his knees.

Spanish prayers silently flowed from Antonio's lips with fervor. Eventually he adapted, but still felt uneasy as Brendon led him down the rickety stairs that creaked with every step loud enough to wake the dead, but apparently not the living. Somehow, and shocked to shit, Antonio noticed the stair light barely reached the bottom of the staircase. He watched as Brendon disappeared, just for a brief second, to turn on another bulb, and he swore that it was just like what Mr. Thorwald must have felt like after Jeff kept flashing him.

"I don't know why I'm struggling with the dark and the light so much," Antonio confessed.

"Dad finally told me years ago the reason he insists on super bright lights was in case of a vampire or werewolf attack. Overwhelms their senses briefly, but that briefness could be the difference between life and death for the prey."

"Dad's pretty smart. Hot and smart is a lethal combo. Must be why I fell for you."

Brendon smiled the faintest smile, but it was there nonetheless. He turned toward the back wall where an old washer and dryer that had been out of commission for years still lived collecting dust next to a painting of a middle-aged woman that gave him pause. "Great-Great-Great-Grandma Jessica. Don't worry, her eyes won't follow you… anymore. She finally died the day you died."

The way Brendon was so casual about this felt both haunting and sexy to Antonio. True, his death was a traumatic event that led to so many questions he still had, but the bits and pieces he was picking up along the way, knowing now that it was Brendon's sister who unintentionally caused the accident after birthing evil, Brendon's great-great-great grandfather who insisted he be turned after that accident that he was mere seconds away from everlasting death, Brendon's family had been entwined with his fate without him even knowing it, and now Brendon was his lover.

His.

He'd almost forgotten that Brendon also convinced him to commit. Something about protection? The bright lights clouded his recent memory as he spotted something familiar. Something lost. Something he never wanted back.

Holding the jar close to his heart, Brendon's hands concealed the contents.

"I've been the owner of this lonely heart far too long. But now you are ready to have it back."

Antonio seemed taken aback. What was he supposed to do with the damn thing? He obviously didn't need it! But there it was, in a jar since the day the branch rightfully ripped it out of his cursed body the night his Sam was taken far too early. He knew now it wasn't his fault, but for years he felt the guilt, the pain, the constant quest to find out what the purpose of immortality was if love was forbidden.

And then a red leaf begged him to find out.

And that red leaf led to Brendon.

And Brendon had his heart.

In a jar.

A fucking mason jar.

So quiet.

And as Brendon opened the lid, tilted the top, he noticed something damn peculiar about his old organ. It should be ash. It should be stone. It should be anything but bloody and fresh and pumping? Yes! It was alive! His dead heart beats! Loudly! But how?

"Let me explain. No, there isn't time. Let me summarize," Brendon said—shaking his head slightly, knowing he'd already explained this, but knowing Antonio's fractured mind was still just that, and not all memories were sticking like flypaper and that he needed the patience he'd have with someone suffering from Alzheimer's or dementia—before telling Antonio how the night he drank from Song's End and fell down the cliff Song's End created as part of his death slash ascension, the heart started beating again.

"So that's what I heard? What we heard?" Antonio asked, his confusion a blessing in disguise.

"I wanted to tell you then, but knew you weren't ready."

"How did you know I wasn't ready?"

"Song's End told me."

"He found time to tell you, but couldn't bother waiting for me to wake from the bloodlust?"

"Yes. And we did tell you, but you forgot. It's complicated."

"Doesn't have to be, what with my family keeping secrets about me with you."

"He's basically family, what with him being my great-great-great-grandfather's lover and all."

"He's my dad. Well, second dad. And boy do I have a track record with dads abandoning me."

"Truth."

"Harsh."

"Not as harsh as this is going to be."

"What?"

"You need this back."

"My heart in a jar? Nah, you can keep it. Glad to see it's beating again, as I haven't heard that since, what September 2000?"

"Labor Day."

"Day before."

"It was after midnight."

"You know an awful lot about the timing of my death."

"It was the most traumatic day of my life, so I'm pretty sure I'd remember most of the details since my brain refuses to allow anything like that to happen again."

Antonio felt the tinge of guilt for not knowing all the details. He had always focused his thoughts on his own feelings, his own trauma, his own truths that the feelings, trauma, and truths of the man he loved came in second place in a two-person race.

"Stop it."

"Stop what?"

"Being you. I'm fine. I'll tell you more about it later. Right now, I need you to have this."

Brendon handed the beating heart over to Antonio. Antonio held it like a tired housewife holding her husband's limp dick because he wants sexy time but she's been dealing with the whiny kids he wanted but ignores. What he wasn't expecting was to begin to feel a weight lifted. His heart. In his hands. Close to the place it should be. Close to the hole it once occupied.

"I'm not supposed to. Not yet."

"I'm telling you that you need it. Now."

"Sam said I should wait."

"Why would Sam say that?"

"Said it's the only way we all survive."

Brendon paused. "Sam… may not have had all the information he should have had before saying goodbye."

"What?"

"With Rex and Deschutes gone, it changes things. I know this is a lot, and I know how difficult this feels right now, reeling from the second loss of Sam, rediscovering the second birth of your heart, and me telling you to dismiss what you were told, but…"

"Please tell me that it won't hurt. That I won't hurt anyone. That we all make it."

Softly smiling, Brendon assured, "I can only tell you that this is our best chance, with you at full capacity. I just pray to Lilith you heal from this quickly."

"Wait, that I heal from…"

"This is going to feel a bit spicy," Brendon said before his hands started getting sparkly.

"Wait wait wait!" Antonio shouted, almost dropping his heart onto the basement floor covered in dead bugs and dust bunnies.

But Brendon didn't stop. He chanted as his hands glowed. Teal light forming a ball that grew and grew and grew as he spread his hands apart. Growing brighter and brighter. Bigger and bigger. Louder and louder Brendon's voice chanted in a language he didn't understand. Was it even a language? Was it a tongue he should know?

Before Antonio could answer his own questions, Brendon locked eyes and said, "Remember, I love you forever and always," then released the glowing teal ball straight into Antonio's chest.

Floating nearly a foot off the ground, the glowing ball dug its way into Antonio's chest, digging and digging and digging so deep he had to clench his teeth from the pain. Pain! Pain he so desperately wanted to feel again. Not that he couldn't feel pain, but this was real pain. Suddenly it got to be too much and his arms flew out. Where was his heart? His open hands were empty. Did he drop it? Did he lose it? Again?

The pain made him shake.

The pain made him scream.

The pain made him beg for death.

Then POOF! it was gone.

Like magic.

More accurately, it was magic.

Antonio clutched his chest like he couldn't breathe, which he didn't technically breathe, so he found the sensation familiar and foreign. And then he heard it. His heart. Beating. Beating again in the empty place it once called home.

"How do you feel?" Brendon asked.

"Alive!"

"Good, because now we might have a fighting chance to survive what we have to do next."

"What's that? The coming evil? Psshhh! We got that!"

"Don't be cocky. We don't got it. Not yet."

"We have you and Fuzzball and Falls Apart and Ghost Whisperer and Fucking Fairy and stronger-than-ever me. What more do we need?"

"We need to break someone out of prison. Or maybe she's in an insane asylum. Haven't really figured out all the details on where she's being kept because the case is oddly very hush hush for how public it was when the whole thing went down."

"You're not talking about…"

"Ami."

"You are talking about."

"Yep."

"Call me confused, but what the fuck?"

CHAPTER 19

Mad World

"No."

Brendon didn't even have a chance to explain before he got shut down. He knew he had to tell his sister Sheree and sister-in-law Courtney about the plan to break Ami out, and he knew it wasn't going to be easy, but he didn't anticipate the complete lack of understanding that it needed to happen to save the whole fucking universe.

Antonio sat on the Hollins's sofa as patiently as a vampire could, and as he sat, he felt the emptiness, the loneliness, the complete absence of a huge part of what made this house a home: the missing dogs. The dead dogs. Brendon's dogs. The dogs who gave their entire lives protecting him from as much harm as possible, though only of the supernatural variety because, let's be honest, no matter how much someone loves you they can't protect you from everything that life throws, and it sure as shit likes to pitch.

"Da fuck, Bren," Courtney said in what anyone who knew her would consider a normal volume, but for those who don't, basically a shout.

"There's a connection between…" Brendon started, but as usual when it came to his sisters and the black boy's sister, never fully had a chance to finish.

"…between this new threat and Ami? We got that. But what help do you think she'll offer? She wasn't even the chemist," Kayla, his other sister and Courtney's lover since the day they met, but really not the day the met, but the day they actually met corporeally. It's complicated.

And then it happened. The look. The look Antonio swore he'd seen a thousand times before on Sheree even though he'd only officially met her mere months ago that fateful day in the woods. The slight-head-tilt-arms-crossed-left-hip-lowered look that layered so much meaning words were completely unnecessary, and honestly, would just make the matter completely lackluster like when someone actually says goodbye on the phone in a TV show. Only this time, Brendon gave it, and Antonio couldn't decide if he was turned on or disgusted or both. His dick held the truth.

"You know damn well that her, Kori, and John all came up with the formula together. True, Kori was the real chemist behind the final product, but Ami and John were there, making the shit that killed…" Brendon started to say, but seeing the murder in Courtney's eyes, stopped.

A massive sigh escaped Sheree's mouth as her body loosened faster than their mother after a bottle of wine on a Tuesday night when she'd make googly eyes before heading to the bedroom followed by their dad with a grin knowing what's about to go down. The hurt that struck nearly fourteen years to the day they lost someone close yet so soon after they met smacked her down to the seat next to Antonio who shocked the shit out of Brendon when he put a hand on Sheree's back and said, "You can't keep blaming yourself for other people's decisions."

Courtney nodded before bursting into tears that almost flooded the living room and joining Sheree on the other side. Kayla crouched into back of the couch to hug from behind. Brendon stood his ground.

"Listen, if there was another way for her to help us develop some kind of, hell, I don't even know what, but she's the best chance we have right now. I just started living, I mean really living, and sure my boyfriend is dead, but is he? I mean, damn! If that's dead, what am I? For fuck's sake, just let me try something before the rest of my world falls to shit!" Brendon yelled through tears and pain and heartache.

"I mean, yo man fine as hell, so yeah, I get you," Courtney said.

"Plus the dead guy did finally take Brendon's virginity, and we all know what happens to nonvirgins in horrors, so now he's gotta be cautious," Sheree said bluntly.

"And his man's got that vampire thing, but like, super vampire thing going on, so..." Kayla said with duck lips and nodding like a goddamn bleach-blonde bobblehead.

"Everyone gets a hot guy but me," a voice from out of nowhere said, causing Brendon to jump as if a tiny spider crept into his Cheerios. Again.

"Jennifer! You sneaky Asian, can't be creepin' up on people, yo!" Courtney shouted, and this time was an honest to Baby Jesus Courtney shout, so there was damage. "Damn. Shit. Fuck."

Shaking his head, Brendon had to pipe in with, "Maybe if you weren't into the hot guys who were only into hot guys, you'd have better luck."

"True true," Jennifer said. "What's with the pile onto Sheree and why was I not invited to be the cherry?"

"Sheree's having a moment. Also, it's supernatural shit and we all know how you feel about that given your history with, well, me," Kayla said, blasé as fuck.

Ghost possession was so 1999-2000.

"So, are we just going to walk in and grab her?" Antonio asked, just now wondering if there was a plan or if this was one of those action-only plot holes he abhorred.

Head tilt. Rex and Deschutes. Sheree. Brendon started nodding back and forth ever so slightly, but enough to cause an irritancy not unlike spicy diarrhea after thinking Thai spice level was a good life decision before he said, "The plan is to do what I say."

"Ooh, Action Mode Brendon has been activated. God, I want to…"

"Later."

"But…"

"Later. Time to go in."

They walked with ease into the compound. Past a garden. Through the well-lit courtyard. Into the building from an unlocked side door. Down the hall. Left. Left. Right. Another left. Down another long hallway until they reached a door with her name, turned the handle, and walked in.

"Wow, that didn't take long, Hollins," Ami told them as she stared at the ceiling from her bed while tossing and catching balled up socks.

"So easy," Brendon said.

"Yeah, it's easy getting in. Getting out? Not so much. Who's the hottie?"

"Antonio," Antonio said.

He held out his hand for a shake which he immediately regretted, especially knowing her history, her sick and twisted history that, now that he was beginning to calm down after the 0.02 seconds of rage hit him, was nothing compared to his own sordid past. True, Ami was a killer who killed not one but both of her lovers mere hours apart—including one's entire family—but the reason behind those deaths. The reasons behind that poor teacher's demise. The reason she threw caution to the wind. The serious plotting and planning and patience to stir up the storm over a minor slipup that had no consequences, yet had all the consequences in the world. And for what? Some notion of empire?

"Back off, bitch. He's mine," Brendon said, puffing up his chest and flexing his biceps through clenched fists.

The tight black t-shirt hid nothing.

"Relax, he ain't really my type. Not into biters," Ami said, biting her teeth a couple times before adding, "So, where're my street clothes?"

Brendon tossed a bag onto the bed. Ami quickly changed, not even asking the men to turn around. No modesty. Of course, a year in prison and thirteen in an insane asylum kinda has a way of forcing one to let go of Puritanical ideals made up by men to shame women for being human. As Ami dressed, Antonio couldn't help but notice the scars in places scars shouldn't be, which she noticed.

"Mommy Dearest," she whispered as the sweatshirt paused over her breasts before pulling it down and giving it a good tug to hide inside of.

"Ready?" Brendon asked.

"I hope your plan is solid, because this place isn't to keep people out, it's to keep people in," Ami said, feeling the sweatshirt and thinking it was familiar.

"I know," Brendon told her.

But they didn't leave the room. They didn't go out the door, down the hallway, take a right, left, right, right, and walk out the side door, through the well-lit courtyard, past the garden to scale the ten-foot wall to freedom. Brendon just stood like he was waiting. Waiting for what?

And then it hit. Ami cried as she punched Brendon in the chest over and over, and he just took it like a man. His man. Antonio thought about intervening, but knew his instinct was to kill the woman punching his lover, and knew that no matter what, they needed her so they could fix or stop or do something about the coming evil. Yes, they needed The Chemist unharmed so she could do her promised duty Antonio was still in the dark about even knowing she knew about the plan to break her out. Did Brendon tell him and he forgot? Again? Could he even forget still? What was this trickery?

All Antonio could do was watch and wait for the hysterics to die down. If Brendon wasn't telling him everything, he knew there was a reason. It still pissed him off and made him angry as orchards, but the intent had to be part of the game. Only this game was new and he wasn't the only one playing, but felt like the only one who didn't read the rulebook and trust the person winning.

"It still smells like him, fucker," Ami said quietly as she softened her punches to taps. "Like John."

"Those are Kori's jeans," Brendon told her blunt as butter knives, yet slicing razor sharp.

Ami fell apart.

Great! Just what we need! A fucking psycho getting all blubbery! I hope he knows what the hell he's doing.

I do, asshole. Trust me.

Wait! You can telecommunicate again!

Apparently.

Get out of my head.

"Get into my car," Brendon said out loud.

"What?!" Antonio and Ami shouted just before hands grabbed theirs and they were whooshed away into the abyss.

It took a few seconds to realize Brendon had transported them to his car just outside the compound. He was already speeding away. Antonio's stunned face that even he had to admit this was not something to get stunned over, was a bit much. Brendon gave Antonio a wink as he shifted into fourth. Ami vomited in the backseat.

"Sorry, but every time I've prepared someone to teleport, it ends up being worse," Brendon told them. "Sorry about the plastic lining the seat and floor, but, you know, had a feeling you'd puke."

"Asshole," Ami said, wiping her mouth. "Now what's so important you need me for?"

"You didn't tell her?" Antonio whisper-shouted through clenched teeth.

"Tell her what?" Brendon asked, mischievous grin firmly planted.

"Tell me why?" Ami asked.

"Ain't nothin' but a…" Brendon started singing as dramatically as a middle schooler.

"No! No Backstreet Boys! Tell her!" Antonio shouted, totally unamused on the outside but laughing hysterically on the inside and completely and utterly ashamed he knew the song.

Covering his mouth, Brendon's hand traveled up to his hair where it pulled the thick brown locks into clumps as his eyes closed and he let out the longest breath humanly possible. A couple strokes and pats later, he let go, opened his eyes, and said, "Well, no sugar-coating it Ami, but your drug is bad."

"98.2% addiction rate says otherwise," Ami responded.

"Thank you for mathing?" Brendon said.

"Kinda my thing," Ami said.

"We need to know how to make it," Brendon told her.

"What? Hell no!" Ami said.

"Because it's proprietary?"

"Because it's lethal!"

"And suddenly you care about that shit?"

"Yes! No. I mean, ah hell, I don't know. But no. I won't."

"You will if you want to live."

"You fucking broke me out to make drugs, Boy Witch?"

The sting hurt more than it should have. How did she know about that family joke? Who would've told her about him being a…

"Listen, COLD has some, shall we say, serious side effects."

"Yeah, which is why I wanted to stop making it! John insisted we keep working to perfect it. Kori did whatever I told her to do, so no questions asked on her end. But John knew. He knew! He knew and he didn't care! He thought it could be a cure! A fucking cure for his goddamn mommy!" Ami hurled and continued hurling truths that unexpectedly painted her in a different light. Several minutes later, the shouts became speaks which became soft as John's sweatshirt Ami kept rubbing her fingertips over the cuffs of. "If only she didn't take it, she might still be alive. They all might still be alive."

"What are you talking about?" Brendon asked.

But before she could answer, Antonio said with realization, "They died and turned into…"

"…demons. I… I… I don't know what else to call it, but once I knew what was happening after we watched Hot Chocolate OD and then sprint into the fucking air, I wanted to put a stop to it. To all of it. We failed. Or reached a point where we had to start over from scratch. And John? My John, he just wanted to find a cure for his mom's stage 4 cancer so he'd have more time with her. The chemo made her miserable and lifeless. And I hated my mom, not just for what she did to me but for how she made my dad believe she was good long after she died, and how she never once showed me an ounce of love or compassion or, fuck, even a fucking hug after losing my dog, so I didn't get this whole mommy love bullshit John waxed and waned about. After Hot Chocolate, I had to make something to counteract COLD. The problem was that the cure was permanent."

"Permanent is good."

"Tell that to Sky."

"You mean…?"

"She didn't die from an overdose of COLD. I slipped her the cure in her last bag. I couldn't let what happened to the others I saw happen to her, so after finding Hot Chocolate, judge me all you want, but that bitch is crazy as fuck, I convinced her that my new stuff had an even better high. She snatched it out of my hands faster than going down on a cop behind the quickie mart after he caught her shooting up out front and swallowed it just the same. It took a few seconds, but she died. Really died this time. Burned her body in the dumpster. But Sky never turned. She was a moody little bad ass on wheels, but she never turned, so I hoped the cure would just reverse any of the shit COLD caused, but that didn't happen. She died too. Everyone died. Everyone!"

Antonio kept listening, waiting for that feeling he was being punked, but it never happened. He sensed she was telling the truth. Catching Brendon's eye for a moment made him realize Brendon also knew she wasn't lying.

"Why didn't you…?"

"What? Tell the cops, 'Hey! I'm a teenage drug maker slash dealer, but my shit's turning people into psychotic murderous demons, so, my bad!' Yeah, that'll go over well."

"I didn't mean the cops, I meant…" Brendon stared, but didn't know where else she could have turned. Not everyone knew the small-town horrors, and not everyone wanted to know, and those who did tended to keep it to themselves or pretend they didn't exist despite all the evidence to the contrary. "Goddammit. I have to ask. John's mom?"

"Yes."

"Did she turn before you…"

"Killed her with a hefty dose of the cure? I was too late to save John's dad. She'd already gotten him. But John? He… he… he'd been taking COLD on the regular and I saw the rage in his eyes like I saw in Hot Chocolate's right before I thought it was an OD. Oh gawd, she tore his dad apart! I brought two guns with me just in case. A dart gun with three doses of the cure in case I missed, and a Glock in case I really missed. Didn't even have time to think as John rushed toward me, so I fired the cure at his mom and she fell to the ground, then as John looked back to see what happened, I reloaded and fired at him. Dead. Both dead. So, I unloaded my Glock on them all. They were already gone, but I felt like I had to make it look like a murder not some supernatural demon shit. Gawd, child brains, right?"

Brendon had never given much sympathy to Ami. Ever. Sky was like a rock to his sister when she needed it most, and those four months of friendship changed her entire friend group forever. And when he found out it was Ami's fault she died? Unforgiveable. Or so he thought.

Antonio was calm as cucumbers throughout the villain confession monologue. Only now she wasn't so much a villain as an anti-hero. He knew the type. He considered himself to be that type. And as he bent down to where she sat in his living room, on his leather couch in front of the fireplace that gently popped as the flames danced inside, he met her eyes and said, "So you know how to make a cure?"

"I do."

"That's the most important thing we need to know right now."

"But there's a problem."

"Of course there is!" Brendon said, losing patience faster than a teacher in late May, or the day before when he asked Wayne's magic genie who's not really a genie to fix the issue, but the genie who's not really a genie answered that he couldn't possibly interfere with the natural course of the world again, and he went ballistic and almost killed the poor green guy with a single word.

"I'm sorry, but one ingredient isn't manufactured anymore," Ami said, staring at Kori's jeans wrapped around her legs. "Discontinued in 2001."

"Fuck me gently with a chainsaw," Brendon said.

"Don't quote *Heathers*," Antonio demanded.

"Huh?" Brendon asked.

"Never mind. Okay, so we can gather all the ingredients but one. Can't you, I don't know, witch magic something for the missing one?" Antonio asked Brendon, serious as all get out.

"That's not how it works."

"What do I know, I'm just a super-powered vampire with the blood of Song's End running through my veins and my recently reinstalled beating heart that'll one day soon activate some witchy powers of my own."

"Shit's getting freakier by the second," Ami said, rubbing her thighs and leaning back into the sofa.

"About to get freakier," Brendon told her after realizing something Antonio brought up. "If I know the chemical makeup of the discontinued ingredient, I actually might be able to whip it up."

"In a cauldron?" Ami asked with a snicker.

Brendon lowered his head and quietly said, "Yes."

"Oh shit, you're serious! Um, uh, well, the issue is that I don't know the exact chemical compound. Chemistry is so precise that one wrong molecule, and poof, bye bye bangs!"

"That's awfully specific," Brendon said.

"It was horrifying," Ami admitted.

As they talked about the missing chemical and how to possibly replicate it, Antonio felt his senses blur into oblivion. He never was good at Science. And Chemistry? The worst! Listening to Ami speak in Periodic Table of Elements made him nauseous from deficiency in what Brendon seemed to understand in abundance somehow, which only made him feel more nauseous and more deficient. The elements swirled and swirled around his head for what seemed like hours, but alas, mere seconds until he couldn't take it anymore and had to make it stop. But he didn't know how to make them stop talking about the very thing they needed to survive this threat that was about to overtake not only the town he'd grown to love and call home and was home to the man he loved and called home and so desperately just wanted the talking to stop and the fucking to start so the elements would stop spinning, spinning, spinning around and around and around and…

"No. Oh shit, guys, maybe?" Ami suddenly interrupted Brendon as he was trying to think of a way to replicate the one ingredient they couldn't get.

"Maybe what?" Brendon asked.

"Kori," Ami said, laughing as she rubbed her thighs wrapped in Kori's old jeans.

"Dude, she's dead," Brendon said.

"And you've got a fucking medium! Anna! She can ask her, right?" Ami asked.

"Wait, you know about Anna being able to talk to the dead?" Antonio asked.

"I've lived in Ravenwood my whole life. You pick up on the obscure, even if you don't exactly know what it is when you're younger. I remember thinking she was cuckoo for Cocoa Puffs back in the day, but now that I think about it, she definitely has the gift of being able to talk to dead people like that creepy kid in that one movie."

Still not convinced, Brendon asked, "What gave her away?"

"She told me once during Trig that my mom wanted to talk to me, which totally threw me off since she'd been dead for two years by then. But what really shocked me was that Anna said she told my mom to fuck off and never get inside her head again because she knew what she did to her own daughter. And in typical Anna fashion, she smiled that creepy little doll smile, giggled, and said she wanted to know that she knew and that I'd never have to worry about my mother haunting me again. And she was right. Shit, she was right. Didn't even know what to think because later that day my dad mentioned how much my hair reminded him of her and I cut that shit right there in front of him and threw it in his face. Jesus Christ, I'm a horrible person."

"You are," Brendon said. "But you're a horrible person who had horrible things happen to her, and no they don't excuse your actions, but you have a chance to make things right."

DING DONG!

The front door flung open.

"Heard you need. To talk. To Kori. Bitch." Anna walked in like she owned the place. "She's not here. But John says happy. Birthday. Bitch."

Ami laughed. "Sweet thirty-two."

Realizing what day it was, Brendon wrestled with all the details that came flooding in. April 21st. The day Sky died. The day John and his family died. The day Kori died. It was Ami's birthday. Ami's 18th birthday.

"Last time I was not locked up for my birthday I killed a family, went to a Foo Fighters concert with Kori, then threw her down a cliff after injecting her with the cure. Jesus, what a day."

Ami laughed. Not like the insane asylum laugh one conjures up like, say, The Joker, but a genuine lighthearted laugh. How long had it been since she was able to laugh like that? Antonio couldn't help but stroll down the rabbit hole of wonder, pondering the chance that maybe the killer in the room—okay, the other killer in the room—okay, so everyone in this room at this very moment had killed another at one point, so maybe clarification was in order—Ami, was finally free of her own demons, just not the ones she created by accident.

"Wait, you saw Foo Fighters after killing John and before you killed Kori? That's so high school," Brendon said.

"John doesn't think. It's funny," Anna informed the small crowd.

"Tell him I'm sorry. I didn't have a choice," Ami told Anna to tell John, wondering why Kori wasn't the one Anna conjured.

"John says he. Knows. Now," Anna said before continuing with, "But you need to break. Into Kori's. House and go. To her basement lab. To find what. You need."

A couple redheads walked through the open door.

"Hear we need to do a little larceny," Kwirk said, twirling picks.

"I'm always down for B&E," Anni said, wringing her hands.

Wayne walked in full werewolf and nearly scaring the Beelzebub out of Ami and said, "I'll make sure the coast is clear."

And then someone else walked into Antonio's house that made him furious and filled with so much rage, so much anger, so much hate yet sickening intoxication and want to abandon everything he loved just for another taste. It was Vulgar Sam. Bad Sam. Fairy Sam. "I'm only here because we might have a chance. What we gotta do?"

"What a freak show," Ami said, scanning the room filled with supernatural beings and some random redhead boy pretending he didn't have a soul when he was obviously the most sensitive soul in the entire town. "This really is a mad world, isn't it?"

"Sure is. Bitch," Anna said. "That was John. Bitch."

"You know you can stop saying bitch after everything you say to me," Ami said to Anna.

"I know. Bitch." Anna giggled, gave her the creepy doll smile, then said. "Let's do this."

CHAPTER 20

Fight the Future

No matter how hard Anna searched, Kori Myer could not be found. No matter. The crew searched Kori's basement lab her mother left completely intact, and stocked as though Kori had moved everything from the backyard shed down before her inevitable demise. Turned out there was no need to break into the house since the door was unlocked, and there was no need for lookout since she lived in a quiet corner lot, which disappointed the redheads and annoyed the werewolf. The vampire, the witch, and the fairy helped the human find what they came searching for.

"What's your deal?" Ami asked Sam as she pulled a bottle from a shelf to add to the stash of ingredients.

"Ain't interested," Sam shot back.

"Wow, not either, just you don't seem welcome in the Island of Misfit Toys," Ami shot right back at him.

"He's a fairy. Don't trust him. Don't listen to him. Shit, don't even talk to him," Brendon said furiously, eyes twitching.

"Wow, intolerant much?" Ami asked.

However, instead of defending himself, Sam chuckled and said, "No, really. You should listen to the witch. He tells the truth."

"Always an Other," Ami said, rolling her eyes, annoyed, thinking back to her high school days and the gossip that would surround her scandalous relationship with both John and Kori and how the three of them never hid the fact that they were a throuple before the concept had a name.

But Sam had a sadness about him that Brendon noticed and Antonio pretended not to notice, which irked him to no end. He knew what could happen if he engaged in so called small talk, but also knew that he needed Sam to be present and ready to fight, and if he was distracted, that wouldn't be any help.

"What's up with you?" Brendon asked quietly, reluctantly.

"My Edgar gone missing," Sam said. "My oldest friend. Like, we ain't fuckin', but he my man, you know?"

Without even a word, Antonio left the Myer's basement. Swiftly rushing down the street to the main road through the forest toward the cliff where he smelled Edgar but not the same Edgar he encountered so many months ago in the back alley where he sucked off Fairy Sam before tearing him apart. Something was different. Odd. And no, sunflower seeds wouldn't be dispersed for distraction.

"Please don't come near me," Edgar said, holding his stomach and backing up toward the cliff.

Then Antonio smelled the difference. The taint. The thing he feared was about to happen to the whole goddamn town then state then country then fucking planet. But why now? Why the sudden surge? Surely the drug would've shown signs that it was dangerous back when it was popular? Yeah, it was a localized thing a few high schoolers did to make bank, but it had a decent following. Something wasn't adding up, and he didn't need a calculator to know why.

Ami specifically mentioned she needed Kori's help. Anna didn't conjure Kori but John instead. Anna could conjure up anyone she damn well pleased whether they wanted to be or not, so why not the very person they needed? Why the auxiliary boyfriend and not the main cast member? True, John did know enough about Ms. Myer that she wouldn't have the heart to clean out Kori's stuff after she died. The basement didn't look like anyone had been there in over a decade, which tracked mathwise. But Kori was the one who, if they couldn't find the ingredient they needed, which was probably expired and useless anyway at this point making the whole ordeal that much direr, knew how to replicate it to a tee in order to create the cure.

Staring at Edgar who looked like he was also in dire's straight, Antonio couldn't shake the unease. He was certain that Frank had performed the autopsy as the town's only medical examiner at the time, but could he have missed something? Was there something he withheld? Did he… lie?

"Please leave. She's here," Edgar pleaded.

"Who?" Antonio asked.

Before Edgar could answer, someone flew up from the inside the cliff, the giant hole his blood father birthed from and he himself was reborn in and for some reason up until now he completely didn't comprehend, Kori Myer died in. Falling down this cliff made him stronger. It made Song's End an unstoppable force. But no. Couldn't be. She was just a human, whereas Song's End was a vampire witch and he was vampire. More than vampire.

"Guess what happens after a blood exchange?" the person who flew out of the cliff said as they clawed their hand through Edgar's chest, holding his beating heart.

"No. Can't be."

"We need to go! Now!" Antonio shouted so loud a bottle fell from a shelf, which he prayed wasn't their magical key to unlocking the cure they so desperately needed yesterday.

"The fuck, man," Sam said, but then he smelled the blood. Edgar's blood. His Edgar's blood straight from the heart where a droplet landed on Antonio from at least ten feet away based on his perception and knowledge of spatter. "No no no no, not mi amigo?"

Without so much as a thought, Antonio found himself holding Sam, vulgar Sam, keeping him upright. "I'm so sorry. He knew something was wrong and that something wronged him in return."

"What? What happened?" Sam asked, tears flowing so endlessly in slo-mo like a goddamn supposedly emotional scene but it was directed by Michael Bay, so it was shitty at best and humorous at worst, but the humor was lost like Edgar on that cliffside missing his heart that…

"Kori."

"Kori?" Ami asked, not sure she heard right.

"Kori's not exactly dead," Antonio told the group, head down and staring at his shoes where he found the blood droplet Sam smelled and wondered why he didn't notice it earlier.

Wasn't he supposed to be more attune to the world around him? Wasn't he supposed to know when this shit was about to go down and be ahead of the game? Wasn't he supposed to be better? But no, he wasn't. Sure, he knew where Edgar was based off his scent, but had no idea, no inkling, not even a fucking clue that Kori wasn't a splattered mess of bones in a coffin next to his house.

"No, that can't be. My dad wouldn't…" Brendon started, but found himself in the same dilemma of what ifs and supposed to bes and wondered what else his family was keeping from him after they all made a pact of no more lies, and here, now, a lie that was coming back to bite them in the ass and destroy them all.

Seeing the hurt in Brendon's eyes made Antonio want to rush to him, console him, make him less sad, make him happy, make him forget. But no, he was too busy consoling some fairy he didn't even like, who smelled sweet like candy, too much though, and tasted even better. He gnashed his teeth, fangs begging to come, release the flow, satiate the desire, need, lust.

"Your dad may not have lied," Anni told Brendon out of leftfield.

"But how would you know?" Brendon asked.

"Because when I, uh, okay, remember when my dad tried fixing me and it wasn't working and I wasn't all that alive because too many of my parts failed to stay on?" Anni asked, knowing that Brendon was her good friend, but wasn't exactly the prying type into her constantly needing new parts to keep her going.

"Yes, and Dad, uh, hooked him up?" Brendon said, disgusted with the way it sounded when he realized the morbidity of it all, the way his father would supply the demand from those deemed to go to the crematorium after his examination for the po-po.

The way Anni fidgeted reminded him of the time she got so excited about Brendon revealing he thought he could heal people when he was nine that she bit off her own finger to test it out. And yes, Brendon healed it, but Anni didn't even seem to flinch at her biting her finger off, but the excitement before? Oh boy! Crazy pants! It was the first time he told anyone about thinking he was a witch and the first time anyone realized Anni's "Handle With Care" bracelet that was permanently attached to her wrist had more than one meaning.

He was new to town. They were still somewhat new to each other. But they knew they'd always have each other's backs when shit got real, and so many times did the shit pile up and the shovels start doing the dirty work to keep their worlds moving.

Anni knelt down. Brendon didn't even notice that he'd collapsed to the floor.

"Your dad saved me more times than I can count. Well, I can probably count if I mathed, but who's got time for that? What I mean, what I want you to know, to realize, to understand, is that your dad is good people, alright?" Anni said, putting a hand on his shoulder gently.

Antonio just watched as Sam sobbed into his jacket, staining the leather with salty tears. Why now? Why was this happening in this moment? All at once? They needed to leave quickly. But where? Where could they go that would be safe from her? Was safety just another myth?

"But there is a reason your dad took this job when so many others left. You know Ravenwood by now. You know what goes on in the shadows. So does your dad. This is his hometown. Your family's hometown. You may not have moved here until 1999, but your parents grew up here. And anyone who's lived here for a time knows the shady shit that comes with small-town life," Anni said.

"True. When my mom told me I was a werewolf, it was like a lightbulb went off. All the weird stuff suddenly made sense. Well, not exactly made sense, but, uh, you know what I mean," Wayne said.

Ami shook her head. "Yet your dad proclaimed Kori died with COLD in her system, just like John, his parents, and Sky."

Hearing Sky's name brought back so many memories of the joyful, free-spirited girl who came to town after the first nightmare of his life ended. Sky may have been bound by wheels, but she could fly every time she entered a room. Until those last few weeks. The weeks her parents decided to hide her away. The weeks she sought something, anything, to feel again. When Ami and Kori and John said they had just the cure, just what she needed, just what her family wanted to keep her away from. Only she didn't react to it like she should have. Interaction with her prescribed meds. Deadly. But does that mean Sky also…?

"No," Ami said, seeing Brendon's wheels turning. "I made sure of it."

"But, Kori?" Brendon said.

"I thought pushing her off the cliff and watching her body splatter at the bottom would be enough. And it looked like it. She was found. Your dad did his examination on what was left. Hell, they had a funeral!" Ami said, suddenly realizing an error in Antonio's logic. "It can't be Kori. Her mother buried her. Gone. Dead!"

Finally feeling like he was ready, Sam let go of Antonio before giving him a shove in the chest. Antonio snickered, knowing that the gesture was appreciated but also knowing that fairies weren't allowed to show such appreciation without demanding something in return.

"Dad was shaken up that weekend, but he was probably exhausted. So many bodies. And then my sister coming back from the dead? Too much. He had to have missed something," Brendon said, shaking himself up after flashing Anni a smile.

"Or he didn't," Kwirk said out of nowhere, causing Wayne to jump, and everyone else to wonder just when he snuck off.

"Shit, bro! Why?" Wayne asked, checking his crotch for leakage.

Covered in mud, Kwirk said, "So, her casket's not only empty, but also appears that something clawed its way out. Yay!"

Swiftly tossing a few things into a beaker, Ami said, "I've got what I need, but gonna need some heat and it appears Kori's all out."

A small fireball flew down the stairs, hovering just above Tommy Fucking Gufflebacht's left hand. "I bring the heat."

"You bring pain," Brendon said, clutching his left arm.

"And I promise to find a way to make up for that, but right now, we need to protect our town," Tommy said, holding his hand below the beaker. "Let me know how much heat you need. The more precise, the better."

Ami told him, and Tommy adjusted.

Antonio made his way to Brendon, clasping his hand, not wanting to ever let go. It hit him how this group of complete outcasts, here, now, working together to fight off something so terrible, that, should it be completely unleashed, would end them all without blinking. And the how? Fighting drugs with more drugs? The 1980s would be so displeased with him breaking his D.A.R.E. pledge to save the world. Reagan's probably spinning in his grave.

Kwirk glared at Tommy. And why shouldn't he? True, Tommy was helping now, but when they were younger? Such a bully! And now? Tommy not only was a warlock but a fag? The self-hatred he must've had that he inflicted so much pain on anything that reminded him of himself had to have cut so deep, piercing the flesh, straight for the veins to stop the blood flow and pain and misery and guilt.

"Almost…" Ami started, but never got to finish as the beaker flew against the stone walls of the basement, shattering and splattering more than just the contents of the cure, but their future.

"Bitch, you never could deal with me being better than you," Kori said before tossing Ami aside like a natty chew toy.

Tommy fell back, but just before Kori struck, something hit her.

"Ooh, fancy!" Kori said, gently tapping a fingertip onto the bubble.

Antonio looked around, seeing they were indeed inside some sort of force shield bubble contraption. "Shit, I don't know what was in that vial that exploded by us, but I think I inhaled."

"You didn't inhale, dummy," Anni said.

"It's me," Brendon said, winking.

Moments ago, he was broken and tormented. Now that the world was broken and tormented, he was cool, calm, collected. What sorcery was this?

Tommy backed away from Kori even though he was well within the bounds of Brendon's bubble. Antonio watched him make his way toward Brendon, slowly but quickly at the same time. And then he grabbed Brendon's left hand with his right and pushed out his left hand to mimic Brendon's right and the bubble somehow grew stronger, even more impenetrable. And larger, getting closer and closer to Kori where Antonio knew that if she stayed, it would kill her for good this time, not that razzle dazzle shit her pretend cancer cure slash blissful tingly high COLD offered its users.

But the hands. Brendon's. Tommy's. Holding each other. Tightly. His fangs quickly protracted.

Don't do it. We've got this. We know what we're doing. Trust me, Brendon's voice said in Antonio's head.

I shouldn't be so jealous, but I also know he shouldn't have been so mean to you and made you feel the way he did when you were so young, Antonio thought back.

Shame forces us to either confront our demons or go into survival mode. Tommy was in survival. Now he's not. And he's proving he's here to help.

But he tortured you!

No more than he tortured himself.

But...

"Help Ami," Brendon said aloud, breaking Antonio's fixation.

Taking a glance at Kori backing away. Was she floating? Flying? Was he tripping? He couldn't be sure, but he knew where Ami was and couldn't believe she was still breathing. Barely, but breath she had.

"Help her," Brendon said, firmly, sternly.

But what could he do? Kill her? He couldn't save her, make her keep living past the next few seconds she had as her heartbeat slowed almost to a complete halt. He was no doctor! He could kill her, though. Was that the help Brendon wanted him to give? Mercy killing?

"She's not ready to die," Brendon told him.

Antonio fought back the anger, the rage, as Brendon was busy still expanding the protective bubble further and further, still holding Tommy's hand, still working together, joining forces, joining powers, joining in ways he never could. Why did this feel like such a violation? A break of trust? Infidelity?

But then Antonio spotted the solitary tear falling down Brendon's cheek. That he, too, was struggling with this situation he was forced to be in, where there was a break of trust, a break of fidelity, a break. But what? Men hold hands! It isn't some moral dilemma, some mass Christian hysteria of Puritanical bounds from generations past binding them to forbid pleasure at all costs in favor of anti-masturbation cereal force-fed at sanitariums before being mass-produced and marketed as a healthy breakfast. These were enemies joining forces for the greater good! Still, Antonio couldn't help but think how much he wanted to tear Tommy apart. Yet the tear continued to slide down, spill over his chin, onto his neck, and hide somewhere inside his tight black t-shirt he wanted to rip off his chest, yank down his pants, and swallow his manhood whole.

No. Now was not the time for such thoughts. Antonio shook his head, trying to make it go away, but it lingered like Taco Bell.

"I really wanted to be your first," Brendon whispered, conjuring up a smile as best he could.

"You mean?"

"I mean."

"But how?"

"Song's End."

"Song's End?"

"You drank from him almost completely. And now you have your heart back. In essence, you have his power, his strengths, his… uniqueness."

"I… I do?"

"Yes," Wayne said. "I felt the change when you came up from the cliff."

"And it made you hotter," Kwirk said. "Like, way hotter."

"Gonna have to disagree to a point, but, yeah, your vibe definitely changed and has only gotten more complex since then," Anni said. "Which is saying something, because if you had only had the foresight to suck off your daddy earlier, my brother might still be alive."

"Anni!" Brendon shouted, losing concentration for a brief moment, but Tommy was able to compensate, which he found both impressive and annoying because it was, after all, Tommy Fucking Gufflebacht.

A joyful burst of laughter bounced off the walls. "Red's right." Antonio looked into Brendon's eyes and spoke volumes of nothing and everything. "Is this what you want?" he asked Ami, who nodded in the affirmative. "Who am I to fight the future?" he said before lunging his fangs into Ami's throat, slitting his wrist, and forcing it down her mouth before she died in his arms.

CHAPTER 21

Runaway Train

As Antonio held the dead woman in his arms, afraid to let go, afraid to look up into her unblinking eyes, stare into the abyss of emptiness and fear and loneliness and pain and suffering, someone's leg smacked him in the right eye. An actual leg, bloody stump at the broken femur, marrow seeping out the bone.

"Son of a bitch!" Anni cried, looking down as she bounced on one leg while the other was quite missing. "Girlfriend's gonna be pissed."

"Shit, not again!" Kwirk said, rolling his eyes.

The calmness surrounding the rest of the Supernaturals Only Club held a queasy uneasiness about the whole scene. Antonio couldn't help but stare at the disembodied leg missing the thigh up, but still holding onto an orange slip-on and ankle sock bearing blood stains. He knew the girl was fragile, but didn't know her parts could spontaneously fly off. Turned out, they couldn't.

"I said stay behind me!" Brendon shouted so loud a few vials fell to the floor, shattering into a thousand pieces.

"Dude, I thought I was!" Anni shouted back. "But then I spotted the rest of my sandwich and, well, you know how food motivated I am!"

Wayne reluctantly picked up her leg, gave Antonio a slight head shake, and walked it back over to Anni. Not that it'd be reattached automatically, but rather just so it was returned to its owner where it belonged. "Try not to lose anything else."

"I'd ask why you're not dead yet, Red, but I smell something off about you," Kori said behind the veil.

With all the commotion, Antonio nearly forgot she was still there. Still a threat. Still waiting to harm for harm's sake. And for what? Forgiveness? Revenge? Legacy? And yet proof of her hatred lay in his arms. True, Ami pushed Kori off the cliff that fateful night fourteen years ago practically to the day, but Ami had her reasons. Nobody knew it at the time, but she was trying to atone her sins best she knew how, which, yes, involved murdering several people after taking down several others in the process of glory and fortune and unprocessed trauma her own mother inflicted for years before she finally died, which made Antonio wonder if that death, too, was suspicious, all things considered. But no. Couldn't be. Could it? Could he now be creating an even worse creation?

Ami twitched awake, eyes red, fangs out. Swift as wind, she rose to her feet, grabbed a syringe to suck in the antidote, slipped through a crack in the shield, walked right up to Kori, and said, "Ready, babe?"

"Bitches forever," Kori said, taking Ami's hand.

"Bitches forever," Ami said before pulling Kori in for a bloodthirsty kiss.

Then they were gone.

The shield fell, along with both Brendon and Tommy.

"Why? Why would she do that?" Brendon asked the universe, but in true form, the universe stayed silent.

"I think I'm going to be sick," Wayne said as he transformed back into a human.

"I knew this whole thing was a fuckin' joke," Sam said.

Sam. Antonio forgot the fairy still existed, yet there he was, waiting to take action in the way of doubt. He fought back the little voice telling him to go in for the kill, even though he knew he'd never be able to kill him because of this little thing call magical fairy blood.

"So, was this all for nothing? Now we just, what? Wait to die?" Tommy asked, tears streaming down his face.

It was enough to make Antonio want to rip out the bully's throat. Especially when Brendon put his hand over Tommy's and said, "I hope not. But I don't understand. Ami wanted to eradicate this virus, this evil, this thing. Why would she join it?"

"Join Kori? They have history," Wayne said. "It's sordid and raunchy, but it's history."

Kwirk and Anni were uncharacteristically silent.

"What are the redheads not telling us?" Antonio asked, inching closer to them, but keeping his distance from the detached leg in case it decided to fling itself in his direction again.

"Oh, fuck," Brendon said, wiping his face as he stood and walking toward Anni. "Hold it still this time." Using both hands, bits of teal sparkly things popped between him and the two parts of Anni's leg. "That should hold for a while."

Anni smiled as she wiggled her reattached leg, bending the knee, and kicking the foot up into the air like a ninja. "Good as new. Well, I'm assuming good as new. Never met the leg's owner, so maybe it isn't so new, so, uh, good as used?"

The annoyance on Antonio's face filled the room. And why shouldn't it? The two loudmouths stayed suspiciously quiet during most of the last several minutes before Ami and Kori ran off to do Godknowswhat to Godknowswho for Godknowswhy. He could tell they were hiding something. Something big. Something important. But during the whole ordeal, there was so much going on, so much at stake, maybe they just decided to shut up? No. They wouldn't, couldn't, shouldn't take their silence for compliance.

"Wayne, why'd you transform back? I need your ears," Kwirk asked. "Whatever. Antonio, you hear them in earshot?"

Deciding, what the hell, why not play into the supposedly soulless young man's hand, Antonio perked his ears. Kori and Ami were far enough away they couldn't hear what was about to go down, and go down he hoped would be happening sooner rather than later because answers needed to be given or heads will roll. "Nothing."

"Whew!" Anni said, wiping her brow, though one would be hard-pressed to find sweat.

"Everything is going according to plan," Kwirk confessed.

"Wait, what?" Brendon and Tommy shouted.

"Seriously, the fuck, yo?" Sam said.

"What he said," Wayne said.

Antonio, on the other hand, burst into laughter once again at what seemed like yet another inappropriate time. But this time it wasn't for lack of understanding, but just the opposite. He knew what was going to happen now. Knew that there was no stopping it. Like a runaway train, never going back, but going the wrong way on a one-way track, he laughed and laughed and laughed.

"Think your man's broken, dude," Anni said to Brendon. "Too bad, cuz, you know, you kinda wasted yourself waiting for him to take your hole."

"Wow, Anni, thanks," Brendon said, but couldn't help but chuckle.

Wayne, Tommy, and Sam did not look amused.

Suddenly the windows shattered in the basement, glass flying in tiny shards to break up the laughing and chuckling and replaced it with screaming as the whole basement lab suddenly burst into flames before swishing out the windows as they unshattered, leaving nothing but chaos in its wake.

"Jesus Christ, man! What the hell?" Sam asked, staring at the emptiness.

"Well, my work is done," Kwirk said, brushing his hands.

"Tell me what just happened?" Wayne asked.

"Ami," Antonio said.

"Ami?" Sam asked.

"Ami," Kwirk and Anni affirmed.

"So, I realize the frosted tips thing is, like, a decade in the past, but the blond still remains, but, what?" Tommy asked, scrunching his face.

"I told you, redheads have no soul," Kwirk told him. "Thought you knew that by now, Gufflebacht."

The jibe hit Tommy where it hurt. "Yeah, I deserve that. And more. I still don't get it."

"Oh, son of a motherless goat! Kori couldn't read you! Like Antonio can't read either of you!" Brendon revealed.

And it was true. Antonio couldn't put his finger on the button that was the unease around both Kwirk and Anni, and that was it. He couldn't sense them, read them, hell, even smell them. But how?

"Can't be because of your red hair, because I could sense Sam, smell Sam, feel Sam," Antonio said before realizing the hurt in Brendon's eyes, yet knowing Brendon of all people would understand this pain, this loss, this sense of needing to feel. And then something else hit him. The others he could read, couldn't sense, couldn't smell. "You?"

"Me," Brendon said. "You probably figured out that Sheree could see you when she shouldn't. That's because she's unmagicked. But it also means that magic can't affect her, good or bad, anymore."

"But you can still heal Anni with magic, yet she can't be sensed," Antonio said.

"Unbound."

"Unbound?"

"My healing unbinds a certain string, so to speak," Brendon told him.

"Oh no, so that means…" Wayne said, eyes widening.

"Yep," Kwirk confirmed. "But we don't talk about that."

"But when did Brendon…?" Wayne asked.

"After Jeremy left, I may have done some irrational… things," Kwirk confessed, hiding his left wrist.

"Why didn't you tell me?" Wayne asked, pulling Kwirk in for a hug.

"Embarrassment?" Kwirk told Wayne's shoulder. "I mean, what twelve-year-old tries to kill himself because his boyfriend moved to Canada?"

"That's what happened?" Tommy asked. "I knew he left end of sixth grade, but didn't know he left the country."

Stomping his feet, Sam burst out, "Great therapy session, fuckers, but what the hell is happening?"

Without missing a beat, Kwirk and Anni bounced off each other as they explained the plan. The plan they concocted with Ami before the whole thing went down. The plan Ami approached them with when she realized that Anna tried conjuring Kori, but couldn't, and knew that could only mean one thing: Kori wasn't dead. So Ami said they'd need to make the cure, she'd have to "sacrifice" herself so Antonio would be forced to "save" her by turning her, but there was a problem about making sure

Ami had both the cure and the original drug, the drug hidden in Anni's shoe, but she was on the other side of the room, and Kori would certainly notice a person meandering over to a dying body and handing something off to them, so Anni did the first thing she could think of, which was get just a little too close to the shield to slice through the bone so she could rip the rest off and toss it over to Ami so she could get what she needed while distracting Kori just long enough for her to take it.

"How did I not see that?" Antonio asked.

"Probably because you were busy wiping my blood out of your eyes. I did aim the bone stump toward it," Anni said, reenacting the pitch. "Softball finally paid off for more than just meeting other lesbos!"

A bright flash erupted, turning night to day.

"Uh, I wasn't expecting that," Kwirk said.

"Neither was I," Anni said.

"Of course not!" Wayne said, throwing his hands in the air.

"So that wasn't part of the plan?" Brendon asked, shielding his eyes.

"Nope."

"Well, fuck."

CHAPTER 22

I Melt with You

The problem with plans that don't go the way they're anticipated, is that when the situation seems resolved, who really gives a fuck how, right? But that's the problem. The world appeared like everything was all hunky dory, but in reality, nobody really knew for certain if that was indeed the case. It's all about appearances, which, let's face it, are more important than reality this day and age.

Talk about fucked up, yo.

Plastering Brendon's face with more cum than he ever thought possible, Antonio stared into his puppy dog brown eyes, one partially closed due to the white, and smiled like a goddamn fool before licking it all off, not daring to swallow, then pushing his tongue into Brendon's mouth, filling it with everything that didn't make it in there in the first place. Why waste it? Brendon craved his man juice more than any other bodily fluid, and he didn't see the point in pretending that wasn't the case. His boy was a cum whore, but only for his, and that was all that mattered in the world, his world, at this moment, this time, this place, this reality.

Even though nobody knew what really happened to Ami and Kori, the ending "i" girls, nobody really cared to find out since, as far as they could tell, the threat, the fear they all clung to like wet toilet paper at a sketchy gas station in the middle of nowhere, was nowhere to be felt. It was almost as if the plan actually did work. Only, deep down, they all knew that something was amiss. Something didn't add up. Like the sum was short a few cents, even though the scents were missing too. Two girls. Two vamps. Two beyond vampires. Vampires with extra powers, extra strengths, extra abilities, flying around somewhere, possibly gone forever, possibly plotting their next move, possibly all for nothing other than finally being together again after all this time apart.

As Brendon swallowed the hefty load, Antonio tried sneaking a little back, wiping Brendon's left eyelid, but knew he'd never be allowed. His insatiable boy wanted all of him, needed all of him, craved all of him, and greedily snatched his thumb and forcibly licked it clean before reconnecting, rejoining, becoming one, blended, melted together to form a single, yet separate, entity. The sway. The motion. The rush. The pulsating, vibrating, exhilarating thrusting, pushing them closer and closer and closer to yet another climax.

Bliss is ignorance.

The moment.

The exhale.

The clarity.

"I fear I'd stop the world just to do this with you for eternity," Antonio confessed.

But instead of answering, Brendon just confirmed the gesture, the moment, the eternal factor of it all as they switched gears, changed positions, honing the versatility of their lack of inhibition with each other. Antonio got so used to being the dominate factor of his conquests over the years that having someone who could dominate him, penetrate him, with so much ease and confidence made him feel both vulnerable and safe all at once. It was the life he wished with Sam but knew it'd never be able to happen, and it was at this moment, Brendon felt the disconnect and pulled out.

"I'm sorry."

"I'm sorry."

"You have nothing to apologize for."

"But I'm with you."

"Only because Sam's gone."

The bee may have died, but the stinger was firmly embedded.

Stopping to think about the situation, the whole situation, that he had going on with Brendon, he couldn't help but wonder just what it was, when it was, that he found himself not just infatuated with the Hollins boy, but in love—truly, madly, deeply in love—with him. Was this witchcraft?

"It's not witchcraft."

"I never…"

"You don't have to say the quiet part out loud for me to hear it."

The kicker. The issue. The problem. The reason this wasn't going to work out no matter how much he really wanted it to. Brendon's ability to sense truth. And the truth of the matter was that, no matter how much Antonio loved, really loved, this boy, a significant piece of his heart still belonged to someone else. Someone who, yes, was quite dead, and true, not exactly dead the way he thought for so many years, but dead nonetheless. And now gone. Forever. But what is forever?

Yet Brendon never made him feel less, feel guilt, feel like his love of Sam tainted his love of him. So, why the disconnect? Why cause the one he loved so much so much pain? Pain. Pleasure. Such a thin line between the two.

But then he heard the thumping of his own heart that he hadn't heard in years, over a decade, not since the moment before crashing into that tree Labor Day weekend in 2000. Okay, so he heard it when it was in the jar, in Brendon's hand, reinserted into his chest. But now, this moment, he heard it like he was alive again, living again, human again. Only he wasn't alive, living, or human. He was vampire. More than vampire. But what? He still didn't know, even after sucking off his daddy until there was nothing left his father could offer. The truth. The knowledge. The everything of his new reality. What did it all mean?

And then it all didn't matter again as Brendon's dick slid back into Antonio's puckered asshole, still tight after all these years. In. Out. In. Out. Brendon kept pulling out and pushing in like he couldn't make up his mind until he thrust so deep his balls nearly sunk inside as well.

"Quiet your mind, fucker," Brendon whispered before biting Antonio's ear, pulling his hair, and picking up the pace. "Now cum," he commanded, and Antonio obeyed, spraying his load on the sheets while Brendon kept fucking him until he came so deep inside he thought his reinstalled heart would be smothered.

They fell onto the bed, Brendon still firmly inside, and shrank into hallucanative hypnagogia. They were two, yet they were one. Asleep yet awake.

"You have to let me go," the red leaf begged.

"I can't," Antonio cried.

"It's time."

"But how can I be without you?"

"I'll always be with you, I just can't be with you."

"I need to know you'll be okay."

"I'm finally me."

"Finally."

When Antonio opened his eyes, he felt the pressure behind him and instinctually pushed back. The response answered the call and pushed forward without missing a beat. This is what Sam knew all along. What he'd been trying to tell him since that day all those years ago after he died but he wasn't ready to listen: Brendon was actually the one he was meant to spend eternity with. As much as Sam wanted to, he knew he was temporary somehow. Some transition between monster and humanity. And as much as Antonio wanted to remember, to contemplate, to figure out the whole of it all, his hole was busy getting pummeled and that was all he could think about.

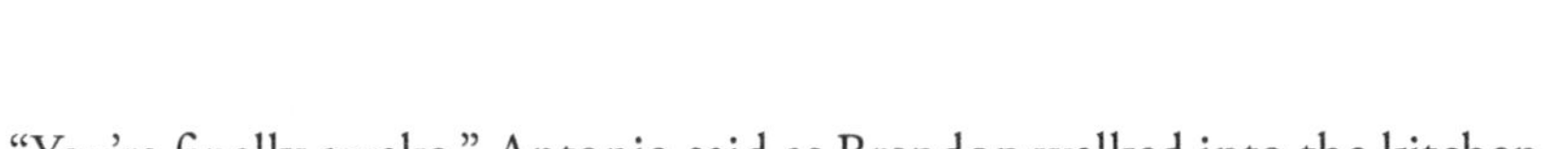

"You're finally awake," Antonio said as Brendon walked into the kitchen.

"Somebody kept me up all night," Brendon said mischievously, yawning with a stretch, flexing muscles that rarely get acknowledged.

"Somebody was up all night," Antonio said before kissing him.

Nothing else mattered.

But then it did.

Brendon sighed.

"Fucking kangaroos, my sister needs me home. Now," Brendon told Antonio, shattering the moment into a million tiny shards of glass.

"Fucking kangaroos indeed. I heard her too," Antonio said, suddenly realizing something new, something he shouldn't.

Shaking his head, Brendon revealed, "It's happening."

"What's happening?"

"The next phase of you."

"Next phase."

"Remember how I said you are so much more than you realize?"

"Yes?"

"This is one of those things."

"It is?"

"It is."

"What if I don't want it?"

"Too late."

"Too late?"

"Shouldn't have swallowed nearly every last drop of Song's End and taken back your heart then."

"How was I supposed to know?"

"You weren't."

"But why?'

"Because you are the beloved. My beloved."

And then they kissed.

But like all things romantic and sweet and good about this Earth, it was over long before anyone was ready for it to end. In a flash, Brendon was dressed and out the door and on his way back to his home, his childhood home, to find out what his sister needed. And it was all so eerily uncanny that Antonio knew what she needed. Knew her question. Wasn't she immune from magic? Unmagicked as Brendon called it? What sorcery was this?

Oh my gawd, calm down! Brendon shouted in his head.

"How can I?" Antonio asked, naked and afraid.

Put some pants on and come over. Sheree's got a bad feeling about what went down last night, Brendon said as he walked through his front door.

"No shit, Sherlock!" Antonio said, opting for yesterday's outfit rather than finding something new to wear before quickly making his way two doors down to the Hollins house.

"As much as I trust you, I don't trust you," Sheree said as bluntly as your mother's favorite knife.

"That slices," Brendon said, clutching his left elbow.

"It should!" Sheree shouted. "You said this was the only way! You promised me that Ami would fix everything! You fucking promised me!"

Her hurt was palpable, pulsating, not like the pulsations he and Antonio experienced over and over the night before well into the early morning hours. Yet they were just as real. All Brendon could do was become flaccid, small, plunged into ice water. Shrinkage.

"He promised you what he could," Antonio said as he walked through the front door like he owned the place.

"Thought vampires needed an invitation."

"Only when they're not fucking one of the residents."

"You're not fucking me," Mrs. Hollins said as she poured a cup of coffee.

"Or me," Mr. Hollins said with a wink before slapping his wife's ass.

"Jesus Fucking Christ!" Sheree screamed.

"You know good and well the Lord's middle name is not 'Fucking' young lady," Mr. Hollins reminded his daughter before chuckling.

Antonio had to admit the family dynamic banter was something he'd always hoped he'd be able to experience with his own family, his own parents and siblings. But alas, that was never the case. And never would be.

Sheree lightly punched Brendon's arm. "You promised."

Her tears flowed like spring rivers.

But there was nothing Brendon could say to alleviate the hurt, the pain, the reality of the now. He made a promise, and yes, it was the only way they possibly could defeat Kori even though he didn't know it was Kori they needed to defeat, but still, defeat her all the same, and he couldn't keep it. He could explain to Sheree that Ami knew the magnitude of the problem long before any of them had an inkling of a clue, and yet it wouldn't matter. He could tell her about the drug, about John, about John's mom, about what Sky would have become, and it wouldn't matter. Nothing would matter. He broke a promise he swore he could keep.

"Oh my gawd, stop blaming yourself," Kayla said as she flew through the door.

"Dat shit gone take a number on ya' soul, boy," Courtney said as she followed her girlfriend.

"Tru dat," Chad said, walking in behind them with his husband, Joel.

Brendon couldn't help but smile.

"Ah, Brendon, I see you've finally gotten the tooth," Sheree said.

"The tooth?" Brendon asked, wearing confusion like last year's Versace. Again.

"The tooth," Kayla said.

"Yep," Chad said.

Then they all pulled down their lower lips to reveal a solitary crooked tooth, just slightly out of alignment. The left lateral incisor. For the rest of his goddamned life he'd never be able to see his mouth the same way again.

"Oh, did Brendon finally get my tooth?" Frank asked, innocently pointing toward the offending one as he walked up the stairs in his boxers and nothing else but a cup of coffee and his penis tip saying hello as it peeked through the flap every other step.

"It appears so," Brendon said before rubbing his index finger back and forth over the tooth in question.

Antonio felt the love of family. He also felt the sadness of imperfection, and knew he'd never be able to compensate even though he was well aware that perfection was nothing but a fucking illusion perpetuated by imperfect people who want everyone to believe they are better than everyone else. Losers.

And yet, overwhelmingly, the feeling that those imperfections were what bound them together and make them unique. Not unique as individuals but unique as family, as a unit, and goddamn, Mr. Hollins certainly passed down his unit to his son and probably his other son based on the smile plastered on Joel's face every time they've met.

"I hate you all," Brendon said with a slight smile on his face.

"We know," Sheree told him as they all closed in for a group hug.

CHAPTER 23

The Future

Ravenwood General was about as classy as the name alluded. I mean, don't get me wrong, it had all the typical hospital stuff, just, you know, you never knew which life-saving treatment device was going to be broken at that particular moment. Need an MRI? Sorry, it died last week, and we'll conveniently forget to inform you that we even have one or that it is an option. Sorry about your kidney, though. If we had a working MRI we might have detected an issue after your car accident. If only you hadn't been in a coma, you could've requested a transfer to a hospital that had one. Oops. Sorry. Here's your bill.

"Abuelo, I wish we had more time," Antonio cried, tears carving canyons into his cheekbones.

"Time is a concept. Love is forever," Antonio's grandfather told him, patting his cheeks and gently wiping the tears away as he smiled. "Besides, looks like all those Catholic boys prepared you for the one."

Brendon blushed.

"Of course, didn't think you'd take a virgin," he said before falling into a coughing fit. "Specially since you a tlahuelpuchi."

"He's more than that," Brendon told the old man. "But surprisingly accurate for his maker."

The room started spinning like a top as Antonio tried to steady himself. Windows and walls and machinery blurred together. Swirling. Mixing. Blending the flavors like a milkshake. Instinctually, he started tapping his thumb and middle finger on his right hand to stabilize.

Tap tap.

Tap tap.

Tap tap.

"You… you know?" Antonio asked.

"No fucker stay that sexy and not be turned, fool," Antonio's grandfather told him. "Sides, ain't like it changed you. Not where it counts. Not where it matters. You no monster, Antonio."

"I can…"

"No, sweet child. No. My time now. Time to go, time to go," he said, coughing again and spitting up a little blood that frightened Antonio, but he just waved it away.

"I want to stay."

"What, and talk to your mama and papa?"

"Well, no, they…"

"Damn right they no understand," he said before grabbing Antonio's hand and Brendon's hand and hold them together. "This your family. This is all I ever wanted for you."

Unable to fathom the love he felt, the love that filled the room, drowning out the incessant beeping machines and wheezing ventilator and squealing air vent that all threatened to swallow up everything in its path, Antonio fell into his grandfather's arms. His abuelo kissed his forehead.

And that was it.

The end.

The flatline made Antonio inconsolable for weeks. Eventually, with the help of Brendon and the distraction he offered more times than he could count, he broke through the barrier. The deep. That seemingly impenetrable place we go to when loss becomes too much to bear. And yet, he moved forward.

They all did.

"You really have no clue who I am?"

"You'd think the confused looks and blank stares would have answered that for you," Antonio jested, not sure what to make of the short stout woman in front of him, so incredibly sure of herself.

"Fool! I'm Preeva Hicks!"

"Girl, ya need to calm yo' titties the fuck down."

And, shit you not, the bitch quite literally grabbed her breasts and swung them around while shouting, "I can't calm them down!" before bursting into the most uproarious laughter imaginable and continuing on her way.

It was just what Antonio needed. This. This random connection with a stranger to make him feel worthy. Not that Brendon didn't make him feel worthy, but that was different. Brendon was different. He nearly forgot the joy of humanity. The spontaneity. The—albeit she was obviously high as a mother fucking kite—bliss of tiny connections, even if just for a moment before they flutter away like leaves in a gentle breeze.

Antonio had to remind himself that for every prick, there were at least a dozen Preeva Hickses out there making the world smile.

Normal seemed like it was just around the corner. Good versus evil. The morally gray man replaced. Right?

Antonio continued to tell himself that as he watched Brendon tear apart three men from the inside out. He recognized the men in question, even now all these years later and several months before tried to take him down until he recognized the leader. The ones who bullied Brendon as a child. Beat him up. Left him bleeding on the Fourth of July as fireworks blazed the sky. All because of a fucking handmade shirt the then ten-year-old was so proud to wear out in public that said 'That's Mister Faggot To You' in rainbow marker.

Not that that was the reason Brendon was violently murdering them. No. They'd apparently evaded the police for too many crimes far worse than just his own hate crime nearly fourteen years to the day.

Daddy's a bit corrupt. Brendon didn't even acknowledge that his own father also tended to do some shady dealings at the morgue, AKA, the hospital basement. Nope. Not now. Not when he knew for a fact these three gang-raped a twelve-year-old boy just because they could. Never even had a trial. Never saw a day in jail. And now? That ain't gonna happen.

The last of them fell.

Antonio looked across from him, inside the pile of bodies, and saw Brendon's face aghast. What was happening? Why was he imagining Brendon killing them? To satiate the guilt? The desire? The need to revenge every last person who wronged his man?

His man.

"And just like that, the man I'd been kissing moments ago became the most dangerous person in the world."

"So dramatic, Brendon."

"Would you expect anything less?"

"Admittedly, no. Now I have to clean up this mess," Antonio said, scanning the body parts scattered across the bloodstained room.

"We."

Why was he so chill about this? Was it actually his imagination? Did he just take out one and not all three? He felt darkness creeping back in, claiming the spaces she vacated. It was only a moment, but she was there, skulking, waiting.

Antonio awoke to find Brendon at his side, sound asleep. A dream? A nightmare? Or was it later that night? That week? That month? That year? Time!

Brendon's hand rubbed the small of Antonio's chest, the little divot cum tended to pool. "I'm right here," he said.

"I know. But my mind is…"

"Healing."

"Healing?"

"All those years without a heart, and hell, even the years you had one but it never beat, took a toll on you. But now you're whole and your body and mind are trying to reconcile that."

"Still?"

"Still."

"I don't know how much longer I can take this."

"You're stronger than you think."

"I'm weak."

"Liar."

Sometimes quiet is what the doctor ordered. Only no doctor actually ordered it. Some self-prescribed medication bullshit. Antonio couldn't shake the feeling, the awful feeling, that the worst was yet to come. So instead of waiting around to find out, waiting to fully heal, to fully be aware of his actions and inactions and immense imagination that flooded his psyche with crazy, he left. Just hopped on his bike and rode off until the gas ran out.

The problem with this half-assed plan was having a witch for a boyfriend.

"You can't just turn into a bat and fly away when you don't want to deal with things," Brendon said quietly after grabbing Antonio's arm, squeezing tightly.

Antonio yanked his arm free. "Watch me."

Brendon watched and waited, but all Antonio did was walk away. "I knew you couldn't turn into a bat."

"I just need… time."

Then he disappeared into the black.

But the thing people tend to forget is that the dark is also temporary. Light pushes itself into the crevices like a predator because he's a nasty little bugger. And while the darkness helped Antonio prepare to welcome light's embrace with open arms, he couldn't shake the comfort dark held, like a weighted blanket. By contrast, light doesn't let you hide anything, leaving you naked, lying broken on the floor even when you want to get up, grab cover.

Sometimes we have to be naked and vulnerable and afraid so we can pull ourselves out.

Eventually light won the battle. Antonio felt his head cleared of fog for the first time in years. Every thought, every memory, clear as day. He suddenly remembered everything his brain tried to make him forget, buried deep in the shadows. He finally saw reality where his memory played tricks on him. He finally saw the truth, and the truth of it was simple: he was loved.

In a flash, he was back home, back in Ravenwood, Washington, back in the loving embrace of Brendon who fucked him so hard, so deep, he felt like a virgin again. Raw. Carnal. Tender. Sweet.

It also wasn't long before the gang was back together doing supernatural shit. This time, a rogue witch who'd just vanquished her entire coven for the sake of power. Which, to be fair, seems like a legit reason to kill your family if you're so inclined. The rich do it all the time. "Oh, what happened to Mother?" one child asked, and another answered, "The stairs. Father's burying her in a bleak alcove on his golf course come morning," and the third says, "Oh good, with the weeds. Mimosas?" Fucking fascists. Like this witch, stealing power, taking lives, all for herself, no remorse.

She was easy pickings for Brendon.

"All that blood looks good on you. It really brings out your eyes," Wayne said.

"He's right," Antonio said.

"Because it brings out the murder in them right now?" Brendon quipped through heavy breaths.

"Yep," Wayne said.

"Ditto," Anni said, picking up a finger that had fallen off and pocketing it for later.

"You say that like it's a bad thing," Antonio said before kissing him. "Mmm… tastes like cherry pie."

Brendon licked his lips. "Huh."

But the problem with complicity and normalcy and getting the old gang back together is that it doesn't account for the natural evolution of things.

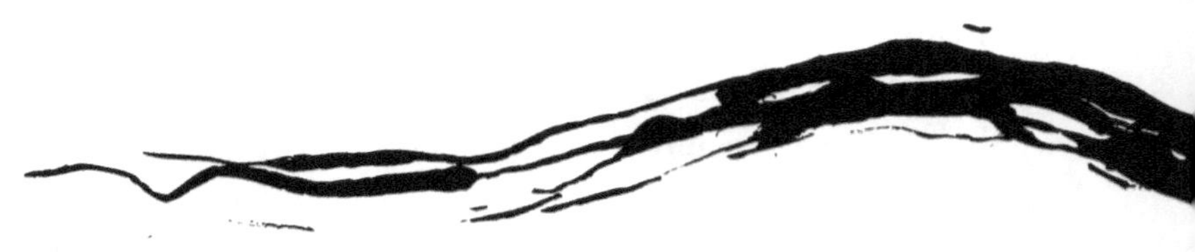

"Most of the world doesn't even know we exist. We hide amongst the shadows and try to live a quiet life."

Antonio stared at the audacity spewing from the vampire in front of him, mouth dripping with the blood of his latest victim still in his clutches, and said as he shook his head, "That's a load of horse shit."

"I got hungry and she offered me a snack."

The woman's eyes looked wild and wide, breath fast and furious, and scent full of pure fear.

"Somehow I doubt Sheila was as willing to offer herself as you suggest," Antonio said to the dark man, face still hidden on the opposite side where the street lamp's glare cut through the night.

"Sheila? What, you know her?"

"Her name badge."

"Shit, man. Didn't even notice that."

"Let me guess, hunger took over and all you saw was a pretty piece of flesh ready for biting?"

"I'm just so hungry all the time, man."

"Newbies," Antonio said, rolling his eyes. "Let her go. Promise I'll find you another meal soon."

The dark man's grip loosened. Sheila stood up straight, smoothed out her skirt and hair. "For the record, he wasn't lying when he told you I offered him a snack."

"You mean yourself?"

"Well, technically I meant my pussy, but apparently he had other plans," Sheila said.

Antonio noted her voice was without any hint of sarcasm. No qualms either. Her fear had completely vanished. As the dark man slowly made his way into the light, Antonio could see why. The Greek god before him was the stuff of wet dreams, right down to his chiseled marble ear lobes. Unfortunately, at least through the tight jeans he sported, his manly appendage was also quite in tune with Greek gods whose only promise was being a grower not a shower. "Wait, do people still call it 'pussy' these days?"

Sheila laughed more heartily than he expected, her guffaws echoing in the alley off the brick buildings on either side of them. "I do."

"Cool. So, back to you, youngling…"

"Wait wait wait wait wait, did you just call me a youngling?" the dark man asked, a crooked smile dimpling his cheek.

Goddamn dimples.

"Yes, because that's what you are."

The dark man snarled.

"Sheila, you might want to head home."

"Damn, cuz I really need to get laid."

"I apologize, but this man is not for you."

"Whatever. Guess I'll have to figure out how to cover up this neck wound before work tomorrow, and come up with a…" Sheila said as she walked off, pulling out her cell phone to take a selfie.

Suddenly, a foul-smelling black liquid shot from her mouth. She hit the pavement head first as her body convulsed, a sickening **CRACK!** indicating her skull crushed itself on impact.

"Trust me when I tell you I am no newbie."

"What are you?" Antonio asked, eyes rapid-firing between Sheila and the dark man.

"THE FUTURE."

The dark man flew away before Antonio could find out what he meant. Sheila continued seizing. As Antonio approached her, she suddenly screamed a torrential animal-like cry before her body burst into black oil, slicking the asphalt and making it look like a new patch job.

"What the fuck?!

AUTHOR BIO

Cory Blystone lives in Vancouver, Washington with his husband Greg and their dogs. He's obsessed with collecting tiki mugs, building LEGO, and taking an absurd amount of selfies.

Antonio will return...